STRANGERS AND REFUGEES

Also by John Fraser
and published by
AESOP Modern Fiction:

Animal Tales
The Answer
Black Masks
Blue Light / Starting Over
The Case
Confessions
Down from the Stars
The Ends of the Earth
Enterprising Women
The Future's Coming Everwhere
Happy Always
Hard Places
An Illusion of Sun
The Magnificent Wurlitzer
Medusa
Military Roads
The Observatory
The Other Shore
People You Will Never Meet
The Red Bird
The Red Tank
Runners
'S'
Short Lives
Sisters
Soft Landing
The Storm
Thinking Scientifically
Thirty Years
Three Beauties
Tomorrow the Victory
Travels with Strangers
Wayfaring

STRANGERS AND REFUGEES

John Fraser

AESOP Modern Fiction
Oxford

AESOP Modern Fiction
An imprint of AESOP Publications
Martin Noble Editorial / AESOP
28a Abberbury Road, Oxford OX4 4ES, UK
www.aesopbooks.com

First edition published by AESOP Publications

www.johnfraserfiction.com

A catalogue record of this book is
available from the British Library.

First edition 2020, revised 2024

ISBN: 978-1-910301-66-1

CONTENTS

THE REFUGEES

'DON'T THINK of changing your name, Khalil,' says Zenobia from the chaise-longue, naked on her back, thrusting with her legs upwards, urging on an upside-down horse, or donkey, into a gallop. 'They'll put you straight in jail. And you won't have a document with either name to show. To get you out or keep you in more accurately.'

'I'd be ready for anything, suspected of everything,' says Khalil, 'And innocent.'

'Well,' says Zenobia. 'I for one shan't visit. And if you've done nothing, there'll be no one to lie for you.'

'These rooms,' Khalil says, 'are built for rent. See the angles – you look right down over to other rooms built for rent, same smell – same scene on the divan! You can see the lino ageing into bark: there's guys above looking down on ours. If there were hundred-franc notes beneath, you'd not want to burrow down for them.'

'They'd be worthless anyway,' says Zenobia.

'Just big words,' says Khalil, 'and drawings. But the smart ones here, they had a continent of bourgeois, squabbling for them – the notes, the words, and sounding off. "I'm an ephemeral and not too discontented citizen...." That nailed it. No pictures, just "*la magie bourgeoise*", from Le Havre to Kitezh. Then it was soiled or blown up, the massacres ... and these crap rooms were left. I don't have a bourgeoisie behind me, Zenobia: just guys in uniform, smoked spectacles in place of eyes.... We should leave at once. We know where our next port is, there must be cash that waits for us.'

'We can do anything at all,' Zenobia says. 'Here, in this city. You don't seem able, Khalil.' She's angry, putting on some clothes.

'The others should have come,' says Khalil. 'Zenobia – say goodbye to the guy over the road, up in the sky – the show is done, you're ashamed and clothed.'

*

'I was a democrat then,' Khalil recalls. 'Was it yesterday? It's easy when there's two of you and you're about to separate.'

'They say in any group, one in three's a spy,' Zenobia says. 'The spy – it could be you.'

'In a group like ours,' Khalil says, 'it could be two of three. Maybe that's why the others stayed away. We could be the two.'

'The people here,' Zenobia says, 'have twice what we might want – and yet they'd like to throw us out. Even if we had twice more than them, we've lost it, so it's just too bad. No rancour, just "move on".'

'That's it,' says Khalil. 'If we had the same as them, they'd let us stay. Inside – we know we once had more. We'd not spoiled it quite so bad ... except we couldn't do the politics, handle the cash, the arms, the visitors in all their shapes. The hopes, the scorpions. The exorcists.'

'Thinking it over,' says Zenobia, 'it's better that we both are spies. Only one – brings complications. Anyway – how would you want things back there to turn out different?'

'Oh,' Khalil says, 'I didn't come from there.... I want to be left to myself, and see the bad guys hung up high. But that is incompatible: changing things and being left unchanged yourself. We've learned too much. We people, who have only half of what the guys here think they possess – we travel round, we go everywhere we can and can't.... It's even in the religion we're supposed to have.... The world is ours, because what's right is right all over. I've already been all round one world.... I know how it ticks and tocks.'

'Don't ever say that, Khalil,' Zenobia says. 'It's jail. Travel incriminates. They'll know you are a spy, but won't know who it's for.'

'It's true,' says Khalil. 'Suppose you're a philosopher, then I should go to jail for doing nothing. For being suspicious. Well, I am a suspicious type – so, you are too. But – since I've run in order to escape, it might seem a kind of failure, don't you think, to shut me up? If you do something – what then? What should be the punishment? Run for ever?'

'See?' says Zenobia. 'We look like everyone else here. Even unclothed – the same. Similar. You must never look the same as anything. That's conspiracy. Somehow, you must be indistinguishable from other people who look the same but are conclusively not the same.'

'I don't see this,' Khalil says. 'It will be hard, for sure, living in a place where we don't want to be, that reads so well in books but when you're here, it's dull and big, you never find the interesting things that other people do.'

'It's so for everyone,' says Zenobia, weary. 'It's the children who don't think like that...'

'I don't want your children, Zenobia,' Khalil says.

'Whose then? The choice is partly yours,' says Zenobia, not wanting kids with anyone.

'Genghiz,' Khalil says. 'He had a patrimony to leave, and all the children had lives quite remarkable; most existences and legacies you wouldn't want, but theirs were neither dull nor skimped.'

*

The stair – as they go down, it uncoils like a tree, its growth.

'Wait!' says Zenobia outside. 'Need five minutes ... my tattoo.'

In the street, she takes off her shirt and shows – the main gate of Palmyra. It's already infected, and she's swollen, red.

'I told you it was dirty,' Khalil says. 'You slow us down, we'll have to see you cured.'

Her shirt has a design of mammoths, on a black ground. She's very hot – if she gets over this, she'll be cooked hard like a pot. 'I'll grow round you, Khalil,' she says, 'as a tree grows round an axe-head.'

'It sounds as if it's love,' he says, not at all convinced.

'No,' she says, 'nothing to do with that, you'll find. Be aware, be ready, don't fuck with me, and don't go your pathetic way without me. I'm round you like the fur coat on a wolf. I'm to stop you dying of the cold, not to keep you warm.'

That may be so. She's hot, very hot, hotter than cats always are.

'There's a free doctor in this shop,' says Khalil. 'Get him to cure you, then we'll be off.'

'Oh,' says the doc. 'I'm not concerned with her. It's self-inflicted. She'll get better, or get worse. It's you, Khalil, the subject....' and he stares down Khalil's throat, drops a long worm down through his ear – 'It'll eat up alien tasty bits,' he says, 'And leave you inedible. But – there's a battle going on, Khalil – your organs are in perfect state – too much. They battle, climb all over. Your coward heart – as usual tries for threat and ransom. The liver crowds over, eats what's in the gut, the lungs scoop up dark bags of stuff – it's wonderful, Khalil, but it can't last. Do you do cannibalism, or maybe have ancestors who were shipwrecked or besieged? – maybe it's not acquired, the taste for human flesh, but innate, part of our evolutionary kit installed and ready.... Those last days – remember, "take one with you" – I'm sure there will be recipes.'

The clinic sign says 'Biovit – Mangetout. One for two'.

'We should have known,' Zenobia gasps. 'People got interested in exotic food when there was enough. Now ... it's evolution. Like autophagy. We'll self-consume, till there's just two, or maybe one that's left, and start again. It's repetitive, but who's to care?'

'I'm not a freak,' says Khalil, sitting in the road. 'Your tattoo – it's a tribute to the Navajo – an orange desert, all slump and blear.'

'My friend needs a place to die,' says Zenobia.

The lady says, 'That's up to him, but I want no reminiscences, no writing on the walls.'

'We'll manage,' says Zenobia, doubled up with Khalil's weight, her heat: 'It's an internal matter.'

'Zenobia, Zeno dear,' Khalil gasps. 'Tell me, what will it be like, on the other side? Do we shades stand and watch you, while you grapple and trip each other? Will we all be voyeurs, Kandaules, with our flags and slingshots, trying to dent your armour.... you living guys, defending your frontier from our pebbles?'

'The other shore?' Zenobia. 'Like the wild side: oh, nostalgia, perhaps.... You've no one you can blame, Khalil. Don't howl – the lady wouldn't like it. Just let it happen. I read once – some experience a rebirth almost at once – you die, a new creature struggles forth, not recognising you, pulling on your clothes, down the stairs and out.'

'And do I sing?' asks Khalil, quite amazed.

'Everybody sings and no one hears,' says Zenobia briskly, peeling off a folio of skin.

'There are people I could blame,' says Khalil. 'But it's useless, or maybe it's undignified – to shout out what you couldn't change.'

'No one can see higher than their knees,' Zenobia says. 'Then there's clouds. Don't blame yourself, Khalil – you don't know how it would turn out.'

She picks at her back. 'Perhaps the needle went right through,' she says. 'It's all pictures, all the way in. What am I supposed to do? Say one's better than another? Paint them – some of them – right out, like the books do, and put in bones instead?'

'Oppression, Zenobia,' says Khalil. 'I have been oppressed.'

'Yes,' she says, 'let your passion out. Revenge. Even – hurt someone, be hurt. Hurt again, and win. At least, don't surrender. Pretend there is, but no end. Maybe there's not. For you, of course, but if you are not satisfied – then on it all goes.'

'Suppose it's a birth?' says Khalil, 'and – of course, we must oppose the oppressors. No, it's not us created them, nor them that created us. Except, of course, there must be some kind of order. Interest too, and keeping a strong face, a firm presence with the neighbours.'

'If it is a birth,' says Zenobia, 'the lady, the landlady, says it's just the same. Birth, death. No excess. We're just foreigners, dirtying the sheets.'

'The truth is,' says Khalil, 'when we were all honest – there was no profit. It was hard, impossible, to make a fortune. I went to work, Zenobia, in places where people were to congregate, people I think were not worthy, for entertainment, luxury real or counterfeit. I was employed by people who should have helped me, instead ... they took a cut, ten cuts. Something must be done....'

'You're wrong about the history, Khalil,' Zenobia says. 'But right about the now. It was fear, back then, that got the profits invested in religion and wise men. Now, it's just there is no limit, no pretence.'

'It started bad,' says Khalil, gloomily. 'Our age. We had the truth. Machines – nature's a machine, and we do philosophy because we're animals. We're flies in the machine – we'll never go beyond the revelation. We work through our obsolescence, we play, beg for a tickle and a stroke – philosophy can't go further, nor can we. Vanity, Zenobia, and soldering irons. It didn't need a genius, just a wanderer to figure it all out. We reached the back wall – it's high as the sky, and smooth, a new alloy we have found.'

'I must get you well, Khalil,' Zenobia says. 'You must forget. Forget what being ill is like, and then you're on the flat again, no crazy up or down, just potholes.'

'The parts are at war, Zenobia,' Khalil says. 'Instead of destruction – maybe they just combine – to tell the time. A time.'

'Well,' she says, 'you must think your way out of this one. Your body's yours, I can't get inside. Nor inside your thought, but I can watch what's happening to that. Don't try playing with yourself – the pleasure, if any, fleets, and the battle goes on. Thinking's independent of everything – you'll be fine, Khalil. When the butcher comes with her knife – be absent. Remember the sheep in the field – one goes to the table, the next day there's another one, indistinguishable, in its place – same baa, same trusting eye. Be convinced.'

'You're right,' says Khalil, winding an unclean sheet all round. 'I'm better already. Better – it's a view, a preference. I'm on track. You didn't pay in advance, I hope, Zenobia? There'll be a backstair... That's where they watch. Down the front, unseen, and out. Back from exile – set up two large Ricards, change the water into fog and hide in it....'

'I knew you'd recover,' says the lady. 'Here's some tofu in a bowl and my honey, my bees....'

'I can't finish it,' says Khalil, 'though it's excellent. There are legs, maybe you should filter more...'

'Oh, they're all mine,' says the lady. 'If you'd finished it, you could have struck a note from the bowl – as it is....'

'Fish,' says Zenobia. 'In the market – it's a cemetery. I don't go along with the spiritual stuff. I see them execute the creatures – every soul weighs just a gram, it swims round the world, and comes back in the market, dies there.'

'There!' says the lady. 'You've seen it all. That's the way it is. Now, pay the room. I'll use those sheets again.... Someone else, I mean,' and she laughs.

*

'Would it have been different if I'd struck the bowl, heard the note?' Khalil asks when they're outside.

'Probably,' Zenobia thinks, and says. 'Oh no. She's a collector, doesn't believe in cleanliness. You're cured, Khalil, the war is over, the conflicts in your gut are normal and they'll kill you – think of me, my back. I can't reach over even to take a squint.'

'We're lucky to have got so far, Zenobia,' Khalil says. 'It's true, these are days in monochrome – but these chancers, granting your three wishes – they can't be up to much, not if it's chance. Think of all the others on the raft – if the wind blows for us, they'll be overboard...

'We're lucky. Everyone has ruins on their back, though the fever sometimes passes.... Look at the people in this sreet – they all need help. Cash or coddling. We have everything we'll ever have: our lives....'

'While we're together, Khalil,' says Zenobia, 'we feel free, feel whole. Each on his own – it won't seem good. A game of ping-pong with no adversary, roulette that spins and there's no ball.'

'I remember,' Khalil says, 'a scene of a bombardment – real hell, not like they say or write it down. Film stock – you have to polish it, it comes up better than a memory. I never read the book – Böll, how'd he manage something so bombastic, explosive, fire and devils red and black.... In ten years, we'll have another version, but we'll remember only the movie – that at least, it moves. It's a scene, like the creation of the world, that ends with fire trapped underground, the roaring in the clouds.... The Torment renewed, end and beginning identical....'

'It's so, Khalil,' Zenobia says, rubbing her smouldering back against a wall, 'But now – there's many ends, the accent's on fresh starts. Reconstruct – that is the word. You see the houses split apart, but all they say is "afterwards, the future comes and sets it up again, better, more solid, nicer people, pacified and cruising on their screens..." Hell comes – and then it goes, there is tomorrow, think of that, suffer, recover....'

'What keeps us two together,' Khalil says, 'is not our bodies, but our stickiness.'

*

They think of making it alone, without the other as the scenery, the plaster column you can lean on and declaim.

'I feel I should protect you,' says Khalil.

'Don't,' says Zenobia. 'Don't protect, don't feel. If you're a guardian, guard what will last. Don't bother with ephemera. If you must be pure, seek clean water, not a body that needs washing. If you want a cause – read the book, don't take the bow and arrow.'

'It's not you that needs protecting,' Khalil says. 'It's that this city has too many dangers. Lurking. Like monsters in the tunnel. Everybody needs safety and we know – no one will have it. Not for a second. Zeno – it's a man's name – it means friend....'

'It means "stranger",' says Zenobia. 'A man's name is fine. It makes no difference.'

'Ours is a mystic union, don't you think, Zenobia?' wheedles Khalil.

'Who'd buy into that?' asks Zenobia. 'You want to contemplate, is all. My body, which I agree is as close to perfect as they ever are – it needs polishing and rubbing down, of course, but yes – if you paw it, sprawl all over, it tarnishes and rusts, the fault is yours. Dirty hands – leave dirt on everything. Contemplate, imagine, fantasise – and then forego. Yours, Khalil, is even a defect, they call you *voyeur*, you don't touch, and don't want someone else to. It's cowardice, Khalil. You don't want things as they must be. It's good. It's even very good. It could be the fashion, though alas for you, I'm real, not a fiddled figure, a golden number on a screen.'

*

That's all good, but you can't stand forever on the pavement. If you paid the room, you walk away, confidently. If not – you'd better run.

'Life is full of traps, Khalil,' Zenobia says. 'But, you've made your own. All those rote beliefs – they're traps, for sure. Just don't fall in – mumble the prayer and grow the beard – no sweat. Yes, you get beaten if you stray. But you're an idiot – misbelieving, attracting *takfir,* is the biggest trap of all. They'll beat you, but there's nowhere else to go for you, when you're in the hole you made, you-sized, all by yourself. Can you hop out, all by yourself? Seek another faith, or be content with none? Either exposes you.'

'Forget it,' says Khalil. 'There's no answer if there's no question.'

'I don't trust you,' says Zenobia. 'That's fine, it's normal, it's general. But you've made the wrong choice. Everything or nothing. Even if you believe neither. What you've done is uncertain. It's not for me.'

'Wait! Zenobia,' Khalil shouts. 'We just said – no money and no documents – better in two than running scared alone.'

'You may have misunderstood,' Zenobia says. 'Two derelicts are squalid.'

Cinema

'All you do, Khalil, is stand on the edge, the roof. They take photos, and you wear wings, or nothing, hold a kite. You are the city, you play her – you don't need documents, you're paid something: from each according to their snap,' says Heinz. 'You've a fine body. The right kind. We do shoots like this often, different: you must be supple,' and he touches Khalil on the shoulder. 'We want you to make poetry,' Heinz says. 'Let others make their poetry from you – as apple blossom made the *Lied.*'

'Something heavier,' says Khalil. 'More time. More hours, more pay. I don't want to fly. A gust – you're in the street with broken wings.'

'A longer sentence? More punishment, more lustre to your conscience – but you're locked in, alone, much longer,' Heinz says.

'I could act,' says Khalil. 'Do stunts. Those deeds – they're not the dirty ones, and you can get a prize.'

'You wanted it....' says Heinz, laughing loud, as the snappers rush to the roof's edge. He pushes Khalil off; he plunges down, his tutu flares, the parasol's a chanterelle – he spirals, all metamorphoses progress – from spore to gliding lizard, the leaping lemur, flying fox, the bat, the cat – and lands.

He's jarred. No one ever's done a stunt like that. As he went down a hierarchy watched – the offices – first the top poppies, than descending to the lickspittles, the brown-nosed – and the hopeful – all watch Khalil, fluttering, twisting down, skirted like a sufi, an evzon – up to his ears. His furry legs don't let him fly, nor go smooth on four paws. A marvel.

*

'You're perfect, Khalil,' says Heinz, hugging him. Heinz is bonier than Zenobia, but cooler, much much cooler. 'Perfect in what you do. Angelism – falling angelism. Of course – you'll do the stunts. A life not quite of Rimbaud, but full of derring do. Even fuller, that's what I mean. You'll write the poetry, and sell the arms, bewitch, renounce, and make your bucks. People – we all come from Africa, but civilisation – comes from the great river. Syria, Iraq, like you, Khalil. With all its spates and droughts – like you, Khalil. A great disappointment? As far as it can go, and then – is it a gift or theft – to show we cannot go beyond? The scale in seven parts – and then the omnitonic – just a fiddle on the first.'

'Do I sing?' asks Khalil, enchanted. 'You open up, dear Heinz – a prospect. Rosy cities in the sand...'

'I see you're trained, Khalil,' Heinz says, not listening. 'The sport: it sets you up. What brings you down's the piss-ups after in the bar, the pills your coach has you take....'

'And is it true, Heinz, you burned those people out in Africa?' Khalil asks.

'We compensated them,' says Heinz. 'They'd seen the whiteys trash whole provinces before – they took the cash, went on the razzle.... But you, Khalil, you'll do it all in your own flesh. No tricks...'

'The falling doesn't bother me,' says Khalil, 'But the poetry ... how'd I play that?'

'Oh,' says Heinz, 'that's prologue. And besides – whatever's in a head that writes and fancies things that don't exist – it's not contractual. Whoever wrote those lines – is unrecognised. How can you finger inspiration? Is it a he, a she, an in-between? Have paws or gills, a beak, or quills? It's feathers, Khalil, drifting from a tree, a dusty moth-wing. And – you get to choose a partner – and of course, back then, the men were all in homosex. Empire and wars, painting and symphonies. The noise! dear Khalil. And the smell! Of course, the trenches gave you time for sonnets, lounging in your hole...'

'Villages, Heinz. That takes a lot of thinking,' Khalil says.

'Oh,' Heinz laughs, 'that wasn't for a movie, it was something else entirely. Of course, if you want balance, you encourage the superfluous, more people than can prosper – but then you kind of make it happen. Or it will. Patience. I'm not that at all. For me – yes, the old guys thought the cabinet of marvels was a dictionary, of the language of a God, that classifying all the wonders gave you a story of how it fits together, makes a sense. Put the animals in their orders – makes a hierarchy, who eats who. Same with history – you find the early things – they're primitive – and so, the more you find, the higher up the scale they go. We know it isn't so – the thoughts are from the start – the same. History – oh Khalil! What a nonsense – the ever-rolling stream, the upwards, ever upwards, the elephants who grip the tail of ignorants who at the front turn into mammoths with their tusks unmanageable – what fables! Order: cramming everything in order. But – that was all. You could collect – I should have, had I had a castle, been a prince – but once you had a sample of nearly everything, and you had cracked the script – you're done! There's nothing more. It was a lexicon – so, they thought, there's a language, speech, a people and a literature. Where? Was or wasn't? You needed to get rid of God before you could compose, make stories with all the wonders in your house. They were the words, every word. That's all. A camera, Khalil. A chamber. A room, a movie. People that move. Why? Where do they go, do they know each other, know themselves? Carve a line, Khalil. An inscription. Watch the sand erase it all. Watch the celluloid – it crinkles, crackles – and the beauty is, you make another movie, and another and another. The things you've done – the burning and the charity ... the daughters trained, the marshes drained, the campaigns with those waspish drones, assassins killed, allies betrayed: collect, dear Khalil. If you don't – you'll be collected. Maybe you are. My labels and my killing bottle – watch those flimsy wings! – who knows what you'll be taken for....'

'Villages,' Khalil insists. 'They've no defences. Just huts and houses...'

'Machines for living in,' says Heinz. 'Herdsmen: they need the space. The green, the ochre – all those plants. What a lot of room, those shacks, that animals could fill. The herdsman dosses down, and sings, transmits the melodies from plain to upland – and remember, mmmm – those animals: the spit, the sauce, the steak and then the skeleton. More wonders for your chamber.'

'You won't tell about the villages,' says Khalil. 'Move on. Then there's the poetry. Do we put that in?'

'Oh, you don't listen, Khalil,' says Heinz. 'What I say – that's it, the poetry! Think back – I've told you everything. A season in a paradise. Finished! Dull exposition, nestling down with people making you feel good and tickling your neurons: enough! Do something quite different. Choose something else, a warrior who eyes your scalp, your skull, who'd hug you, love you so's to get a tighter grip, or turn you so her blade will strike the softest part ... the part your parents said "don't ever show it, not to anyone", your secret garden, Khalil....'

'Oh, you mean Zenobia?' Khalil says and laughs. 'We've done the poetry? I didn't hear it come or leave. Not included in my life, not in my character's....'

'No,' says Heinz. 'In mine. I'm an awful greedy type. Now, start making up your script, Khalil.'

*

'Movies?' says Heinz. 'I love them, of course, you can't say you didn't love your lovers or that movies didn't move you. It's the cadence and the badge on those shining rads – "The house burnt till dawn".... "he climbs up to the sixth step, looks down on the fire, and waits". "There will be a tremendous explosion, but no one will hear it...." I could do all those, Khalil, old stuff, makes a ripple. I wouldn't sully you with it. Something absolutely different. I shan't make you a tiger, nor put you in the senate, or on the central committee, or drop you from a plane, make you a hermit or a caliph.'

'That's all good,' says Khalil, 'Very good. I can't wait to start.'

'I fell, Khalil,' Heinz says, holding Khalil's bicep and squeezing, like deflating a balloon: 'From a thin world – pinched and cold, but very tall, like those old figures born of a tree, a lone tree growing from the silver ground. Two colours are enough, too many, Khalil. This polychrome nauseates me; black, white – that's about right. No greys. These fat tints – it's all empires. Conquest and pushing in. People in line for the massacre, the marches militaires. Feeding the livers, stuffing down the widening throats. The first people – they could do it all. They were black, Khalil, black as black birds, they lived in trees, in stone, basalt for choice, those basalt rings where the dead would return, resurrected, straight twigs.....'

'We shan't go back,' says Khalil. 'It's tricks now. I could jump from an aeroplane – but I don't. Two takes, and the camera says I did.'

'They worked it out,' says Heinz, 'Knew all they needed – not the late flowering, the hatch we have now, knowing nothing, doing everything, misbelieving, surrendered. Agnostic. You must believe, Khalil. If you're wrong – who cares, who sees? It's us. We're that way. Rites, myths – that's our invention. It won't survive. Those big fish – a single song goes round the world. We shan't rule the earth, the universe. It's good. We'll disappear. Who would be sorry? It's not that we didn't do so well, it's that we did worse than we should.'

'That's the movie, Heinz?' Khalil asks. 'The truth? To hotchpotchy guys, sitting there, ticketed, with eats?'

'After, that's how you feel,' says Heinz. 'You start off thinking it's right to tell the truth. And then – so what?'

'Of course you're right, Heinz,' Khalil says. 'We must believe in something, something that does not exist, at least not like lions or earthquakes do. But, from that belief – metaphor is born. We don't live by belief in nonexistent things – we sail on metaphor. We bring the others in – we're queen, they're kings or knaves or jokers, you can use those as you wish – discards, a pair of undistinguished nothing-muches... Metaphor is our disaster, the trap of language, juggling with our brain, trying to enter in those checkpoints, the synapses – and in turn the brain, fluid as blancmange, tries to hold the language firm.... It's a struggle, like Turkish wrestlers, slippery with oil, two combatants – one wins, there's never resolution for the twain, nothing ever is resolved. And metaphor – a joke, approximation, rhetoric, the executioner who says – it will not hurt a bit, be patient for a year or so, we'll sort you out, the things you fear will melt away, your enemies will scutter off into their holes... It isn't so.'

'That's true too, Khalil,' says Heinz. 'For me – it's worse. I have a script, already charged with metaphor, and I must make another jump, turn it to pictures that you never dreamed of, will never use again. It's hard, so hard, Khalil, it makes me weep ... although, it's what our business is. There's worse – once you take ship in metaphor, there's waves of real things – up and under you. You believe you owe a reverence to the dead, they bore you up, the order's theirs, you wear their face, your prick and tits are handed down, and you will hand them on – the sun is good, the moon a little less.... If they weren't there – how would you see to hunt, or plant....? I turn them into portents, poetry – suppose they stay that way? Suppose the realism I court transforms the world, turns seasons inside out, and ghastly things come down from rocks out there in space where nothing is, though it is filled with hard stuff quite invisible... And as you know, Khalil – it doesn't end like that. Into the death pit, on the memorial ... the names are sketched when we are born, the space reserved – a niche for slaves, a bed for nobs – a death is a serious thing, it stands and will not move aside and let you through, not for a day, until you pay it with another death. Not yours, if possible, not a metaphor – first a sacrifice, then you work it out ... you send a postcard. A mobilisation, the scything of the young – conscription, by politicos or friendly nature with its germs and tidal waves.... An office to report to, an emergency, a judgement: death is insatiable,

Khalil. However many bodies you can offer up, it's always harder to evade – "move on, move out, just let me past" you cry in vain.... Unforgiving, unmoveable. Quite insatiable.'

'Is that the story, Heinz?' Khalil asks. 'It's quite magnificent, you tell it well, but....'

Heinz laughs. 'No, it's a bit late for that, don't you think? This is old hat, we've known for centuries, the prayers, the incantations, shamans' drums ... quite useless, made the fraudsters rich. No one thinks of saving other people now: the point today – is saving a few animals, cooling the crust so we can walk on it, turning off the lights so we can see the stars are still somewhere, maybe they twinkle, though what for....? No, the best for us, we think, is some good deal we get from other guys, and have them cogitate how they can get a better deal at our expense, and on and on. No, the movie cannot deal with things that in a minute everybody recognises; you must invent a mystery, a derring do....'

'Zenobia's not made for this. Not for the serious that we all know, and try to dodge, nor for the passing time,' Khalil says. 'The tickling and the bussing in the dark...'

'You do realise, don't you, Khalil, that it's not about a story, or huge fortunes chasing larger ones by way of showbiz hokum, nor about you falling off a beam or Zenobia screaming wild?' asks Heinz. 'It's an adventure, and you're a character, a prop: – for me alone, the sole creator. My use. Like my chair, my name that's stencilled on. That's you, your mark, your brand. You're dead, Khalil. Enter my bower, my scenario – you're filleted and boiled, your projects become mine, your women and your men ... hug and surrender. You think you sold yourself for cash, but no, I have your quiddity, I only care about the tell and show, and you're a piece of painted wood and shabby cloth, held vertical by strings.'

*

‘The problem,’ says Zenobia, ‘is not your monotheism – it’s your mind, Khalil. If there was once a big god, omnipotent, who lets you do exactly what you want including insults from you, and denials – it’s clear. He left us, deserted centuries ago. Omnipotent but impotent – it happens with those steroids too, the ones you take.... Our species – quite unnatural – grew like a magic beanstalk, or a mould. We shot up fast and hit the ceiling – down we go....

‘Find something new, Khalil.... We didn’t last.’

‘Oh yes,’ he says, ‘I have. There is this guy who’ll write me in the script, and maybe, if you implore, Zenobia, he’ll put you in as well.’

*

‘Ah,’ says Heinz. ‘Zenobia. Fit you in? Well, we finished the first one, the movie. No, you can’t see it, dear! It’s real, you never see that twice! We need capital to make you see it, a whole fund-raising, with chairs and usherettes. Why are you curious? You’re not there, the material’s all new, the technology as well. You’d not believe it, what we can do, what we’ve done. The real – inexhaustible, and in this case – exhausted. You can’t have it over, it won’t be the same. Worse – much worse already has been done. Too bad. The movie that you didn’t see, won’t see – it was the best thing. Khalil did it all, kicked ass, even his own, chased the good with the bad, bad with the good. Beat me down with sharp ripostes.’

‘I wish I’d seen it,’ says Zenobia. ‘I’d love to be in the next one.’

‘Love?’ asks Heinz, impressed. ‘“Love is a spark. Lights up the dark.”’

‘There’s nothing like that between us,’ says Zenobia, vaguely, ‘Anyone.’

*

'Let's not argue,' Khalil says. 'Making movies – up to Heinz. Being in them – me, maybe Zenobia.'

'Oh,' Heinz laughs. 'I know you, Khalil, you hound! Champagne cocktails at the première! You think that should be the end!'

Khalil and Zenobia try to drift away, unnoticed, they hope, but Heinz stops them. 'After the première,' he says, 'they might saw off the top of my head and peer inside. That would be an atrocity – with motivation, but no diagnosis. Your country, Khalil – it's been quite devastated. Like my silent brain, a junket – but a country, much bigger, grey dust, dried lymph, of course.'

'Oh,' says Khalil, 'Apart from – I don't believe in countries! Where I was – they invented it, the boundaries. It was a project – to be a country. Like your brain, Heinz – an atrocity. Round the corner...'

'My place too,' Zenobia says. 'You won't even find it on a map. As if a mistake was made, and they'd cut off my feet, looking for my brain.'

'That's smart,' says Heinz, admiring. 'Cut off your feet! Yes! What a thought. But of course, it wouldn't stop them, once they realised – they'd go on looking for your brain. Just change direction. Once the knife takes something off – it's irreversible, best smile and hop along....'

'Yes,' says Zenobia. 'That's what you do. I discovered – you start without your work. What you find, so's not to starve, is like slaves do, although it's paid. The work – it isn't yours. The next stage – is slavery. Once I thought – it's more intimate, you roam, there is escape, there always is.

'It isn't so. There is no manumission, and if you run, if they don't catch you, you are valueless, a worn coin falling down a drain. So, you find work again. It's not done well, it's never yours

– it's paid until.... you have no work. You see, it's circular. Khalil's on steroids – I'm an asteroid.'

'They don't circle, dear,' Heinz says. 'They crash. Sometimes they go in movies. That's the better choice – it isn't intimate, but, yes, it is a choice.'

'Once there's been intimacy,' Zenobia asks. 'Where does it go next? And, Heinz, how many movies have you made? That we could see, I mean, without you being there and us falling off a bridge?'

'Classics?' Heinz asks. 'That you wait twenty years to see and then they're trite? Warriors – they're instant. Artists take longer. Mostly, they don't fizz.'

*

There's scores, waiting. 'Extras' – that's correct, but as a title, doesn't exalt... 'Hopefuls', Khalil says. 'Gullible,' says Zenobia.

'When you make a movie, open a goldmine,' Khalil says. 'It's always so. You strut or dig – it's just the start, and you are at your end before it's all begun, the real story, that ends in golden statuettes.'

'You must concentrate, Khalil, or it will all drift by,' Zenobia says. 'Who cares if there's a movie at the end? It's not owed to you. See what's here! Like an auction. There's window arches – my, how strong! And stoneware pots, and people with wall-eyes and ships on shoals. You must translate the shapes, Khalil, the facial scars, the blocked dancing slippers, it's up to you to discriminate and make your sense. Then – that's your horse! Ride on! It was built for that....'

'Oh, that's dull,' says Khalil. 'I see clowns' baggy pants and mongolfiers, maybe a sun yellow as an egg, or red as a spaniel's rubber ball....'

'Yes,' says Zenobia, 'They're all here, but don't enunciate, they'll think you're a fantasist or a snob. Take it all in and don't expound.'

All around are people – Heinz's friends, people met in field and kitchen, hucksters from Jerusalem, Accra carpenters, reciters from Kiltarlity. All in for fame and a buck, filling out expenses claims. Waiting for their script.

'It's not at all like that,' says Zenobia, holding tight to Khalil. 'They're already in it. This is it. There's no camera, but there'll be anger when they find there's not, and that all they do's intense and unrecorded.... Nothing's reimbursed, not ever. The stars.... you'll see them if the lights go out.'

'Suppose I understand,' says Khalil. 'Will my understanding be recognised?'

'Who would you have in mind for that?' Zenobia asks. 'Someone you don't know, clearly. If there's nothing to be done about anything, you can assume there's many ways of understanding that lead to nothing at all except that they are only, exactly, what they are.'

'It sounds like understanding the world but not living in it...' Khalil says. 'And this dust...!'

All sets are like that, even interiors. We're all cowboys. We're all Indians. There's dust on the quays, and there's dust in those back sets by the Roman sea, murder mysteries, you bet – they say it's sea mist, but it's really dust. It's the dancers and the crowd, the extras in line for extras' food and extras' pay. One day there'll be no need for all these people, they'll be painted on what comes after celluloid, and then dust will need be invented over again.Their feet, makes it fly. Heinz knows how it can end – rough. Go deep into the past, they lived it up, there were more animals in antiquity, you could just eat the tasty bits. It's an illusion. They're all gone, the oldsters, but the danger – that's still there. The appetites, fear and vendetta, all theirs, multiplied.You can end bad in rough play, or in your bed, under the indifferent, the flyers. Drop the load – and they are off – into the horizon, gold and silver, so fast, your foot's down, on the metal, and there are more horizons, flicking past, like scrolling down a stranger's pics. This time – it's your room that's gone to dust, maybe you too – but flight is wonderful. A miracle. Those sharp-nosed planes – fighter-bombers, they are everything you'd ever need, attack, deterrence, first and second strikes. Defence, intelligence.... Or just a drop.

'If it's a war movie,' Khalil says, 'I want nothing of it. They're always old, old stuff, where everyone's identified, the good, the bad, the sexy.'

'We don't have helmets, so it's not,' Zenobia says. 'If nothing happens, I don't see the bus that's to take us somewhere else. I'm not sure we're interesting, Khalil. You have to be – the three cards you play with – are justice, reason and belief. One of those is a discard. I don't mean faith – that's tranquil – I mean belief, in improbable things, that everyone should have, or else...'

'Oh,' says Khalil. 'We'd all be fine if we were all sceptical. Or liberals. Or anything, all of us, potatoes in a sack. But – I'm interesting in myself – I took positions long ago, extreme and loud, made friends and enemies. I've done what you could do, changed the world. The point now is – to understand it. And then – do something else. You don't represent something, Zenobia? Just trommeling down the road, your drumstick legs...?'

'It makes you sound patrician,' says Zenobia. 'Maybe if you wore some giveaways, some clues, clothes that you choose, not picked up somewhere...'

'A statement?' Khalil says. 'Fashion? *Facho*? They're never clear, and often you do it so's you don't need enunciate or say what your mission truly is.'

'It's rather passive,' Zenobia agrees. 'It means you don't need explain to strangers. In any movie – you'd need people of all sorts, left and right, heretics and zealots ... but you almost never find a cast like that, not like the one's a-milling round us here.'

'You're soft, Zenobia,' Khalil says, losing his little patience. 'Don't try philosophy, it comes out soft and reasonable. Forget the ideal person – she's a bore, talks moderate and packs a gun.'

'Go, Khalil,' says Zenobia, annoyed – 'There are some walls – while we're stuck here, go practise falls....'

'It's jumps and rolls,' says Khalil. 'But it's about limitations, not leaps.'

'My tattoo,' Zenobia complains. 'The fever's gone – but look!'

The outline's lost, her back, the thin legs – are a tumble of rocks and shards...

'When I sit down,' she says, 'I feel a crumble. There has been a fall.'

It's believable. Her buttocks are a mass of powdery stones....

'Concentrate!' Khalil says. 'Hold firm. See – the people: – now, it moves!'

The crowd is shifting, a wave, like on a field of corn.

'We're off!' says Zenobia. 'To liberate, perhaps, to bring justice, revelation, at least. Your trouble, Khalil,' and she pulls up her pants, berates him, 'is the ideas you have – they're wrong, distorted. Important guys have had them first: you don't understand, or didn't study them. So – how can your feelings have a weight? If you don't understand what is natural and true – how can you guarantee yourself?'

'They say if you do a trip,' he says, irritated but impressed, 'you find your brain may have a spot that if you finger it – it tells you: love is everywhere, and you have a non-religious god there, permanent, in your head. It's all natural, Zenobia – but it doesn't seem to work. I don't feel love for you, or even tolerance. Is it a failing? It seems quite arbitrary and hit and miss.You don't stick, Zenobia. Maybe I'm wrong about the natural world, what's in it, what might be left outside ... for sure, it's tough to grasp. I'm not sure what grasping it would do....'

'There!' says Zenobia, as the immense crowd starts pouring into buses, like new wine into clean bottles: 'You can't articulate.

If you don't know how deep – how can you know how far? Where do we go – and is it good? And am I with you....?'

'Heinz knows,' says Khalil, 'where we'll end up, though he's not here. Every driver of a coach – has orders, I suppose.'

'Get in, you idiot,' says a guy who's pushing him. Khalil's a bulky packet, primed with those pills and other stuff, the muscles specialised and made for showing off: – he lets himself be pushed ... up the steps, to somewhere new.

'Sit here,' says the guy. 'Don't crowd me. Your woman's standing up ahead, she'll get off with someone new. You should be glad.'

*

They travel, up and up, there's stumpy trees, clefts by the track, up to a plain, some scrub. And then – a field of snow. Magnificent. No one has paints, but they explore – the buses leave. It gets dark here – so in a while the summer's sure to come, but it doesn't seem there's food.

The guy who'd sat next to Khalil says – 'The nature here is wonderful – those buses, they pollute. It's fortunate they've left, but I don't see cameras.... Meanwhile – those geysers! I'll take a boiling shower!' And so he does.

After some days, they're weak. All of them. Khalil is suffering.

'It's clear,' Zenobia says. 'The others – technicians – they are lost, perhaps. Or else we're here on an experiment – to see how we adapt. We've conquered everything, our species – it's up to us, our ingenuity.... I know you're hungry, but, Khalil – it was your vanity pumped you up. See this as a sign – be moderate....'

She weakens. Her thin clothes – they don't protect. It's good she's not a fox with foxlets that she cannot feed. She lies there naked, catching the sun, her body a long tumbling of ochre rubble ... they all lie around, extras, like gulls marooned without an egg between them. Khalil tries to make her laugh, resign herself, have hope – or think – what of? Philosophy is not a help. The sun is hot, the snow is cold – it's hard to know which way's the best to take, and hope you will adapt.

'I guess,' says Khalil. 'Heinz was inspired. You put an ad – for extras. Experience is not essential – and there's daily rates. They flock like guillemots. Some will mate. The drama – is extreme. It's an experiment, you'd say – the ultimate, maybe it's parascientific, more a social ploy, and then, when it is done, you'll have a story quite remarkable. It doesn't end quite there, of course, there is philosophy – that doesn't starve to death, besides, Heinz is a creative, not an undertaker...'

On it goes – some blame, some say be patient – all are feeble with the cold, the heat.

*

'There's always people scanning the publicity,' says Heinz. 'Ready for anything, experiments and such. It's not about the climate – it's adventure, seeking something new. A buck or two.... I'll take some snaps – you guys, you suffered and you didn't, any of you, adapt at all. Some laid down to die, others complained. Is that the best that evolution does?'

Heinz is a genius, for sure. If anyone should ask – the cameras, all that stuff, they just got lost – no casualties, but a drama, certainly, and – he's made no friends.

'And now, Khalil, Zenobia, you understand the kind of movie I'm prepared to make,' says Heinz. 'How did it seem to you, the experience, the white field? The snow – nothing arty about it; no black snow...' and he laughs. 'Challenge? Joke? Spectacle? Or stunt? You didn't aspire to any of those – I was the creator, and I enjoyed the scene. You must admit – you were completely at a loss. How far, how deep? – that was just the start. You weren't adapted, not evolved. What have we done? I bet that's what you asked. A punishment – that maybe ends real bad. I didn't need to, but of course, I didn't send the buses, not until you'd all lost hope, or failed to find a sense, way in, way out. I knew, of coure, what there was to know. Someone will write it up and speculate. Millions will fantasticate. The simplicity – it's lost when you hypothesise, of course.'

'Bad taste,' Zenobia says, rubbing at her frozen front.

'Exactly so!' says Heinz.

'Pointless, except as an endurance trial,' Khalil says. 'You might have bombed us first.... Made it political....'

'That's not a fresh discovery,' Heinz says. 'It's always how you manage. Existence: you expect the suffering, and in the end it all falls down or disappears. Theatre – it's curtains, then there's nothing left at all. Film – persists, but fades and lurks. In those pizza cans – it sleeps. They're minor arts – like books that make no sound and stand in silence for a generation, go uncomplaining to the tip. No, the major arts – jewellery, ceramics, bells – they tinkle, sparkle; when you're dead they tell the tale, having tolled your life away.... Those jewels proclaim you as a rich guy or a flashy thief, plates hold your food, humble scraps or humble pies ... the rest is passive. The statues and the victory arch, the art they say's the top we leave for humanities to come. Pictures – like an umlaut or a tilda, an eyebrow or a smirk, strung up between the floor and ceiling: music that rumbles on like carpeting, as you walk shopping round the stores. But, Khalil – that snow: it isn't art. And nor are you! My show: it doesn't calculate, it seeks to signify a something else, a something without shape or recipe. At last, I told myself, some guys dumped clueless in the snow, no claim to be performers, artists, agents or subjects – no communication ... a chance, instead, to find the spiritual, the mysterious, that isn't life, and isn't art. And feel instead – it's cold, cold, colder – until some benefactor sends the bus.

'And did you realise, you were in what isn't anything you've seen or want to see – a future disconnected from the past. The familiar, turned upside down. Shaken – what a flaky swirl! Snow

– now you see it, now you shovel – then a flame! Call those obedient three dogs. Always ready for a frolic – they'll bring some warmth, a breath – a zephyr, *libeccio, fœhn* – and ... the snow's all gone! And back it comes! Original and unrepeatable, unstoppable and meaningless!'

'It's quite ridiculous,' Zenobia says. 'Unless you really want us as the stars. Back to the movie, Heinz! We have survived. We need the work.'

'You need the pay, I think you mean,' says Heinz. 'I want to show you: don't expect you're capable of handling a situation. You're not. Maybe I'm not too – but, I set the scenes!'

*

'We must sign on,' Zenobia says: 'The office. They are always there.'

'We need to cover you?' Fenella asks. 'With scrip? You're the stars? – shooting? Falling? Snow becomes ice, I know, it sticks around, like you exactly. I must make up a story for you, you're illegal here, and while you wait for Heinz – whoops! you're in the glacier like two cod. How slowly now your lives pass by. How those eyes show they resent it – the snow – or is it salt? If already you're not dead, prepare to die. Death is serious – that's your Noh. Kabuki makes it simple, explains it all. "Actors pretending to be animals". That's the picture. We putrefy: but animals – pinned on doors, or hung on racks – they're clean and irreproachable. We – we leave slurry. They dry waving in the air – we need a box to hold our fluids, keep them from the earth.'

'Yes,' says Khalil, trying to ignore her. 'We're the actor types. Let us in your world – we have no documents, make us your citizens.'

'Oh,' Fenella says and laughs, 'not a world. A colony. You escaped the shooting back home, Khalil, now you'll wait for more!' And she laughs and laughs. The joke – untranslatable – a chance; taken on the fly.

They wait. It's miserable – actors, animals, it is much the same: the cage.

'Zenobia likes the waiting,' says Khalil. 'She's not satisfied with what she's been – time given free while you wait gives her a chance to be something better. Less sceptical. Sceptical about other people, that is. Me – hanging around drains me out, whitens me. I get my muscles back, but my soul's slipped off and that too is hung up somewhere. If you see it....'

'Oh,' Fenella says, 'for me it's all what you call waiting, what I call work. There's no drama. I guess being fired would be, and then – more work, with luck, more nothing in particular. Weeks and years.'

'Being a couple with Khalil,' Zenobia says, 'means I've always something I can watch – but it's a wager. Racing without a prize or finish-line. Like the three-legged race – one stumbles, both go down, still tied together.'

*

'You've trickled out, Khalil,' Zenobia says. 'When you're empty, you can re-inflate, become a doodle-sack. Like a cartoon bag of SWAG: badly drawn, forged notes – but copious. I wonder who'll be playing you. Strange music – those Jordanian bagpipers.... The quarter tones, that don't make you think of home. Where shall we end up, Khalil? With us two, there is no ageing, no maturing...

'You're not militant nor victim – what's left? What I am? Spying on people, on you, seeing what is normal and not wanting, not being able, to do it. A change of sex, perhaps....'

'Another one?' asks Khalil. 'It happens to us every day, and no one cares because they know we're extra-odd already. Foreign – it explains everything.'

*

'Oh no!' Fenella says, she's prepared what she will tell them, Zenobia, Khalil – it is her work. 'There's a condition, very fashionable – called "smalling". Heinz retreats, denser, talks less ... compressed. All deals are off. He'll blow up again, more japes – but.... Right now – no movie, and no promises. You won't see him. He won't come here, not ever. What did he promise you....?'

'No undertakings,' says Zenobia. 'Frostbite and inspiration. A critique – forward from art, and down with life as it's been lived.... For us, not much. A snowball fight, then hunger. We couldn't eat the penguins – salt and oil already in abundance, made them inedible....'

'Oh, I agree,' Fenella says. 'We must eat leaves and grass. There is a kit, they say, and our gut adapts....'

'We're there already,' Khalil says, 'with the diet. We're ready for the end of everything, but not for Heinz's smalling. For us – a disaster.'

Fenella smiles: it's good not having talent: – no one lets you down.

*

'I don't care,' says Zenobia, 'when something that doesn't exist, doesn't happen. Meanwhile – if we were at home, we'd have had lives mostly separate. That's good. Here – it's spur and trip, a brief gallop, then yanks on the reins to turn the head... It's said that's perfect. And it's ordinary....'

'Maybe so,' says Khalil, reluctant, not liking Zenobia much. 'If we're riding two horses – are they pulling something? Something big – a sleigh? A mail coach? A dray?'

'Oh, a hearse,' says Zenobia, impatient.

'Everybody here's the last of their tribe,' says Khalil, 'And we all want to go home to search for the rest of us. But home when I lived in it, it wasn't home. Nothing to feel nostalgia for – it's good. While I was there, I escaped all the time – but now – how can you escape a desert?'

*

A little failure – makes you forget the bigger ones, some past and some to come.

*

'You're clumsy, Khalil,' says Zenobia. 'People who have the same work all their lives – they are skilful. You gyre about, Khalil – it's your fall-down. Try to work with Fab and Alex. They do debt collection – it's central to society, and states. Without collection – there's no lend. It's logical.'

'I expect you need to drink a lot,' says Khalil, quite forlorn. 'I guess this is the bottom that you have to start at...'

'I don't think they'd be so keen to have you climb,' she says. 'But – you're an imposing size. They'll test you out, I'm sure, to see you're suitable.'

They're polyglot, Fab, Alex.

'Here,' says Fab. 'Get rid of this,' and there's a bloody packet.

'What is it? Was it?' asks Khalil, quite ingenuous.

'Oh, *filet mignolo*,' says Alex, and they laugh.

'What would be my job?' asks Khalil.

'Place it where it won't be found, and never be forgot,' says Alex.

'First, let's be clear,' says Khalil. 'Is this a joke, requiring a Bergsonian laugh? Or style – a language joke? Not transgression, not anomaly – and maybe it may make you laugh, but leave me cold, which rather knocks psychology and the social on the head....'

'Oh no!' says Fab. 'No knocking! We're in a spot in time where transgression's problematic. Disposing of the pieces – it's what geopolitics is all about. We expect everywhere will become similar – even make a picture, in the end. The question is – whose finger is it?'

'We know that.' Alex says. 'A friend, who was unfriended, then became a friend again, a little sacrifice – enforced, it's true, and so it enters as a ritual. A saying, *hapax legomenon*, perhaps...'

'Whose finger was it – is it – ?' Khalil says. 'Maybe that's the joke. Pass the parcel – if there is. A tidbit, a finger found, over and over, as God gives the touch – or one that writes, on the wall, or just stops ... unlikely, especially when it is the weakest of the bunch.... Maybe it's violins that come to mind – *le soupir long des violons* – the pain of severance, no devil's trill, farewell, farewell – a hero, warrior; when it's chopped, would limit her response, to, yes! – a sigh. A music amputated, though the sound persists, the faun amid the silent reeds, hear! o hark, o hear – the horns ... the call returns to nature.'

'No, no,' says Alex. 'Of course it is a language joke. The incantation, the summoning. You, Khalil, are the neophyte – this is your test, initiation, disguised, of course, a mystery for those who enter in the solemn world of cannibals and Yakuzi, and yes! anomaly. The *filet* that you mustn't eat. A fillet round your head, a circling of flies. Carrion – it's tabu, but how it tempts. A mystery. False pairing that reveals exactly what's occurred: a delicacy, a little finger, raised from the cup or glass ... but where's the rest??'

'The tea ceremony? The French might do that, not Italians,' Fab objects.

'I'm not quite sure,' says Khalil: 'I was prepared for crime – not honour, sacrifice, self-harm – and not ritual. My task – it is without depth. God – or Alex – proposes, man disposes. The cutting, though – goes too deep. Conclusive, irrevocable. It severs.'

'That is it,' says Alex, 'That's exactly so.'

*

'I didn't pass the interview, Zenobia,' Khalil says.

They laugh and laugh as he recounts, and jazzes up his puzzlement. 'Too complicated, too uncertain,' Khalil says.

'Work is like that,' says Zenobia. 'Perhaps redemption, punishment as well. All they asked was – a hiatus, a new paragraph. A change of scene. The body carried off – the action can resume. Cut – on to something else. As for anomaly – the secret services, they do that stuff: dismemberment. The bits are sundered, then pieced back – always a bit's not there. It can't be done in secrecy. Secrecy would lose the point, the edge.

'Where has crime gone? Evidence, induction – the criminals, the whitecoats, and the toga'ed – not just among us, they are us, we pay them, they keep us safe, they say. What you were asked, Khalil, was "put the waste into a bin". Food, crap, indifferently. Crap is food that's passed on to a higher state ... the thief's hand, the captive's ear, the frieze of skulls ... the parchment for the worthy dead....'

'I see where you are leading me, Zenobia,' says Khalil. 'I messed up, the job interview. And now – what if they finger me?'

They laugh some more. They have no cash, but much intelligence, too much. 'Was I too squeamish?' Khalil asks.

'No, Khalil, not at all – just too curious, and you didn't laugh,' she says.

*

'Do we suppose,' asks Khalil, 'that it was voluntary, the guy that lost the hand? Or...?'

'If it was honour – for consistency. If your convictions lead to where you lose a limb, a life, from principle – then it is voluntary,'

Zenobia says. 'If you've convictions, all your destiny is voluntary.'

'Too honest, and too abstruse for me,' says Khalil.

'Too witty,' says Zenobia. 'You don't appreciate baroque.'

'I study hands, to see who's missing,' Khalil says. 'No one would put those flappy things on robots – it's poets who find them acceptable.'

'Maybe you're looking at the wrong part, Khalil,' Zenobia says. 'Fingers aren't filletted. Language takes you on a slide, suggests that anything is possible. It's worse than jokes and wordplay. Speech is just a bouncy crust.

'The bloody deed? Look elsewhere: look for what deposits an impression, not a print. Think reproduction, iteration, repetition. Fab and Alex – I met them in a club – those could even be false nicknames.'

Khalil is nonplussed – jobless, is how we're born and end; but say that language is elastic, a suspension bridge ... a bouncy castle: ... a chasm opens....

'If you don't pay for women,' says Zenobia, 'the punishment is fierce. Friendship, all that, the meanders and the spats – when you jump in, trust other people – you never know what's the expense, how you're exposed. I mean sex, Khalil.'

'Maybe I'm not right for crime,' says Khalil, quite appalled, 'I can be bad without that kind of risk, I'm sure.'

'You've borrowed that from Heinz,' Zenobia says. 'He runs through good and bad like through a field of flowers, and in the end his shoes are clean – but full of dust. I take our money where I can – it's you who's called to tidy up....'

'I'm indifferent to what flesh does,' says Khalil, flexing a muscle big as a parcel of sausages, 'So long as there's no suffering.'

'Then crime and riches are both out for you,' says Zenobia, climbing on to classy shoes, ready to go out. 'Intended and unintended – I don't think intention impresses you....'

'Oh, it comes in,' says Khalil, 'but slippery as worms on a fishing pole.'

'We're well inserted in the world,' Zenobia says, at the door. 'It isn't good. We've lost our space. Our homes – knocked down: – to compensate, you have to swell your life. But – Khalil, you've no attraction. And – I'm in debt. Worse – my debts aren't all in cash.

'Try to deflate, Khalil. Heinz can cast you different – maybe as a crack, a rift, a rent ... a slender sort, who knows the everything, but doesn't move or speak. Then – coup de scène – resolves it all!'

They don't believe in Heinz. Neither does. He, though, believes in himself, his plans.

*

'Think how much time you have to work so's you can eat – you and me,' Zenobia says.

'I'm learning that,' says Khalil. 'Home is gone for ever: what am I walking on? Fresh air? It's good that there aren't small revelations. They're enormous, revelations are. I'm waiting for them – not false prophets like poor Heinz....'

*

'Zenobia's in the entertaining biz,' Khalil tells his friend Bahadir. 'No cash comes home, of course, you spend it all on you, your friends and so, and so, but – you're always reappearing, bigger, more powerful. New routines. And if you don't, you're gone, gone indeed, for always. It's perfect.'

'Forget her,' shouts Bahadir. 'You'll never touch her, even if you want. Be adventurous. Join me! I've just come back – adventurers, explorers, athletes: everybody says it's useful, or a joy to watch.... It isn't so. Adventure's always for yourself. And you must be savage at it – it's not the specie's march to progress – it is regression pure. Eating your sleigh dogs – that is just the start.

'In Cayenne, there's Montagne d'Or. In the past, to get there, you had to do an awful crime – now that's past – you must do the crime when you arrive. There's opportunity – you've guides, there are extended families – they don't count numbers, or ask who's poking for some edibles, down in the jungle. There's tons of gold, there was this person, she was called Richgal ... knew all about the snakes, the creeping things, the sex....' and he describes her feats while Khalil dozes....

'And did you get the gold?' asks Khalil, waking, 'And the girl? Get her? How did you speak...?'

'Oh, Portuguese is just old Arabic,' says Bahadir. 'Not being Arab, I just speak it bad – they understand. Cayenne. You're taken as a worker, you're enslaved – so, you must escape and write the book.

'Of course – you have no honorific, but you get a uniform when you join the Académie; medals too....'

'How much gold?' Khalil persists.

'Aha!' says Bahadir, 'I see you've given up theology and on wanting to be straight. People you meet, they're all criminals or lovers: in Paris, you have to legislate on how to speak the language, otherwise, you're left alone. Then off you go again....'

'I'm not quite sure it's me,' says Khalil, not knowing what he is. 'But if you got a bucketful of wealth.... I'd trade the principles we all must have and no one's seen....'

*

'What should I take?' Khalil asks. 'Nothing,' Bahadir says. 'Except gold and diamonds.'

'Who do I tell?' Khalil asks. 'Zenobia clubs. Knowing's indifferent. There's Fenella...?'

'Come!' says Bahadir. 'Without a mystery, no one will know you've gone. You have to leave the state: evil. Work – someone organises it all, so even more evil. The people? – they've gone under, work and state's on top – all that's left for them is pull your tail, poker-out your eyes.'

'Of course it's so,' says Khalil, as they leave, and he slides the key back under the door. 'We've lived it. It won't change. Who's to change it?'

They scutter down the stairs in three-two time.

'I forgot my boots....' says Khalil.

'Oh, we shan't go far,' says Bahadir. 'It's all come here – palmtrees and beaches by the river, snowstorms, sandstorms. Black suns. It multiplies. Enjoy the suffering, or it hurts. This will be the empty quarter – and we should leave a record. Big cities like this – they're going underfoot and all around.'

'Down into the underground, then the sewage, those canals – fine work, no one can spin like that,' Khalil says dreamily. 'Those tunnels ... a few hungry days – as if we're bombarded.'

Bahadir laughs. 'Whatever is doing it, they don't have planes. They're all ours, or friendly – how long can they buzz around? They're old hats, skimmed: the satellites – those are the all-seeing eyes of God. Maybe they weep – there's not much else they can do.'

'This is Kitezh, Bahadir,' Khalil says, radiant. 'They do everything for us, the wise men from the East....'

There's a parade of camels trotting by.

'Oh yes,' says Bahadir. 'We're used to following rules, and here – we can be set to work. The camels – here, they're reborn. This is the new home. See how they laugh! Their milk's the new delicacy – maybe they'll be trained to pulling loads....'

'We could begin to set our wisdom to making what? – hypotheses? resolutions, answers, ways forward, back or on the side...?' Khalil asks.

'Your question's right,' says Bahadir, striding on. 'These answers ... philosophy – it always rests on going on, a future. At least – a present that holds still, stays in the frame. Hmmmm. Consider well, Khalil. Don't waste your little time; and avoid the quaint! Going back? I don't advise. It's entertainment that is left.... Outpace the modern, the contemporary, my dear friend – kick dust in its face....'

'But, Bahadir, what we are,' says Khalil, panting after him, 'is not a bit an entertainment. Not childish wonder, like the painters seek. We've not a scrap of that.'

'Then silence! Wait and see,' says Bahadir. 'Enjoy being loose. People here, people anywhere – they don't care you've been bourgeois. Your rise and fall – it's monotonous, trivial as the sea. Only you could enjoy it once – if enjoyable it was. When you stop being bourgeois – you don't just slide on to another class. It's not a football ladder: – lose a division – here's another waiting, with its fans. If you can be a peacock, you can have fans, spread widely in the world, wide like your tail.... But you're not at all like them. You turn your back, and make your rose. It's not like being respectable. Having a niche.'

He says it 'having an itch'.

'I'm not like you, Bahadir, I don't have an act,' Khalil says. 'I just read the books.'

'Work on it, Khalil,' says Bahadir, ogling some people sat drinking *kir*.

*

'Whether it's done, whether we do it or we don't – we must not come to judgment. Only you yourself can judge,' says Bahadir.

'What would they say?' Khalil asks. 'If they said anything? Those who comment on what you want to show.'

'There's too much substance,' says Bahadir. 'It dissolves, like every substance, and becomes some disconnected things –

metaphor and allegory. “A smell of empty rooms.” Forget it. If you don’t *do*, you’re a victim. What profit is in that? Remember the line, “our heart alone knows what we are” – forget that too. It never stopped anyone doing anything.’

‘I don’t grasp...’ Khalil says, ‘what we’ve done and what we’ve to do.’

‘Oh Khalil,’ says Bahadir. ‘What we do doesn’t belong to us.’

‘Maybe ... there’s Zenobia...’ Khalil says.

‘Now,’ says Bahadir, ‘there’s something more you could forget. You hesitate because you think she’ll give you suffering. No – she gives you nothing: – it’s all you, you suffer, taking on the suffering of women everywhere. It’s punishment, Khalil, we’ll find enough of that, without we take it with us.’

‘There is no answer, then,’ Khalil says, thinking this is revelation. ‘There’s no answer, not to anything. Or – there’s too many answers – all Muslims are Jews, the Jews are wrong about the only God....’

‘That’s right,’ says Bahadir. ‘Worship the tree, take care when there’s high winds, and thank it when you chop it down.’

‘Fenella?’ Khalil says. ‘I took a shine....’

‘No!’ shouts Bahadir. ‘She’s a slave. Did you strike off her chains? Join her march, prepare for crucifixion with the rest? No. Of course not. Leave her be, forget salvation. You’ve missed yours – let each seek their own....’

‘But – I’m an actor,’ Khalil says.

‘Then pay your union dues, or skip them, like we do,’ says Bahadir. ‘Really – to get you on the road – you are a Hudson tourer – the springs are gone, the muffler works too well: you make no reasonable human sound. Let’s off! The road! But first – some drinks.’

*

'What one must do,' says Bahadir, making a face at their recurring brandies, and engulfing them – 'is to avoid circumstance. Wars, terror, austerity – what they call history. Someone's policy – not yours, and if it were, you'd at once reverse it. Don't say what you are – never; write on no form. Leave that space: – settled on a religion, or on going it alone? – don't ever say! Money earned? Spend it. It has never been. Have no place, origin or destination. No nationality. There's nothing ever to be proud of, and in any case – you did not contribute....'

'Most people say that, and it doesn't work,' says Khalil. 'Discretion. You show up on the screen, you're a red dot, hooded, scampering. It's a giveaway.'

'Well, do your best,' says Bahadir. 'Circumstance – history. Don't climb that step.'

'You – we – must lose,' says Khalil.

'Yes,' says Bahadir, joshing the bar's owner. They don't pay... 'Of course,' he says. 'But losing doesn't count. We're heroes. Epic heroes. Rama got lucky. Mostly, we don't.'

*

'There's this guy,' says Bahadir. 'He'll be instructive. A warrior: had six tanks killed under him like horses. He put on the last stand: the last charge of cavalry, or of battling starships, fighting suspended outside a moon of Jupiter. He never had an enemy – that's what they say. He fought for justice. It wasn't on his mind, though, not much, not often. Anyway, the guys he fought against are on his side today.... And the justice? Well... If you're a soldier, you accept all that, like you're an idiot. Well, that's what you were. What's new is all the memories, your people turned to dusty leaves, hung like a parure on you – like dried apricots, like ears....'

'And he instructs us?' Khalil asks, appalled.

'No, no,' says Bahadir. 'His experience. Is instructive. He's a bore.'

'I know about order, where it went, and how they try to get it back,' says Khalil: 'Don't educate me in all that. Order – it's an animal, into extinction, you preserve the last one, if you succeed, you never see it...'

'We're like soldiers, Khalil,' says Bahadir. 'Without arms and officers, and without a war. They can send us away, the deportation – or rather, they can send you off, Khalil, to anywhere. I'm wily – I see next moves. There is this crash, always coming – the rich ones lose their money, make more poor, and get their fortunes back again. There's resentment, and it turns against you, Khalil. Wide-eyes, like you. Not me – I'm off, running anyway.'

'You've been everywhere, even twice....' says Khalil.

'Oh, I'm not looking for anything,' Bahadir says.

'I asked the good shepherd,' says Khalil, "What are you for?" He said, "Don't worry – the good is good for you." "Where will your sheep end?" I asked. "Not your worry," the shepherd said....'

They sit and wait: the clock stops. 'The pendulum,' says Bahadir. 'Those clocks are never on a level plane – you have to jiggle, lift the edge....' He fiddles for a while, the clock ticks once and stops. Time goes on, it seems.

'Of course,' says Bahadir, taking his seat again, 'we're glad to win some fights. Is it worth waiting? Well, there's those battles, the pictures and the panorama: – the horses entered in the spirit, see the spirits going where they have to go. But now – you can explode your enemy – blow up their economy; bulling your boots is out. There's misery, and saviours sought. It all goes on and on – it's punishment until you sell them stuff again, the rich bring out their gold, you're in the race, it's peace and Adam Smith....'

'This guy we're waiting for?' Khalil asks. 'He sounds like Heinz, though with a sabre by his side.... A voice, no body, maybe a tomb that talks.... A theory, of how he knows everything: "sign up", he'll cut you in...'

'I told you, Khalil,' says his friend. 'It's instruction. If he won't come, we shouldn't wait. It's not our thing. Besides, we know it all. Deployments, millions spent and millions given boots and staves ... an army of some thousands wandering in a marsh, sucked down, every one, those felt boots saturate ... a sandstorm ... all disappeared ... lead poisoning ... those cans of bully beef..... It isn't where we two should end.

'I'll give some precepts. Avoid an interest, refuse a cause. Don't plant perennials, don't cut down trees – you're not the kind that publishes or wraps things up – choose shade, not paper serviettes....'

He rambles on, and then they leave. No interview – the general, the dog of war – he doesn't show.

Of course, we need a hero, bad guys must be taught ... it's not a job Khalil or Bahadir can do. On it goes.... Khalil has a cause, he's born to it.

It's a pile of rocks.

*

The heroes die – infected saddle sores.... Not a clean end.... Bahadir does not intend ... nor does Khalil … an exit so uncouth....

*

'We're in your head, Khalil,' says Bahadir. 'We're balloony – cloudy images, disputing, scrumming. We're well lodged in, my friend, you'll not be rid of us. I've nearly pushed Zenobia out from centre-stage. You'd be best off with Fenella – but she has a job, an office she can't leave, that telephone... What is she, really? You have no idea.

'Heinz – you waited, and he didn't come. Most people don't. I'm here, in all my flesh.

'You're dangerous – you think, and so you could do anything. Usually, you won't. Nothing. That's your likely accomplishment: it's very good. We're better so.'

'I'm not following,' says Khalil, running after Bahadir.

'Have your thought, Khalil,' Bahadir explains: 'Like I do. Freedom, justice, emancipation of our brothers and our sisters. It won't come, and besides, you don't have the heft, you can't secure it. Something else, some other content – must be your life. Understand that – or else ... catastrophe.'

'Perhaps catastrophe....' Khalil says. 'Zenobia – there, yes, you might see its start. She's a fine wine, that takes your patrimony, you hide it in the roof, and then – one evening, open it. It's vinegar. Perhaps it always was. As for Fenella – better some death-defying mates, a group of cuirassiers, republican guards, or first-hour Bolsheviks ... there's comradeship, dossing together, hands by your side....'

'The trouble is,' says Bahadir, 'you're so naive. Your straight neighbours – they live on the edge, with risk and debt, and trading body parts. They sniff and smoke, hardly a one has not been seasoned on death row; they've fled and come to live next door by sneaking down the sewers, bribing a judge.... Everyone you see, a-strolling in the street is, to employ a kind of metaphor, also on the rock, Tarpeian, ready to cast themselves down into the pit, or flap some home-made oilcloth wings and hope to soar....

'You, Khalil, have seen your companions gassed and bombed, have lived in tents and on the sand ... your dwelling pulverised, your cat sucked down a hole ... an existence hard but normal: dictated by the rules of politics and natural laws. You, Khalil, are an everyman. *Echt* normal. The rest of them are freaks.'

'That's the movie, Bahadir,' says Khalil. 'Don't leave me in its mist.'

'Everybody loves a show,' says Bahadir. 'It's comedy and tragedy too, domestic and exotic.... If you try to be consistent – they won't bear with it. Thirty years in jail and then your head's cut off.... Who'd pay to see that? No uplift, no mechanicals. What's different too is – everybody writes her own particular script, and slots the lines in when there is a pause.'

'No,' Khalil says. 'No Heinz! I'll come with you, Bahadir, only if it's for real, no show, no metaphor.'

'That's what I said,' says Bahadir.

*

'This is the beginning,' says Bahadir. 'This is where the emporium starts.'

It's a dusty yard. There's – pipes? Not that you play, or join together. Not for air or water. What's left...?

'They're mufflers,' says Bahadir. 'Exhausts. Every shape there's ever been. We start from here. One day, there'll be everything. The gas – exhausted: it's leaves and animals right from the start, all mulched.'

'No one will buy,' Khalil starts off.

'Oh, buy and sell,' laughs Bahadir. 'I hadn't thought. It's true we'll need someone to keep the books.... Though,' and he laughs more. 'Books will be obsolete like mufflers. I thought of Zenobia ... she can do numbers, knows they come out bad in the end....'

'There's Fenella,' Khalil says. 'She's a Tokay. Zenobia – is Bull's Blood. Too strong for what I have in mind....'

'You think you know what that is?' asks Bahadir, surprised. 'For me, it's not creating, not making anything this time, just gathering. I'll have it. Everything. All here, here in this yard.'

'All knowledge,' Khalil says. 'Yes, it's like they all begin. The watchmaker – wants a monopoly of time. The guy who starts a brasserie – wants every taste, and every fire – the spit, the charring and the cures, the salt, the chimney and the oils ... and then to mute and blur it, every scumble, chiaroscuro, a scrubbing of the senses, into the steam, the alpine fogs, the dust-storms. Every butcher – all dismembered on his slabs. All of us – all's exposed, no secrets hold. The hatters – who circumnavigate all rounds of head and every class, lives in his cosmicity – the dust, *his* dust, that drives him cracked and bleary, like the nappers...then, the chromers, tinners ... each wants the mastery of their trade, their substance, place in the universe's macedonia: and every time it maddens them, or it destroys – the butcher lays his hand, his head upon the block – and that is it....'

'Exactly so, he knows!' says Bahadir. 'Each knows – the limit, the futility, the partial. That's why we want everything. Not knowledge. That's where the madness lies.... Worse than insanity – is obsolescence, Khalil. What you, or anyone knows – is temporary. You know, and everything will change, so's you won't know a thing. Knowledge – comes from things. Things as they are, not as they were or will be. Stuff, Khalil. That's what we collect. We'll travel everywhere to find ... the concrete, the material. Suppose you stay at home and read – expect pure knowledge to pour out from the cold ink, poor tree; its bark, its pulp, the mulberry, the reed, the clay, the slate. It isn't so. If it is so – it mustn't be. Use and fortune, Khalil. That's what we'll have. Nothing that does not exist – no gods, no frontiers, no just cause or evil one, no theory of race or sex, no finalities, no journeys and no ruminations. Only sheep and goats will ruminate, Khalil, and they won't tell. Eschew what you can't collect and store....'

'It sounds, well, a little pure,' says Khalil, unconvinced. Though, maybe, Fenella ... her empty face ... he thinks. 'A little barebones? Accumulation as the end? Medieval book-keeping – those alchemists ... even positivism...?' and he shudders.

'Ah,' says Bahadir, in a huff. 'If you've better to do? If you prefer – die for your religion, for a treaty, for the price of shrimps ... Die for the king, the queen, the president ... for history's tramp, the coronation of the pawn.... No, I shan't store those...'

'Yours is a life's mission,' says Khalil. 'But – in the end ... we come back to ends, ours, everything's – what do we gain, what is it for....?'

'Oh,' says Bahadir, 'apart from the fun: it's use, and satisfaction. You need this stuff, collecting it's a trek – magnificent! Those mufflers....'

'Yes,' says Khalil. 'Crooks and queries. The Pontiacs with back and front divans ... the Dodges – sky ships that cruised among the clouds.... We'll set them running....'

*

'It's "everything" that seems a touch too grandiose,' Khalil says.

'"Everything" is not the same as "all of everything",' says Bahadir: '"All" is limitless, although it seems to have no end. 'Everything's selective. It's the mufflers – I love old cars, or rather, I'm indifferent, absolutely, to them. I don't care for them – let them all rust out. That's certitude, it's finitude. I love the guys who have them, as they're guys who don't like driving. If you drive old motors, you soon find that bits fall off or seize. Best be abstemious. Have some birds nest in your trunk....'

'They're mostly males,' Khalil objects. 'The greasy guys….'

'Well, Khalil,' says Bahadir, 'there's Zenobia and Fenella keeping our tab. As for gender – easy, Khalil! Let nature run. Besides, we're booked into Bolivia for hats.'

'It's starting to seem, Bahadir,' says Khalil, 'a tiny bit – random. Passing the time. Eclectic.'

'Exactly. You are right, Khalil. Those are the benefits. For disadvantages of what remains for you – remember, you're still on the run,' says Bahadir. 'A prisoner of my whim.

'Now – there's grasses on Sakhalin. Beautiful – I must have stands of those. We'll ride, of course – some truckers like fun company. They all remember the big movie – *Waterloo Bridge*. Veronica Lake. Remembrance will take us there.'

*

'No history, Khalil,' says Bahadir. 'The war is over for these guys. The revolution – just sea spray. Don't speculate. With all this grass – so hard to parcel up! We'll take the *paquebot* to Canton, and then to *Indo-Chine*. War is history, my friend, and history is war. You'll object, of course – it's seeds and prophylactics to you. Relax! Our wars too, they'll end, we'll plant the grass and stop the desert stumbling over us – next it's gold weights from Accra.....'

'I love the travel, Bahadir,' says Khalil. 'And meeting people and not knowing them, and on again, no animals, no history, no speculation about where the water goes when it has gone... *Waterloo Most* – we all remember what we haven't seen: but, it's an escape....'

'I know, Khalil,' says Bahadir. 'Adventure fascinates but, you think, there's something more. You want to save a mammal, or a crawling thing. – be useful or be prescient. It will not do. Those limits – they don't satisfy...'

'Explain some more,' says Khalil. 'Use the future and the past....'

But Bahadir, he keeps schtum.

On the road, they sell a lot of surplus stuff. Other collectors, they will buy, though not on Bahadir's scale.

*

'The women?' Khalil asks, and Bahadir's amused.

'You thought,' he says, '– fixing the books? At home? In fairy tales they stay behind. The oldest fantasy – of little boys. They were never there, not Fenella, not Zenobia – not in our plan, not in our minds. If you want – you must chase after them, and then – what? What do you want, expect, Khalil? What can they find in you? It's over, all that stuff, and it is good it's ended so. We start again.... We hope there's time....'

Grass, mufflers, little bowler hats: it is a start, an enterprise.

'So tired, Khalil,' says Bahadir. 'I've had my time, my epic's nearly done....'

'It seems a little scant,' says Khalil, worried that Bahadir.... might leave the scene, quite inconclusively ... the plan forever undisclosed....

'Leave me, Khalil,' says Bahadir, closing his eyes and reclining on some pipes. 'My organs ... let's pretend these mufflers will connect and send me requiem – a *rombo*, the motors roaring, ripping out exhausts, but – my eyes are open, nothing moves. Up through the sky? The race – suspended? Power without movement. Ah, our planet – always moves and is forever blocked into its orbit. A lesson there, Khalil. A race? Ascension? Simply tripping into mould, the fall, the leaves, Khalil – does my colour change? – my sugars, proteins turning into pale pale river gold....'

Bahdir – expires ... he rests ... he sleeps ... he readies for the spring ... he orbits. Round and round.

*

'I'm between gigs, Zenobia,' Khalil says. 'Let me speak.'

'What is it, Khali?' she asks, impatiently. 'I see amassing everything has lost its pull for you. What do you want – repetition? Is that your goal? Being with someone quite predictable who does the actions everlasting, like the budgie picking cards, the monkey – faithful to its string and nuts?'

'It's true, Zenobia,' Khalil says. 'You adventurers ... you want no day resembling every day....'

'Oh, it's not that, Khalil,' she says. 'Multiplying, running offices – some like it busy busy with no end. I'm not for that, and what I must avoid is replication, dull, shut in. It's night resembling eternal dark. It is too late for that. Try Fenella. They say that love becomes a something else – a satisfaction. Try it! Fenella's emptied out. She'll give back whatever you put in. You could try a song, and have her hum. Accompaniment is what you seek? Then try a scene you recognise, the two of you. A bridge – those flowing symbols, small animals – the allegory. How trite! A movie, pulling out a tear from each, seated alone and side by side – the darkness ... softens you. To jelly. Familiarity: be content with that, Khalil.'

'No one could be content with that,' he says.

'Your problem, Khalil,' Zenobia says, taking off a set of clothes and wriggling into others – 'is you've no power. Most people have none, whatever they are told, but you have even less than most, and miss it more. I might seem to be like you – it isn't so. Mine's the power of Kali, and the Buddha too. I choose, and so I have my suitors, and it's like *Turandot* – it never finishes. I'm the mountain no one climbs. If I don't conclude – where I am, what I do and who with – I am the boss. You're a parasite, Khalil, waiting for a hairy leg to pass, that you can jump on.'

You don't get compliments, that's true, not from Zenobia, but she exalts you, in her way.

'Inside, Zenobia,' he says, 'I'm a nomad. I remember the Indians – they worked for the man three days, then quit, and drank. It's what I'd do. The union wouldn't take them. It would happen so to me. They loved the journeying – they lived for that – killing your totem isn't fun, but meeting other Indians – that's the tops. Always a welcome....'

'You never were a nomad, Khalil,' says Zenobia. 'Nomads live in cities now. They get drunk too, but there's no one like them there, no other Indians, the totems – cut up in butchers' shops.'

She's ready to go out – the city, 'These fucking shoes....' she says, and does an arpeggio down the stairs.

Here in the club, you can contribute: children, migrants (not nomads). Even adopt some, and give to mosques and churches. Zenobia is a good soul, and helps her people.

'Snifter or snort?' asks the barman, Ashok.

'My dates will pay,' Zenobia says. 'But I'm not at home to them. There's to sort out, with my Ben.'

Ashok shakes the collecting box at her, in play. 'No Indians left,' he says. 'It's cowboys and first peoples. In my case – Mughals and natives. Ensigns and indigenes.'

'Oh, I'd give to animals,' says Zenobia. 'But what'd they spend it on?'

'Everybody needs cash,' says Ashok. 'Stop the war, buy arms.'

'You're ignorant, my dear,' Zenobia says. 'Trite and reactionary. Like all of us here.'

'If that's you done, Zenobia, I'll start the beat,' says Ashok, heaving on the music, heavy as a protective vest.

*

'There's some guys I want you to see, Zenobia,' says Ben. 'Some guys I want to see you. And some guys I don't want to see again.'

'Oh, I'm the glue, the sweetly sticky –' says Zenobia. 'I'm the queen bee. I'll sort them out, your guys.... Sugar for some, sweet and sour the rest.'

'You're the dresser,' says Ben, not laughing, not at all. 'You put the clothes on the queen – she is a code. I don't need speak – my colours tell you what I feel.'

'You're sure, Ben?' Zenobia asks. 'If you're the queen – the king, then what....?'

'Is impotent. Anxieties of state,' Ben says. 'He stumbles, peg-legged – the queen roams everywhere, every passage on the board, and every square. She has no sex. She's every sex. She does exactly what she wants, Zenobia. She's black and white, partisan, guerilla, on every side, her children reproduce in unisex....'

'I didn't know you played,' Zenobia says.

'Who'd play?' Ben asks. 'A queen is always on the winning side.'

*

Ben has a philosophy – not difficult, but you have to follow closely. He puts forth an image, not a metaphor – he has no interest in varnishing himself, nor in having you pressing on his heel. If he wrote his manifesto – a warning against the monsters like he is –

Most things, you can't afford. Good ideas cost more than bad ideas, but bad ideas – they can cost much more than good ideas. Than any ideas. In the beginning, you need cash. Then you go ahead, sometimes you have the cash, sometimes you don't. Sometimes there's really cash, sometimes not. You have to get results, quick, to keep the world happy, sprightly, so you need money to get a document, an inspector. Those to do and those to fix what the first ones haven't done. Something is rushed through to make something you can't wait to see, and sometimes people quarrel, withdraw, or need their cash for something else. Sometimes they tell you, sometimes not – it makes no difference. And you need pros – who know the law, lie of the land, who's in the way, all that. You know this anyway, saw it in every *polar*, every *noir* – and usually it goes all right, nothing happens you don't want, can't fix, but if you're ready for the nasty turn, it often doesn't happen either.

Ben's philosophy – you might call it vitalism, but that's been done. Lions and foxes – they come in, but they are not philosophy. Usually, things happen as you wish, if you wish enough to make it so.

You have to make it so, because that's what you do, and no one should be allowed to do it for you.

Free will, getting things done, not making messes ... modern centuries went to where they ended up, believing, practising, the philosophy. It doesn't always work.

It's in liberalism, communitarianism, anarchism, fascism – those all have people doing what Ben does. The alternative used to be the church, then it was the state that did it all. Tried to do everything. That didn't satisfy.

*

'My skin, Ben,' says Zenobia. 'It's rotting. Falling off – sheets the size of edicts.'

'See to it, then,' says Ben.

'There's nothing to be done,' she says. 'It's all my doing. My undoing. And to do something ... it must be up to me alone. I alter people's lives, Ben, and never regret it. I'm reluctant to think they alter mine. I keep your skiff afloat – the sea, Ben, it's quite indifferent.'

'I'm not following you, Zenobia, not into all that,' says Ben.

'I miss the grasslands, Ben,' Zenobia says. 'The mountains and the taiga. The desert too – that would cure my back, a suit of leather, new, uncured.'

*

'I'm restless,' Zenobia thinks. 'I could face down an empire. But there's Khalil – so restless, it makes me angry. My world wobbles – it can't take two, thrashing and waving arm and leg to seek a balance.'

*

'There's terrible people,' Ben tells Ashok. 'They have big hit squads – they cream you, when they're told. Make you disappear, or have your motor banged into scrap while you are cruising on the corniche – and for what? They're told: – it's enough, that's what you do. You do it because of what some guy – what he said. Not said to you, or anyone you care about, but to some big cheese who owns you and your connections. These states, Ashok, they are beyond reason, beyond common sense and decency. Their shadow – comes into my room, it lies across my bed, it tries to fuck me, then it seems – it is a sword, it wants to slice me, slow and easy. What can you do?'

'Keep the curtains closed,' says Ashok, who doesn't care at all.

'And that's what you would face, Zenobia?' Ben says. 'Leave or stay, chatter or schtum? The squad comes in, organised, backed by the cops, ambassadors and TV stars.... Deal death, ace of spades, for what guys think, then what they say, and want to do. Five murderers tooled up, they take a plane, and taxis too. Maybe buy perfume for somebody they want, back home. It never ends. It's death, Zenobia, climbed down from his horse, coming up the street, dividing into grape-shot, into black beetles, into every room and under every bed and credence, emptying oatmeal on the floor, crapping in it ... shooting out your eyes.'

'Keep away, Ben,' says Zenobia. 'Ignore them' – calm and terrified.

'I'm not the squeamish sort,' says Ben. 'But those guys – there's no passion, nothing you would call an interest. Taking people out, is what they do, methodical; every guy who has a thought. This side, then that, pinch and punch. It's always been, but now – it's a profession.'

'Just more, everywhere,' Ashok agrees. 'Trained guys. Quarrels you'd not understand.'

'There always were more, everywhere, and quarrels you understood quite well,' Zenobia says. 'The answer is – do what they do where you are. Don't believe anyone. Jail or slavery – the same. When you're caught, remember – if you get away, you can write your story.'

'There's too many writers, Zenobia,' Ashok says. 'I keep a paper for myself to read, behind the bar. I don't want clients suffering, besides, they're maybe not in that mood, not for empathy, not that day....'

*

'I've done what I've been doing, Khalil,' says Zenobia. 'Now, I want something else. Even company, while we look for a new place. Inside or outside ourselves, Khalil?'

'You won't believe, Zenobia,' Khalil says: 'I've reached a conclusion. The more power a person has, the less they think about their principles and other people. And so – after a while, and if you've been handing out a punishment, or settling scores – other people, other principles – they topple you.'

'You could take opponents' skins,' Zenobia says, unimpressed, 'And pin them on the barn.'

'What's in the barn?' Khalil asks. 'If it's empty, it'll seem those skins are an excuse. If it's full – they seem unnecessary.'

'Mortality,' Zenobia says. 'That's God's answer to oppression. You or the oppressor dies – the question is resolved. Once you've invented time – all flesh rots, like mine. Skin withers off your boughs. What can you do – put it in store? Write on it?'

'Yes,' Khalil says. 'I slough mine, then I write on it. It's edible too, of course. Like antlers.'

*

'Ben's stressed,' says Zenobia, 'so, luckily, he doesn't think of sex. Look! – he took me for a ride, braked – and all my teeth, they've finished on his dash.'

She shows what isn't there.... 'All pearls and tiny tusks – like dragons' teeth,' she says.

'You'll need to cover up your face,' says Khalil. 'Avoid the consonants. Do as they do? The people? That's what you said: settle in, accommodate. Be part. But – which people? Here, they make, they send, the bombs that drop on people much like us...'

'Us as we were,' Zenobia lisps. 'I told you, Khalil – don't use thoughts like that. It leads you to the dark.'

'Life and death, Zenobia,' Khalil says. 'We set up as the judge of everything – the animals, the clouds, the trees. No one but us has rights, we say. The judgment is continuous – we must kill those who oppress, exploit, and undermine – and in turn be killed by them....'

'A powerful fantasy, Khalil,' Zenobia says. 'And if it's true – how does anyone go back...? To what there maybe never was. The spirit, *totentanz* – has taken over, you dance to it, or you are swept aside. It's probably a lie – the rights of totem animals, was it juridical, a principle? Or just convenience, a common sense in using a resource....?'

'Oh,' Khalil says, 'I'm for untrue things. Almost everybody is – to them, I am *takfir*. Their falsities I do not share. *My* little lies are useful, the adagio of the world.'

'Too late, too late,' he thinks he hears Zenobia say. 'Those that have hurt us, or who may – we need to stop them first, before.... And – we never shall. Or – in the fighting, we all die....'

'I think it's Ben,' says Khalil. 'Your teeth. You'll never come with me to nowhere, the place, the lie – invisible....'

'Absolutely, Khalil,' says Zenobia. 'I will leave, even with you, but not to go to nowhere.'

'It was a car?' askss Khalil. 'You're sure? You've always talked too much.'

'Listen to what I say,' Zenobia says. 'Repeating is a bore.'

'That's what I think,' says Khalil. 'It's about history. Away with continuity, subjects and objects: it's what happens.

"Fourteen armies" – the French had that and see what happened to their revolution. Fourteen armies – more – invaded to oppose the Bolsheviks ... and then ... and then....'

'I see what you mean,' says Zenobia. 'Where we are and who we are, what we can do, and how it counts – yes, it's history. How we conceive of it. Not a stream, no continuity, not made to measure, but not an accident.

'It isn't about us, though,' she says. 'What to do next – both of us or each their own. What we accomplish, how we evaluate – but it can't just be what we think it is.... Though almost everybody, as they die, thinks that it is ... what's done's their history. And then: they aren't. We must go deeper in, Khalil.'

'Well,' says Khalil. 'What have we done, what will we do? You've lost your teeth, I – nearly my life.'

'We make our history,' Zenobia says. 'What's on the books. But there's discoveries, inventions. Sects and earthquakes.'

'Don't think so much about it, Zeno,' Khalil says. 'It's worth a try. Either make it, or ignore it. Think of it as tapestry, a scene exotic – animals scoffing their muesli and little devils chewing everybody's tail – someone imagined it, and now they've gone. The castle where it hangs – it's deserted – is it yours? I doubt it. Someone else's? Screw them – lie on the floor and watch the spiders, making arabesques high in the ceiling.'

'We could join one of those little bands, going east,' Zenobia says. 'A trickle, maybe one day a river. Against the tide.'

'No precedents, Zenobia,' Khalil says. 'Everything is new. Don't touch the past – look what happened to your back. Finite provinces of significance – don't let in the people you don't like.'

'True, Khalil,' Zenobia says. 'But a province must have others. Cops, tax farmers. Then there's abattoirs. Sleepers in doorways, popes and imams....'

'The invisible city of Kitezh,' says Khalil. 'That is the model. Think of that. Leave the door open, so's they won't kick it down in case we're dead.'

*

But, thinks Khalil, there's Zenobia, the stranger. Whatever happens – there she is, will be. I sat by the river; '*trinken, singen*', I thought, remember the song, and thinking – 'tomorrow.... there will be Ariane, my lover'. Then round the bend comes the skiff – Ariane and the guy Uwe ... it can't be a skiff, you have to work on those against the current – it's too late, like a scene someone else invents, with all the details – Ariane and Uwe, toying with each other, my place usurped. Inexistent. Another future, completely different, written in, no need to bomb your house and kill your grannie and the goat – it's all changed, changed utterly, and a misery is born. It's your choice, all, nothing. That's the past, rotting in its juice.

Someone else's future. From Dufy or Poulenc? – lovers aren't like that. They never were, but now it is admitted. That was an electric power-boat, not a rowboat – they go so fast, the lovers could be anyone, and anyone's. Continuity, originality – be warned – you don't get what you pay for.

*

'Don't imagine sex,' Zenobia says. 'There's no time, even if I wanted some with you.... Straighten your genre, Khalil – we're serious, we're on to something serious.'

A little later, she says, 'I'm determined to leave. Not determined to arrive.'

'I never lived there,' Khalil says. 'Home. My name comes from there – I'm supposed to take it back, like a sword that's survived a battle. It isn't so. Everything I didn't see, didn't live through, didn't die for – it's all been going on, of course. I was saved, saved long ago – but the home I misremember – still goes on inside me, wherever I am lodged. It should be so for everyone

– I have my doubts. They say once history, experience, is done and over – it's desolation, or you go back where you were and start again, like in a game. Mostly it's all changed, or often somewhere is not there at all. We have to avoid those places, Zenobia – make a huge detour, though no one will understand why we are circling round. Cities, everyone's – they're no more ... there's soldiers cheering round about. Armies recruiting. And the villages....'

'Villages are where you park your tank before you reach the city,' says Zenobia. 'And we watch it, like it's water rising from a hole and drowning all the little things, and think – don't think – 'it must come our way'. It's water, Khalil, it doesn't calculate like us. It marches down the road.'

'You're demolished, Zenobia,' Khalil says. 'Maybe you should cover up – the nakba with the niqab....'

'No,' she says, 'I've thought a better thing,' and she has found a mask, a bowl. It's festive, like they wear at *manifs* – no one troubles them. Put one on, you can be a Turk, Chinese, behind it you can be anything – a Uighur or a Kurd, or people nothing's known about.

'You're looking for a home, a nest, Khalil,' she says. 'I want my life, that's all. I'd die for that.'

*

They watch a creature on the ceiling, here in the station. It's ochre, and orange – it puts out its long green tongue and polishes its eyeballs with it. Then it moves off the patch of damp, and turns dark blue, to match the drier patch.

'None of us,' says Khalil. 'Has ever come near to that.'

'We're not a threat,' Zenobia says. 'No one is interested in us. I'm covered up, my mask ought to suffice. The beast up there is not a threat – but we're enthralled, impressed....'

'It's like us, though,' Khalil says. 'With our quotes and loyalties, our stickiness, our lazy thoughts, remembrances so old they can't be traced and seem original. If we want to leave the continuity, we must not change colour as we move, or as the water penetrates.'

'Maybe – we should have no colour,' says Zenobia, playing along. 'It won't end good,' she thinks.

'It could be starring in the movie I was in, that I wasn't in,' says Khalil. 'I expect that beast's the heroine. Time's moving – once she'd have been killed and called a neutral "it": – now she's sexed, she lives, but it really makes no difference.'

*

This is an excellent starting-place – there's trains, pullmans, and a horse. You choose your destination, and the means, accordingly.

*

'Oh,' says Zenobia, 'we've no designs upon the past, nor on someone's claim to mastering a history.

'We'll just ignore it. Start doing something else – and maybe call it history too, its opposite, or any other thing.'

They turn to Piotr – an athletic type, whose name is on his rucksack, and who's asked them what they propose to do with life.

'Zenobia says we two can do it all,' says Khalil. 'Everything we have in mind. But that, of course, depends. We're animals, and someone, something, long in the tooth and claw, has written in a destiny, indelibly, into our bones. But we have strips, airfields, in our heads, that let us fly and falter – like a butterfly, perhaps – above these trite determinations.

'There's teams of guys deciphering the texts, the stones and tablets, assaying coins and piecing frocks together ... the past's a trampled piece of fairground now, everybody's resussed and had a role and spoken lines assigned, even if it's fancy free.... And then – it's all appropriated – sometimes by nobs and hacks, or activists with every stripe, but usually by powerful types, elected, often not, who see what's gone before as bricks to build themselves a pedestal, to raise them up.... Well, I – we – want something else.' He knows this sounds cloudy. He goes on, 'And, Piotr, what do you do, why carry all those painted sticks....?'

Piotr settles down beside them: 'I love simplicity,' he says. 'Your plan. It's even simpler than mine.'

'Oh,' says Zenobia. 'We don't need help. Especially not the patronising sort. I don't need anyone. No companion. I'm in the flow, I deal with everything that comes upon me – that's my strength. I make nothing happen. Now, Piotr – those sticks...?'

'I climb the mountain, plant the sticks. and mark the easy route,' he says, modestly.

'And are there mountains here?' Khalil asks. 'But – easy route? It rather spoils the game. No risk, no luck....'

'All sorts come,' says Piotr, defensively. 'Some manage still to fall. And, naturally – the top belongs to me. I have a special claim. Even a flag.'

'Of course,' Khalil says. 'Glaciers. The down-side. We fall in them, they are the mirrors of our past. When they have gone, there's nothing, nothing left at all. No reflection, no faces, no cods' eyes staring up, up at us, and down they slowly go, like on an escalator....'

'I feel,' says Piotr, tiring of the direction that this takes – 'We are an occupying army. We living ones, the ones who climb. Of course, we have lost millions getting here. We killed the originals, the indigenes – or perhaps they died ... naturally, of cholera. Millions more are putting on their uniforms, getting ready to leave their huts, the summer and the winter alps, and join us, taking their exams, diplomas, looking for – maybe, my mountains. A test, a tryst. A break. A package: bed and snow-board.'

'Yes,' says Khalil. 'I know all that. The question's bothered me – what are the mountains for? And now you've given me a kind of answer. They're so your poor recruits can climb up by the easy way....'

'I know you think it's trivial,' Piotr says. 'This gaining territory and standing on the top. Giving poor people an easy break – they'll remember it, and be thankful when they don't fall down. Not easy: it takes training, training to get in the swim....'

Khalil and Zenobia – they move away – Piotr's sticks take up a lot of room. 'You can be too simple, nearly,' says Zenobia. 'Next to him, Khalil, you shine. I bet he's paid – a state needs a pioneer, athlete – an explorer. Sticks and flags. Starting over – and over, as if everything is renewed. As if we couldn't see the mountains anyway....'

*

Piotr whispers to Zenobia, who stiffens up. She tells Khalil, 'He thinks you're against history because you're a fundamentalist. Or maybe – you reject the past because truth was revealed in it. The past is worthless, ignorance. After the truth is demonstrated, past and future – they don't count. In other words – he thinks you're faith-bound – or else you're *takfir*. Even both. He might denounce you, Khalil. He's secular, he says....'

'Oh no!' says Khalil. 'I wanted a solution for myself, quite intellectual – no one else's business.'

'No one will believe you,' says Zenobia, moving away, down the bench.

'What does he know?' asks Khalil. 'A fucking tourist guide.'

'That horse won't trot, Khalil,' Zenobia says. 'Piotr believes all's encysted in the present, fired like a opal.... He thinks that's what you are – a presentist; ready to massacre for the truth. Your truth. He doesn't think any truth is worth you running after.... Perhaps he's right. Who knows where you will finish up? Or if there really is a place where you'll arrive?'

'Oh no,' says Khalil, terrified. 'I'm headed nowhere, only deeper in my task....'

'Denounce him, Khalil,' Zenobia says, pulling further away, 'before he denounces you. Besides – mountains can't belong to anyone. Coal and sea – well, maybe that is moot. Mountains, though, they don't do anything, except they snare the clouds.'

'This isn't where I want to go at all,' says Khalil. 'I see us, our species, as we roamed from land to land, from red to yellow sand, the lemurs parodying our shambling upright stance – but it's a picture in my head. Like falling in the glacier and travelling for centuries, protected, staring at the sky, and then....'

'There is no "then", Khalil,' Zenobia says impatiently. 'This dreaming isn't you....' and she moves further along the bench from Piotr and Khalil. 'Remember,' she says, 'And be very prudent, silent if possible. The judgement from the great man, lover of mankind and God, is – "Will and intellect are one and the same." What you think, Khalil, is what you want. You didn't realise?'

'Oh Zenobia,' says Khalil, greatly confused, 'I've always thought that animism is, maybe exaggerated, but the only way to give respect to where we live, who we and everybody are, and who we eat, and who we take for walks, have sit upon our knee, and so and so.... A myth that does no harm, requires no sacrifice – to each the poem...the wolf, the rowan tree, their obsequy....Will and intellect are separate, and arise long after peaceful contemplation....'

'That's not the point,' Zenobia shouts across the space. 'Listen to me! Seeing you abstracted and at thought – is seeing what you plot and scheme.....'

'I don't see that,' Khalil says.

'All the others can,' Zenobia says. 'It isn't up to you at all. We're ruled by simple guys – they want whatever comes into their minds ... Small and troubled? Then big and bigger's where you aim to end. Want it? get it!'

'I can't be bothered with that stuff,' says Khalil.

'Then remember – in every group of tourists, climbers, rafters, floaters – there's an informer,' Zenobia whispers to him, closing in, her last attempt. 'Maybe more than one. What the guys gawk at, steal, deface, break off, what sex is bought, what comments made – like when there was the Duce, they report back home. Then, the chieftains wanted no one to escape. Now, they hope they do. Good riddance – pass the suspicious parcel on... The telltales tell on everyone. For the sneak, the trip is free.'

'I have no land,' says Khalil. 'No one to be reported back to, no chief inquisitor....'

'You're ingenuous,' Zenobia says, losing patience. 'You free radicals – you're reported everywhere. You are international, a threat to peace and war.'

*

'It might be friends you need,' Zenobia says. 'A shell, old crabby! an octopus. Friends make a mystic knot, and octopus – they divide you into arms, they are the general staff – or maybe you're a trolley, dashing from the mine, loaded with shale that's bumped off as you race downhill, your mates will slow it down, jumping aboard you, digging in their heels.'

'Yes,' says Khalil. 'I need all that – the bodies, the pricking, the prick of pretension.... And then I need the antidote. What's left when they have steered me down the hill, taken and given what they have?'

'These questions, Khalil!' Zenobia says. 'We all ask them, not aloud, we know they're trivial. You can't reject being lucky, having people on your back, protecting it with shields and nonsense songs... You suck in my patience, Khalil – that's an exploitation. Enough! Trundle on. Nothing is original – all is digested or forgotten: the more you look, the more you find and there is litigation about what it is, who it belongs to.'

'I'm up to that,' says Khalil. 'It's how it goes to other people, as it must, and then they get it wrong.'

'Right,' Zenobia says. 'They get it absolutely right. It's you that don't.'

'I think,' says Khalil, preparing to leave the waiting room, maybe to take a train, a bus. 'Mine is one of the many faces of cruelty in the world. It should be me that's veiled. Contemplation is a nail – in the eye of those who have no time, who can't, who're bound or wandering free and hunted.'

'Spoken like a saint,' says Zenobia, curling her feet under her, a bundle on the bench. 'And no, there's nothing to be said that you've not said.'

*

The silence – it is worrying. No transport has left, Khalil has not returned. Zenobia goes outside –

'Khaleel!' she shouts, a phantom's wail.

'He has his set of eyes,' she says to Piotr. 'He had a mission – to make communism return, but unstable, livable but shaky, a fumbling, uncertain.... the circle broken, but replaced by what new shape...? A polyhedron ... a collapsing triangle...?'

'Horses returning, I expect,' says Piotr, unimpressed. 'Hair dye from soaking covers of old books...?'

'No, no,' Zenobia says, inventing as she peers out into the dark and stormy night – 'Just camels, if they ask – nothing heavy, just exotic stuff, Syrian glass, and lapis, I suppose.'

'I didn't think he'd reached as far as anything,' Piotr says, dismissively. 'He's surely wandered off, will wander back.... It's not a service that you do, Zenobia, making him sound a pioneer, a zombie, a modernist, antiquary....'

'He needs protection,' says Zenobia. 'I love him when he isn't there....'

'It's evident,' Piotr says. 'Come back with me: my group gains and loses personnel... The mountains are still perilous, people drop out and in, the glacier yields old friends.... There is a Chinese settlement, quite discrete, in Siberia ... you'd fit in there for sure....'

'Piotr,' says Zenobia,hugging his right arm, 'How did you know I was ideal for that place? Inhabitants are selected with such care – and it's clear, they supervise our work with finicking, set squares. Few arrive, and no one leaves – immortality is guaranteed....'

'Oh!' says Piotr, in delight. 'You exaggerate, my dear. You bear a noble name – I remember, there were two of them, two Zenos – one believed in the inscrutibility of everything, its purpose, meaning if it had one, quite unknowable – and the other, who saw it all a harmony and interlinked, source of respect, good times, where the other saw only a confusion, ignorance....'

'Oh, I know,' Zenobia shouts and laughs. 'Those ancients! That was dialectic – the harmony and incompatibility of everything! But – that's not me – my root is Zen, or maybe Xein. I'm a foreigner in all parts, so I don't pay taxes, don't go to jail, contract valid marriages....'

'And besides,' says Piotr, putting a numbered bracelet on her wrist. 'Your parents hadn't even read the book of naming things....'

'Oh,' says Zenobia. 'Parents – I had no need of those. I grew myself – a spring fruit sprung not to be harvested but to be the key – of up and down, evil and what's left, the so-so – all the puzzles no one yet has solved....'

'What and why you're called here,' says Piotr, 'is of no importance there. You are all the daughters of a higher power –

when you arrive in the city which doesn't quite exist, you, the builders, will call yourselves, each other, exactly what you please.

'Now, if you insist – go outside, call Khalil. While he doesn't come, I'll lead these people,' and he gestures at his charges, as they drink, play cards, play with themselves or others, ink in tric-trac boards or pare bunions on their feet with Pattada knives, 'Up the slopes. We'll drop them off as we trek back, and I shall put you on the caravan that takes you to the city that you'll build....'

Kitezh

Zenobia calls and calls Khalil – he doesn't come.

In the nights, the train runs over ruined lands, and in the days Zenobia stares from the window at the sand, the grassy plains, the taiga, then the tundra ... grey shapes flitter through the trees when trees there are, and stare back at the train.

At night, Zenobia dreams – the secrets of the memory. The magistrates – they have a school where murders, massacres, on film are shown incessantly – the judges have to witness and recall what they have seen. What is remembered, what is real, what was staged for this exercise, what happens to us all? Each time the victims and the murderers take on a different aspect.... The climax is the mouse, its dream – a huge rectangle of cheese – it could be cheddar – enormous satisfaction. The brain throbs with the joy. The mouse awakes – there is a rectangle in the cage, it's orange – and the satisfaction is immense. The dream comes true. The real – it isn't cheese, but even better, an indestructible brick: – pile them up, and you have Babylon, or Paris. Zenobia wakes each morning from the mouse's dream, she shivers with delight, anticipation ... she remembers Khalil too, but he's not there, of course.

*

In the city that they're to build, you need a friend – one has to fetch the food while the other works on and on, and so the time is filled: 'None of us here is Han,' says Zenobia's friend. 'And the city doesn't exist, of course, but everybody has a good idea of how it ought to be. It will come – it's just for now invisible. We all are graduates from the judges' school, although there isn't time for crime here, and our memory is of the city we must build, Kitezh, we call it.... We're all skilled in judging: heights and weights, and sloping roofs....'

Those padded jackets: – in the snow, you feel the flutter of the tiny birds inside – there's none left in Mexico, they're all here, they have the memory of the grand lake, though here there is the mighty Amur, which the builders learn to love. Naturally, the birds aren't live, but memory is better than the life, their frantic life, and there remains in every little bird the satisfaction of the sweetness, the syrup....

'Turn over,' says Liu the chief architect, best pourer of cement, Zenobia's friend. There's the faded picture of Palmyra, on Zenobia's back, the towers and arches, guard-posts. 'These bunks straighten out your bones,' says Liu, 'and here there's no class war. We shan't need guards. And everyone shall walk.'

It's straightforward – just get on and build.

Zenobia wonders where Khalil went – maybe kidnapped, a troupe of peripatetics, wondering wandering philosophers, with bowls like she wore on her face, now begging with them, making their analysis, then dropping out, becoming station-masters, rent-collectors. Precise.

'My bowl!' Zenobia says. 'It used to be my face – now it's used to fetch *dimsun.* I think, Liu, we're selfless, building a city here when everyone says no! lay grass, build cowsheds, abattoirs, refresh the countryside, shoe horses, castrate pigs.... Maybe we're mad as well....'

'Oh no,' says Liu. 'We're not paid here because, when we're done, each gets a free apartment in a tower....'

'Oh no!' Zenobia says. 'It's true, this city's etched upon my back, but it's not mine, I disown it thoroughly. The exploit here's enough – too much – for me. What we construct – it is my patrimony, but I don't want to own it, not anything at all.... I realise – even good communists must have a bed to lie on, but it isn't me. I'm hard and pure: my flame will travel round, light up the world.'

'Consider the history,' says Liu. 'There's times of trouble, warring states – much more to come. You'll need a nest for raising little copies of yourself....'

'You're right,' Zenobia says. 'My vice – is curiosity. What happened to Khalil? What happens to us all?'

'Look!' says Liu. 'My little telephone! Everybody has a series running, extraordinary tales, everybody, all of us, in real and fiction, looking for someone – stories, Zenobia – someone you want to love, someone who's murdered, mostly who disappear, or go to jungle jails or into landfill. It's not the end that hooks you on, it's all the business on the road – the photos, messages on trees, the files not viewable ... everything is true, it's all mysterious, there is some blood, no flesh ... on and on it goes, with people you don't care about, like voices in a well that draw you in, and pull you down.... Khalil is nothing, dear Zenobia, nothing at all, an absent character....'

*

'Those birds picketing the mud,' Zenobia asks Liu. 'Where do they live? How do they know what's in the sludge, and thrust deep in? If I had time, I'd ring and count them...'

'Well,' says Liu. 'You can't lark about down there – besides, they'd fly away. How'd you ring them – on my phone?' And she laughs. 'You know me, where I am, you can talk direct, all night when we don't work and the other shift comes on....'

'Oh, just heavy stuff, that's all I see,' Zenobia says. 'Concrete and lime, lumpy grey rain down the scaffolding. I don't go for the emotional stuff, life's heavy enough with all the rest. Just blocks – make one; pass on.'

'Some of it is wonderful,' says Liu. 'That Uighur tent with the golden dome – the Kirghiz took it, now we're replacing it, a replica....'

'History is irony, Liu,' Zenobia says. 'While they're doing it, you know what end they'll make: – and what happened to the people they have done it to.'

'Accept it, Zenobia,' says Liu, sneaking inside her friend's jacket. 'Design something, and you can be chief architect like me. Work high up.'

'The fall?' says Zenobia, wriggling free.

'It's still invisible,' says Liu. 'It's inside us all, from every height. It will come, Zenobia, it's not so terrible. Bones beneath the sand – it sounds a fright, but better lay down there a while than be gnawed up top. It's like sex, Zenobia – we have everything within us, whatever height, whatever fall. You're buried, and it's good, but....'

'I know all that, Lui,' Zenobia says. 'I've been to clubs. I don't seek mysteries – find the right person, and the answer's there. To everything. Come! Let's build the city, and be done.'

*

Invisible cities – they're the most imaginative. Zenobia longed to make a concrete something – now, she pours. She's into concrete, wills it: – not like poor Felicidad – her crew turned against her, and made her a foundation, laid her down and covered her....

'Winter,' says Zenobia. 'It lasts nine months, and we can't work....'

'Of course we do,' says Liu. 'We build a wall of fire around the site.'

'How? What?' Zenobia asks, thinking of Khalil, living in the abstract, then becoming it, not feeling the cold, not bothered by those big black stinging flies, night howlings here.... Now, the fire all round....

'Trees! What else,' says Liu, laughing. 'The wolves and birds, they gather round, and watch us from outside the fire. They don't sing or howl, they know it is our gift to them as well, it's not Valhallah. It warms the bunkhouse, not enough,' she says, a little wistful.

'So, we work on?' Zenobia asks. 'And the city – does it have a Russian or a Chinese name? Or both? Or something local, homely?'

'We might remember someone,' says Liu. 'A Russian? Someone forgotten – Smilga? Or a Zetkin? Radek? They're our Indians, our ancestors, living hard in the forest, naming the plants and being poisoned by them....'

'It was maybe tougher than we have,' says Zenobia. 'And what is left?'

'Oh, you know Russians,' says Liu, vaguely. 'For them, everything's a struggle, no one wins. And you must be careful who you name: – this will be an enormous city. They need a name to know where it is they live. Remember, Zenobia – we don't talk about this, but I'm sure you know – this is all for communism. Private ownership of the means of everyone's subsistence – you can't allow it. Tried thoroughly – discarded now.'

'I hadn't thought,' Zenobia says. 'We don't mention it – but even the big poppies, who seem to own it all, or act like everything is theirs – they know what you said is true....'

'That isn't what I meant,' says Liu. 'I'm talking about you, Zenobia. People I love – they must be loyal, must recognise what I've just said is true and right. You don't need chat about it.'

'This architecture,' says Zenobia. 'It corresponds to something. My poor back – almost illegible and under lymph. Like a marsh. Maybe the design – comes out as sonatinas in our heads?'

'You think it's all symmetry?' Liu asks. 'What we lack, aspire to? – look!' And she shows her breasts – not exactly equal, some fingers don't quite correspond on arms a whimsy not exact. Order? or Equilibrium? Is it the right we seek – or the teeter-tilter between good and bad? Oh, Zenobia – do I see you on a plinth, or on a swing, draped? or billowing?'

'That's your fault,' Zenobia says, pushing Liu away. 'You trust in other people – or another person. Be content with just yourself, be curious like me, but don't hook on, give confidences, make an allowance, try to understand too much – it's catastrophe for millions, it will do for you – the ring of fire, it will be permanent, you know! The city will be visible, but you'll be closed inside by an invisible circle, a fire, and if you cross it to get out – there are hungry beasts that wait....'

'Yes,' says Liu, staring into Zenobia's face. 'Beasts.' She pauses. 'You know, we need to make the streets, to finish off. They bring in Buryats, or Nenets – they aren't used to streets: – they have reindeers, yaks. They used to have strong men selected by their ancestors.... Those guys – they slept, suffered – for days they journeyed with the dead, and then forgot.... After that, the ancestors would eat their flesh. Leave the skeleton for dead; and then these guys, the chosen ones, came back to life; a life informed. And knew the poetry, the secrets.... "Be pure: discourse with the dead." Those customs are all gone, besides – I don't believe in them.

'But when they've made the streets, the city's finished, and it's then the bad guys can come in. And after them, like flies that follow shit – in come the cops, informers. And it's like the rest, the everywhere, the hole, the city, ours. Our work, Zenobia, will be polluted, all our architecture, our design – in vain.'

'But Liu,' Zenobia says. 'Without the streets – it's towers, without a link.'

'Maybe,' says Liu. 'We'd work it out. Causeways. Or jumps.'

'But Liu,' Zenobia says, relieved and sad. 'I thought you had in mind we two – that we'd be lovers....'

'Oh, of course,' says Liu. 'I love you, I love everyone, until.... Our city, our creation – see, Zenobia, now it's copied off your back, you're well again.... We need to keep the city safe, now that it's transformed, is visible – pure.'

'The city we have built – it doesn't look at all like my tattoo,' Zenobia says.

'How could it? You were destroyed, Zenobia, when you came to me. I built you too, my dear,' says Liu.

'I was near death then,' Zenobia says. 'But I was strong enough to build the piers and ride the hoists, and put the entrails in the towers. I'm ready, Liu, ready to leave, and ready to use my powers....'

'Those you don't have: – not one reindeer, nothing, Zenobia,' says Liu. 'Even if you knew a mystery – everybody else could look it up, besides – the dead are where they were, and all around. The bad guys ... what do we say to them....?'

'You're stupid, Liu,' Zenobia says. 'But, after all – the question's good, and assumes you're good as well. You're ingenuous – maybe you'll pass that off as being wise....

'We've built, it seems, a prison for the good. There's good guys in each stack – you don't need to make acquaintances further down the street.'

'Well, you can leave, of course,' says Liu. 'But there's no map. And you've no document to say how good you are.'

*

The snow is deep and claggy. Zenobia wades on. 'Maybe,' she says to Sam, a figure with a gun, 'I could winter here, here in your tent, tell stories, in the spring, stiff with frustration, I can leave....'

'Oh no,' says Sam. 'We're not indigenous. We're here to bring them peace and war, or stasis too. We'll house you for your good.... you must convince us that you're good, and then you leave in God's good time....'

'It's Khalil,' says Zenobia, wondering if some tears would help. 'Just a few minutes, finding him, and seeing if he's like a talisman that sets you on another path, gives you new life, a companion ... not lasting, not a contract, that's for sure....'

'We're cosy in our tent,' says Sam, 'and it's not right that you doss down with us. Besides – you might take a gun and do for everyone....'

They nail her in a shed. It's cold. She cannot light the stove, and eating the raw reindeer chunks they drop down through the roof is difficult. 'Oh no!' she thinks. 'I'm growing hair all over – nature protects, but also plays a trick. Suppose I grow a tail and I'm a Samoyed? Is that how they're born, the dogs quite humanoid, the friend of man until they have the time observing him, time to take a distance ... a people with a dog's name, in turn declared extinct, converted to something orthodox and so counted in the mass, dissolved, ignorable....end pulling a sled, cooking a book, a ministrone or a borshch....'

The winter's long, an infinity for speculation. Her back is cured, and covered with thick hair.

Sam and his mates – they remember where she is, they open up the door, she rushes out, and tries to bark. They're mystified – in went a dusty worker, a Mohican probably, used to topping out the towers and pirouetting on the girders, then – out comes a noble beast with paws....

She straightens up, a biped.

There are soldiers all around.

'This used not to be a frontier,' says Zenobia.

'We let you in and out,' says Sam wisely. 'People straggling, and those who scheme and look for work or revelation. It's your Völkerwanderung, it's history. When a place is full, or when the right ones come, fill up their space – the frontier shifts; or we can make a camp, or even bombard some towns whose people don't fit with their lookalikes....'

'I see it's tricky work,' says Zenobia, flattering. 'I don't need find a bundle, though, not a human sample – just one Khalil.'

'Oh, Khalils!' laughs Sam. 'I've lots of those, they come and go, there's some politicos and some with hods.'

'Mine?' Zenobia asks, and wonders. 'A philosopher. A wanderer? Layer of bricks?'

'Wait!' says Sam. 'They're on another page.'

He goes into a tent. Does not return.

*

'Poor Liu,' Zenobia thinks. 'She knows she's powerless. There's a chance someone will stoop down and set things right – there seem to be so many things ... she hasn't found out one of them, except about bad guys. Keep them out. I see everything quite clear – but I know I'll be lucky just to save myself. And who'd I join? Another winter in that shack....! Who'd help me then? Who could I find to stop it happening again? Nowhere's a country now, it's all a frontier. The best would be – to see Khalil, how far he got.'

'Hey!' she says: the guy's labelled, Bela. He could be Magyar, or where the Magyars came from.... 'Where's Sam?' she asks.

'If his contract's up....' says Bela. 'We don't do soldiering for life. We come from everywhere, we're loyal – it doesn't hurt to be a mercenary! The only guys who have a chance against us – are soldiers who do it all their lives. Some of those – some we let in, some we keep out. Some we deal with, some we bomb –

remember, they're the only guys who're good or bad, depending where you stand....'

'I know,' Zenobia says. 'My friend back East, she thought like that. She feared the bad guys – maybe some of them were military, it didn't matter what their contract was, short or long term..... They'd come in, permanent.'

'We prefer,' says Bela. 'Not to get too close to guys – it's shifting sands, sink holes, rifts and fires.... We'd like irregulars fight others like themselves, and leave us out.... People are books, and just as hard to read. Why, you could be a soldier too – maybe beneath your clothes some dynamite....'

He feels Zenobia's fur.

He's mystified.

'My friend,' Zenobia persist – 'Khalil. It's not for me, not making promises or pacts. Just see where he's at and what he's seen....'

Bela shrugs. 'This place,' he says, 'is changing shape. The centre's nearer, nearer by far, than when you went out East. The centre – that means trouble. Trouble used to be sent out on to the edge, now – here it comes. And – dog or wolf? Which are you? Dogs are stolen, wolves are shot. It all depends, whatever side you're on. There's dog in wolf and wolf in dog. It all depends.'

'Oh,' says Zenobia, 'I'm not on any side. If it all changes always, how could I be? It all depends on friends, and trucks of stuff, and pacts – the countries pass from side to side and place to place as if they are on carpets, rolled and sliding, in the air and underground. And, Bela – it's easy to foretell my death if you've a gun.'

'It's not the bullet, it's the blast,' says Bela. 'It takes red meat to look a person in the eye and shoot it out. A blast – is a straight, a flush, that bears them all away. Unseen, it deafens you, and so it is unheard. It hits you like a happenstance. Unmourned, the bits of all of you, like pussy's pieces – the grief is not allowed, you mustn't show, or ask for parts to take back home to bury in the plot. In your case, my dear, a doggy bag would do.'

'You know, Bela,' says Zenobia, 'I'm not interested in tricks, not at all, not in what appears to be or not to be, mental things that don't come out your mouth. Following some guy, reading a tract, pursuing justice or a boss – it isn't me. It's our design, the architecture: – that's what bemuses me. That city – who's to come there? Do they exist, or will they be created by living in the towers, seeing the blue and then the green and yellow on the water, pink snow, grey snow.... We made the city, what makes us?'

'If you don't know how long the answer is, how do you know when it's begun?' asks Bela, playing along. 'Or what you do with it? Does it serve, even if it's for you alone? It stays a metaphor....'

'That's why I want some minutes with Khalil,' Zenobia says. 'He'll have been wafted over an expanse, he knows the landscapes, remembers what he's trudged in caravans, as slave or mago, yabgo or ostler....'

'You could have stayed,' says Bela, leaning on his gun and getting involved. 'Anyway – you are complicit. In whatever happens, and usually it's bad. It's not just the design – you had it on your back....The seed, the sketch, was yours.'

'They didn't follow my print,' Zenobia says. 'I see your point. If I'm just innocent and far away – there's no plot, no drama, no conversation. I'm innocent – who cares?'

'Exactly so,' says Bela. 'You're driftwood. Power? A voice? You won't get it if you haven't got it. That's trite, and it is true.'

'Since you ask,' Zenobia says, 'the city is made of towers for different peoples, different languages. All new cities are like so – towers and emptiness, vast emptiness with shrubs. I don't speak any of those languages, but I have my friend....'

'Who protects?' says Bela. 'Who says they do, and then withdraws? That's what decides your place, the latitude you drift to.'

'All you say, Bela,' Zenobia says, 'makes me long for my hour with Khalil – who would be, as they say, in the grave a companion, in paradise – a friend. What in life he never was. As for your picture – the future.... We live in a fiction, we ordinary, passionate types. We follow our colour, our thread, like someone winked and laid a trace for us, to follow in a maze.

'You see it as it is, Bela: the real – but you squint, like a beetle seeks a route to pick out in the dust. For me – the story, the epic somebody invents, that we elaborate, bringing in our wounded and the dead, our own – fleshing out the tale ... it's full of strange winged shapes above, invading and retreating – the peoples, their archaic names, ideas discarded, ridiculed in school.... Back they come, like seagulls circling, shouting like the damned, throats sore with salt and tiny bones.'

It isn't clear.

Zenobia goes on. 'I see only armies, the planet wholly given over – sharpshooters, nurses, breakers of mules, gravediggers, pioneers and signallers, the cavalry, deserters, dawn patrols, the spies, the guys that burnish, camel-drivers, testers of the ice, killers of tsetse flies, killers for sale and hire, the depraved ... in uniform, in office and in offices, priests of Moloch, priests of Kronos – a roar of tides, of people patched, sent off to fight, and fighters discharged, shaking and slavering on the streets....'

'Yes, yes,' says Bela. 'It is quite like that – even more intricate – there's smelting, packing shells, and sewing wounds and teaching school.... The question is, Zenobia – what do I do with you? You're eloquent, you make me have suspicions.... You should realise – if you don't pass the interview, you are a prisoner.... How long? Who knows. There's judges, there's no judgment. There's judgments, but no judges. Here you stay, Zenobia: think of Khalil, but you are mine. There's rules about that – do they operate? Who knows. Long is a long long time....'

'No, no!' Zenobia says, appalled. 'We talked, you and I, is all. I've been held here, I'm innocent. There's no kind of trial for being innocent....'

'I'm on a contract,' Bela says. 'I come and go. There's places you can't go, Zenobia, and almost everything that you can't do. Most is like you, and many are like me – but here, you're in a holding cage.'

'What must I do?' Zenobia asks.

'There's nothing you need do, can do,' says Bela. 'It's not up to me. You could scrabble, write a memoir, clean the stoop. Watch the sky. Have children so's they can share with you....'

'That's it, then? My life?' she asks. 'Waiting, in between.'

'Lucky if it goes on so,' says Bela. 'And you could grow a thing or two. Have animals. Dogs would love you. Death will not be a drama.'

*

'How long, Bela?' Zenobia asks. 'How long before I escape, and find how thoroughly it's all changed?'

'I leave tomorrow,' he says. 'There's lots of theory behind us being here. Democracy, bosses, cash. School and medicine too. Say – three to five years. It will all have changed, that is for sure. You too. Just walk. Anything else?'

'Peyote buttons. And dog food,' she says.

Those years pass quickly. She doesn't age. She doesn't miss Bela – he's stupid, too crass to be an assailant, let alone a lover. Besides – he's gone, doesn't return. Not ever.

*

'You've had an extraordinary life, Zenobia,' says her friend. 'And now you're free.'

'If you don't resist,' Zenobia says, 'it's all pathetic, or so sad. Pathos and sadness – nothing to be done about them, you have to find a fringe, your space, a season that accelerates ... spins round the time, like a coloured card on a spinning-top, a gyroscope, so quick revolving that you don't get old....'

'It's lovely that you're happy with yourself,' says Aimée, her friend. 'I look at you, and I think of old old Monet, one of the last pics, those shades ... faces a scratched-out rock, an hermetic portal, like the inside of an old blue shoe, a graven stone, fallen off some crag....'

'I don't know that,' Zenobia says, in fear.

'Blue and white, a body like a candle-end,' says Aimée. 'And your face – those salmon's jaws, quite shagreen, and my dear, your face – it *snarls.*'

'It'll warm up, I'm sure,' Zenobia says, shaking.

'What a life you've had!' Aimée goes on –

'I don't remember most of it,' Zenobia says.

'We could push you, somehow,' Aimée says. 'A leader. You're free – you could lead multitudes to freedom – then tell them what they should do next....'

'Oh,' Zenobia says, 'there's criminals, fraudsters – they get in between. And then...' she remembers Mister Heinz, the movie. 'There's what you think might happen next, or who....'

'Oh, not that man again!' Aimée insists. 'Khalil, your obsession. A juggler of non-existent things, a mountebank, a charlatan. He's your bad burden – shake him off! You didn't promise him, I hope....'

'I can choose,' says Zenobia. 'Which of the ways you suggest. But – choosing's all career, or necessity, or taking risks, or following bell-wethers. Khalil was on a higher step: moral dilemmas. That was his speciality. Choosing to do, or not, when you don't have the need. For principle. What a luxury! It never happened to me, not remotely. It must be good. It's rare – so it must be worth a lot....'

'And are you sure?' asks Aimée. 'Was Khalil like that? What was he, what has he become? Besides – we're all rare, but it's evident we aren't worth a lot. Beware, Zenobia – don't appear to be a victim, especially one who's weak... Khalil could seem strong – wherever he has been or what he's done. You'd not want him to win....'

'Oh, Aimée,' Zenobia says, 'I always won. The ones who did me down – they all met awful ends. My strength comes from the martial arts – first, opponents are bewildered – then they're on their backs!'

'Khalil's not here,' says Aimée. 'Maybe not anywhere. How does he stand with us? Might we do him harm? He's hypothetical. An exercise in ethical abstraction: what's our responsibility?'

'Quiet, Aimée,' shouts Zenobia. 'Each day they open up new camps – tomorrow we're at war with obscure peoples, and we don't admit – to starving them or arming them....'

'Yes!' says Aimée. 'That's the way! Shout, Zenobia, and pray! First you lead, then you decide!'

'Of course,' Zenobia says, calming down. 'That is the species' way. We are a band. That's good and bad. We may go on like that, it's in our genes, they say, it's scientific that we climb towards the light – if you don't care, you're pushed aside...'

'That's a fine thought,' says Aimée, who doesn't care.

'It's not for sex,' Zenobia says. 'Before I die, to feel another body held against my body, as if it is a proof. Not Khalil, of course, I know him. It wouldn't be for knowledge, or for familiarity, not someone I'd known, just to show there was another world, going on, indifferent.'

'You're old for that, Zenobia,' Aimée says: 'You're not too old for politics.'

'The project,' says Zenobia, 'requires you feed the cities, all those workers, that there's a kind of order, so you have to take the grain, the land, make everybody equal. There's much suffering for people who are suffering, and so you need a state, powerful and abstract, and a party, concrete and obedient, some soldiers ... all the shooting. It all follows from that. You go on with the project – or you think it isn't worth it, you give up, you abdicate, the big monkeys come back in and skin you and roast you and your friends over a fire, and eat you and shit you out ... and write it down on slabs of rock.'

'Yes, but you don't say it. Not quite so,' says Aimée. 'The project's sure to be eternal, noble even.'

'I never came across people with what you'd call a project,' says Zenobia.

'You're a romantic,' Aimée says. 'That's good. That's very good. And the name, Zenobia – Jewish, I should bet. The city ... and you've ambition, trangressive even.... You're not smart enough to have a project, and it's better not to follow one. Fear and liking: first try for those.'

'Oh,' says Zenobia. 'Almost everyone from thereabouts is Jewish. It's the Book, the style. Don't take it seriously, Aimée – in the beginning there was no book, and there's none now, no one would read it.'

*

'Remember the guy who pulled the boat over the mountains?' Wolf asks. 'I'd never rival him.'

'Mister Heinz?' asks Khalil.

'No, it wasn't he,' says Wolf. 'But I want loads of realism. No stunts and doubles, everybody does what they do only for themselves.'

It's the big Eastern.

No one remembers Revolution – here's their chance.

*

'We're requisitioning,' says the commissar. 'The workers need to have a living space.'

'Not ours,' says Tatiana, the snobby daughter. 'Just fuck off.'

'Fuck off yourself!' says the commissar. 'You've had the good times, Tatiana, now our turn has come.'

'Then there was invasions,' Wolf tells the little band of extras. 'Lots of armies tramping round – then the Red Cossaks invaded Poland. That was probably a mistake. I've brought some mules – they're fiercer-looking than the nags – don't let them kick you in the head....' The actors back away. 'If none of you can ride – we'll do it by a gesture.'

'Where's the hero?' Khalil asks.

'It could be anyone, it could be you,' says Wolf. 'We don't need big egos here – collective effort is the deal....'

'This isn't city,' says Khalil, not impressed. 'It could be desert....'

'That could be a mistake as well,' says Wolf. 'Restoring the imperial lands.... Oases and mountains. It must be shown though ... maybe a map....'

'Why are we all Russian?' asks a guy. 'Weren't there others there and here?'

'It's old style,' Khalil says. 'Wolf wants to be a throwback, shoots everything on plastic, loads it into pizza cans – don't throw any anyway, you guys, no pizza boxes, it could be our work.'

'Nadia,' the American says. 'Write to me. Don't forget the state I live in, write "Conn" on the envelope.'

*

'Tatiana plays Nadia, her granddaughter. The rich guy picks her up – she's a tart, she works his hotel lobby,' Wolf says. 'They get to make the music.'

'It seems a little crude,' Khalil says. 'Do people do their history like this?'

'Of course!' says Wolf. 'And don't dare patronise me – my ignorance is just a con. Naturally, this movie's my catharsis. People who go to cinemas to see a movie – they don't want revolutions, wouldn't know where to begin. It's all me. Once, I was pepped up. Mao jackets, all that. Now I scribble on the scenery.The point is this – the past is caricature, we pull out bits we like, they're cherries in the cake. No one eats the stodge, all the papymashee – it kills you too.'

'There's too much standing round,' says Khalil. 'I guess the biz is all like this, but it's a bore.'

He wanders off, towards the desert. That is real, and hot.

*

It looks barren. Of course it's not – there's no grass or trees, probably no animals. But there's all the rest, all nature, what they call the totality – inescapable. Unless you're dead. You have to learn to read what isn't set down in a script, that's why you invent your own, a series of them – *muhaqqaq, thuluth, naskh* to start with – hands; from China even more, and alphabets, that in the desert are not here, and so there must be another hand to be read, perhaps a forest of them.... Hands read – they say there is the future there, but no! – only what there was.

Beneath the sand – those caravans caught unawares – and sand's so light, so insignificant, like a silk sheet that helps you sleep but doesn't bind. Whimsy. Move on.

The crusts of terracotta, cities, souks – a series of upturned bowls, a form unreadable once you're inside. To see the form, you'd need an aeroplane, or to be God. Each rounded roof a cell, that makes another, and another and becomes a form; the form is life. Start with one cell, it multiplies until there is a thing that eats and loves and writes on clay or birchbark, or trudges, brays and bubbles, carries you to war or summer pasture.

You don't need dig – the life is there, you've just uncovered it. It's symmetry, the single cell that splits into another exactly like itself, and yet the one-on-one produces not a honeycomb but a variety, based on tiny flaws and *sfumature*, an infinity of sports and species.....

*

It's a joke. It's a mystery. The form is only visible from a place that's unattainable, unless you're outside, out of the world, on a hill that isn't there ... and still, you reach your height, your vantage point and – it's gone, all gone. The past is everywhere beneath our feet, it's all been signed off, sanded, sealed ... the fighting to win the territory where other people's gods hold sway, stealing the alien gods and on our knees to flatter them – and they're not there! They don't exist, not ever. There's only ever us, and all the totality, the surroundings. These spirits: don't exist, and yet, there they are!

Zenobia and me – we're not a couple. Like Engels said, one and one don't make a two but many more – for us, our one and one is three.... Who is this invisible third person, always there and inconvenient? Or inconvenient because it's us and isn't there, there where you could see it, turn its pockets out, request its documents....

*

She's gone, because she wasn't ever there, not even half of her.

*

'This caravanserai – it still works,' says the guy, Alain. 'If you're lost, you can sleep here.'

A brotherhood long gone; the spaces swept out, revalued and re-priced. 'No pets, no animals' says the sign – it rules us mostly out. The smell of dung has gone, bundles of lapis too, the smoky glass, the pharmaca ... what would you expect?

'You're off the set?' the officer asks next day. 'Your card?'

'Would be the joker,' Khalil says. 'I haven't one. Maybe – I'm a deserter.'

There's pics – the fierce queen, sometimes in chains, sometimes garlanded.

'Zenobia?' Khalil asks.

'You can have sex here,' says the guy. 'If you've a card. The lady's just to stimulate and orientate, a sign, a probe – a pricking. A pic, a picture show. Or maybe, the prick is you?'

'I've no money,' Khalil says. 'It's true – I was an extra. Maybe the hero. I wandered, hadn't thought it cost so much – a hotel in the sand....'

'He could work, settle his debt,' says Alain, who maybe wants a friend, maybe could be held responsible for such unpaying wanderers of no account, no past or future, just a guy, Khalil, maybe someone could fancy him or maybe not. Ask the boss.

'What can it cost me?' Khalil asks. 'Sleep?'

'It's not the sleep,' the manager, the guy in uniform, laughs and says. 'It's the dreams.'

Pricing things – it's the kingdom of the maybes. Exchange? – no interest, no piling up the bullion, exchange can't make you rich – so, what then? Just work? For ever and for everyone? For service there is no equivalent: service is respect and faith, not a dinar or denarius.

Honesty the worst of policies, if you want jewels, or to open up another store.

*

'I'll work to pay my debt, Alain,' says Khalil, 'but I'm convinced – nothing is equivalent to anything else at all. A debt remains for ever. Never repaid. I work for you – maybe after, you're in debt to me....'

'And so?' asks Alain, already regretting he defended Khalil.

'The world is resemblances,' Khalil says, 'but everything's unique, surreal, juxtaposition – there is a similarity, of a sound, a shape, it lets you make a composition, but there's no logic, no contextual solidity.... Things are like each other, recalling other things. Metamorphosis – has happened, never again. Breasts and pears and aubergines. So what? What's the story?'

'And yet you made that movie with a plot,' says Alain. 'It'll come out clean, unambiguous.'

'But we never did,' Khalil says. 'The hero didn't show.'

'And does it matter anyway?' asks Alain, handing Khalil a mop and broom. 'It isn't how it is, it's how you draw it, Khalil.'

How long, Khalil wonders, to work before he gets away.

Alain says, 'How lucky you are, Khalil. You have no destiny. I, instead, see mine as clearly as I see the dawn and how it rises, and goes around...'

*

Dictators and wars – they come, they go. Some don't go, they gestate. It's exhausting. It threatens.

The past is gone forever, and its shapes keep leaping out, like monsters from a toy-box. Khalil's not the exalting kind. He's a stone in the marching boot. Cities are bombarded, people born wrong disappear. That's Europe. Not to mention how you analyse it all, and get it wrong, or get it right and that lands you somewhere bad without the exit.

Then there's Africa, China, the Islamic lands. The dark birds – where do they nest? They fly north and south, and crap on everything. It's not circular of course, what happens, and there's no saying that being alive is best, or that collecting, placing things side by side that don't seem part of sets – that that's best either, or that there's much chance of finding out anyway, not convincingly. Maybe trying things out, for which you need to be alive is not conclusive, and so not satisfying, but just indeterminate, without a climax, a coda, started, without an end in sight. Your life ends all the same, of course, but be brave! The totality, however much reduced, it persists, so far as you can see ... despite the signs and warnings.

And Khalil works on – he has his debt, he doesn't know when it's paid off. Most people start with a debt they spend their life working to pay off. It won't happen, it clings and moulds. But – Khalil's *will* be settled – one day you set off across the sand, and probably you'll die out there. No one follows you, to save or nurture.

He remembers – 'Nonbeing is a mirror, the world the image, and man is the eye of the image.' It helps him sweep the rooms: 'Who has seen the eye through which all things are seen?' he wonders.

Life – a life sentence...then – the chop.... What more is there? – that mirror's installed in every coffin lid. 'I', he thinks, 'I am that eye.'

'Would Zenobia scoff at that? Putting on her dancing shoes ... that's a good sign. He'd like to go one night wherever Zenobia goes.

Whoever wrote that, Khalil thinks, I don't understand: – they stand with me in these empty costly rooms. 'Away, away' they think – my brother ... my sister.... Spinning abstractions all together....

*

'You mix everything up,' says Alain. 'Stick to your own, and bring the rest in for entertainment, or a lark. Or keep it out. Or bring it in on show to make a buck.'

He's bored with Khalil, putting side by side things that don't belong and don't make sense.

'I don't have a culture,' Khalil says. 'I don't have a title or a building, a civilisation; I believe in nothing except surroundings and happenstance. I represent nothing. It's all mine, though, the world: like postcards that come and stick with you. On your wall and in your head.'

'Dance and magic,' says Alain. 'It's superficial. An owl's pellet. Promiscuity, uncertainty.'

Alain wants company. More than company.

'If you can't agree – then go!' says Alain. 'I thought....'

'What you want doesn't exist in thought, Alain,' says Khalil. 'We were debtor and creditor, perhaps that makes friendship. You wanted something more that you can't communicate to me. And I know I don't want something similar.'

*

'How many more movies do you have in you, Khalil?' Alain asks, laughing. 'After all the years you've passed here in peace – you can play the old heart-throb. In the ruins, looking for the lover ... instead, it's all knocked down, there's severed heads and slave-markets.'

'Oh,' says Khalil, 'I'm ready for anything, like you need to be. Just give me the script, I'll learn it, at once. Getting bread's the thing. What's my fate, Alain? Keeping upright till the last reel – then a bang? Or lovers' meeting? Perhaps – just keep them wondering. I need a new director, though.'

'The things you've missed have made you, Khalil,' Alain says. 'You learn quick when there's disaster, that is true, but best avoid it, like we have.'

'You see,' says Khalil, seeming not to hear, 'I like the imaging. The eye, the "I", the universal person.... I'd like to have the experience underlying it – but ... I have no faith. The whole foundation of the poem, what it promises, the brotherhood – I don't grasp any of it – indeed, I reject it. I do not believe. It's all a metaphor to me, but the horrors – they are not. They are the real....'

'That's awful, Alain says, recoiling. 'I prefer simplicity, but I have the faith. You have to have it, whether it is spiritual, or the politics – you have to fight, resist, construct. You can't abandon your side because some people will be hurt....'

'I didn't quite say that,' says Khalil – or perhaps he only thinks he didn't.

*

Someone called Soraya gives him water. You can die in the desert, though she lives in a row house – no compound, and so no animals. That's quite good. No killings on the stoup. You can see the desert at the end of her street.

'This is my aunt,' says Soraya. 'Don't touch her. She's very religious.'

Upstairs, there's a full-house of grandfathers. They're not the kind sort. They're planning a vendetta. There's guns. They decide whose to be done and who's to do it, and come back if they can when they have done. There's no beasts to quarrel over now, but those in the past, kid- and lamb-napped – they live on like Bambis on a frieze in a newborn's room.

'When this is over,' Soraya says, explaining everything with a single sign, 'We'll start something important. Politics, you understand. It's not China, of course. New men, new women – all raised up. Small things, not the big nineteenth century one. New Soviet Man – abandoned, a foundling, then expired without a tear. Don't cry, poor twisted thing. Oh dear – that was long ago, another age, when there was logic, and things were true or false, you stayed up talking about principles. and what came out? Plutocrats and commissars, liberals and socialists – and that's our side. The not-so-bad guys. The Hybrids: and purgatories: – and what went in? Not stages of development – much stage and no development: kleptomaniacs and torturers. Justice for everyone? If you're ignorant, the puzzle's just the same as if you're smart,' she says, ladling hot liquids from a pot. 'We make this ourselves,' she says.

It's evident. In this house – everything ferments and boils. She says –

'Truth, logic: the individual. There was an order. There were epochs and hierarchies – get them right, you were divine. Then – it went skewed. Revolution in quite the wrong sort of place, of opponents, outcomes.... The heritage tiny, and squandered. A nightmare. Socialism, the last thing you turned to, when all the rest had tumbled, the cells all occupied and ready for another bunch.... More tumble, steps back, forward... prisoners ... those looked just the same as those before, but quite quite different, and.... Class struggle. That brings it down to who does what and sees an exit, a philosophy – the planners, plotters – not doing it themselves, but others taking up the discourse and getting beat instead. The classes – are wind, they swirl, become like mist, a mist like candy floss you buy and sell, it's seasonal, comes out of a machine.... I'm disillusioned, maybe, but....'

'I'm eternally in your debt,' Khalil says. 'The water. But....'

'Oh,' Soraya says, 'you're involved. The old guys upstairs....'

'You can tell they've authority,' Khalil says, opening the front door, wanting to leave: 'Those waistcoats – cherry and emerald. I bet they're significant, the colours....'

'Where are you going, Khalil?' Soraya asks.

'I can't stay here!' Khalil says, appalled: the fusty ponderings.... 'Apart from it being full up....'

'Where else have you got to go, Khalil?' Soraya asks. 'Those guys the old men here are out to get – they're rats. People who've always needled us, stole animals when anybody had some, culled our young, plotted, conspired, and sneaked. A battalion of them. In our family – rich and poor, honest and thieves... we alone – are their match. It should have been the fight of everyone, to cut them down ... cut off their feet. In the old days, it was all paper – paper bullets, paper guns, a novel with grannies and cute kids. Skating and pratfalls. Family feasts and happiness. Scores were settled between dun covers, in serials, in elocution class. It's not at all like that: – that was paper prisons, paper cells. You reached an end, each chapter had an ending, you thought "put it away", then next day....'

'There was energy,' Khalil says. 'They were all buried, you can go and see their tombs....the energy! Released to resonate and wander round. If you're cremated – it all goes, a roman candle, phut and ploff!'

'You're wrong, Khalil,' Soraya says. 'It's class. The servants went into pots, only the nobs got tumulated. Millions, like the communards – they disappeared for good.'

'I was wrong, I see,' says Khalil, 'About the nineteenth century. Most places now, it will never come. It it comes, it never goes. Or else you'll only see the edge, sharpened against you. Or flapping, like someone else's flag. Vultures. Empire, Soraya.

'Truth and stuff – I got it wrong, and now it doesn't interest me.'

'Oh, it will, it will,' Soraya says. 'These rats – we'll bloody one, and have the rest back off.'

'Rats,' says Khalil. 'I esteem them – they don't know fear or fawn, they don't want to take our place ... or anybody else's.'

Just a night. There's a space in the roof – for armadilloes, possums – to be rooted out with sticks and smoke; Khalil's inserted like intaglio. Just for a night.

*

'He's unknown and gullible,' says the patriarch. 'Anonymous. He can do the work. He needs be motivated.'

*

'What am I doing here, Soraya?' Khalil asks.

'Nothing. Nothing's waiting,' Soraya says. 'I had a duty, then I liked you.'

'I know nothing about women,' says Khalil. 'I still feel they're fragile, that they might break, just by themselves. Each one a Zenobia, a princess, shortly to be queen. I guess that's stupid.... But the history of men, Soraya – it makes you shake. They lie, too – all the time.'

'Do you like dressing up, Khalil?' Soraya asks, pretending to ignore what he has said. 'Look!' And she pulls him into her room, tries on fabrics, undressing to nakedness each time, then spinning round, trying cottons and brocades against him, as if she's designing plumage for a drab bird.

'See,' she says, drawing him and her together and grimacing in the mirror – 'You could easily be me. But I'm not you, not by a length.'

'I know exactly what is real,' Khalil says. 'And it doesn't at all fit with how I'd like it to be – but all around, the ever-changing scene – runs on, faster and faster, like barrels rolling down a country hill. I don't have anything left, nothing at all – not expectations, not principles. It's beaten me, Soraya. Things as they are, me as I am – the pairing's horrile, mawkish. I can't exist....'

'Well,' says Soraya, putting on a bib and brace – 'Maybe it's here that you can put your "is" in someone else's real.' And she giggles.

'I have a kind of undertaking with Zenobia,' Khalil says, being drawn along.

'There!' says Soraya. 'That's your mistake. Undertakings are for undertakers! You've always had a debt to things not there, that never would exist.'

'Zenobia said the people spoiled things, anything they started, they fucked it up, and started shooting,' Khalil says. 'It went right back, to the beginning. If we'd stayed with the animals, we'd never have got anywhere, and we'd have settled in. Lost the anxiety, the fear. Once we started trekking, it was certain to end up bad. We're too many things, Soraya – and we like seeing palaces burn, dams break. I think there's something in the plan, the scheme. Each species has a destiny – we think the human one is to transcend. It cannot work ... a contradiction, or a limit no one's seen but me.'

'Everyone's like that, everyone believes that, Khalil, you're the same as everyone in everything. It's what you do the rest of the time that makes us different from one another,' says Soraya, 'when you're not doing the philosophy.The basic has to be the same for everyone. Don't waste time on it. Be obsessed, be addicted, raise samoyeds, make cheese.'

'I'd like to do something for you, Soraya,' says Khalil, 'for being patient with me.'

'Oh,' she says, 'I'll find something for you.'

*

In the small space, the night – Khalil dreams. Of sand, of camels, rocking like galleys or like galleons. The endless song that starts from where you leave and ends when you return.

There's a storm – he's being tipped – a seagull, nipping.... Yes, it's an albatross. But on a stick.

'Come where it's more comfortable,' Soraya says. 'We must get Zenobia out the way.'

And that they do. It's swift, the sex, and dark, forgotten and rewritten – a fork. Fork in the road. 'Now,' says Soraya – 'Put this on.'

Cherry and emerald, a caftan. Two big pistols in a belt.

'Just for show,' she says, 'so's people round will know you're related, not just casual.'

In from the desert comes a guy – he has a caftan too, and pistols. The colours – sparklets, amethyst. The pistols work – you have no choice. You're too encumbered to run away – besides, you were attacked. He isn't hurt, just kidding, that's for sure. That's the end, the end of the scene.

'The ancestors will pay, Khalil,' Soraya says. 'Now, give the costume back.'

'It wasn't what I'd hoped to do in life,' Khalil says. 'I had no destiny – it wasn't this.'

*

'Ask the matriarch,' the patriarch says to Soraya, 'to give him his bundle. We ancients – we won't come down. You could not call him motivated, Soraya. Your body's yours – the pistols, though, are ours. Have him give them back, put things on the stove to boil – we'll have a victory feast....'

*

'Run, Khalil,' Soraya says, 'down the hill. Run like an empty barrel down the country road, till you see "Bar". The bar is full of guys who've done much worse than you, or will do – far, far worse. The boss'll give you coffee, a brioche. Pay him from this bundle.... I shan't forget, Khalil....' And she never does.

She remembers him – explorer, involuntary cannibal – hunter at least ... no scope, no map. No question formulated – everything's a question, or an answer.... Never seeking a partner with another goal or none. Not a Zenobia, no nest-maker she, even of a dirty nest – but nonetheless – she's anomalous. In chains, in victory, or lying by the roadside flayed, her tattoo of Palmyra scissored off, a barbarian's skin, in a royal cabinet and then a collection, public, much frequented.

Khalil – no person inside, just journeying and moving pictures. Hallucinations, he presumes, by their form, by their chill. Transmittable, but not transmitted.

*

And without rehearsal, script; a first take – Khalil has made a movie, or a scene of one – a hero of our time, perhaps. Nothing to do with Mister Heinz. The oldsters film everything, put the proofs in the armadillo hole, up in the roof. You never know ... you always know.

*

Getting out – it's easier than getting in. The hot places – China, Russia, America – you don't want them. They cost too much, you don't resist the being beaten in the street. You could die, and there's procedure, but you'd not know what it was. Everything costs more than you have, and if you've nothing – there's too much competition. There's room down on the ground, but you don't know how not to stick out, not to be a target. Everywhere else – is a dilution of the big ones. Your face is too black, too white, you are a target. A defenceless threat.

*

Here's the bar.

'You'll need protection, friend,' Brad, the barman says. 'Ours. If I were you, I'd move along instead....'

'You look to me like you're dependable,' says Khalil, shaking. Brad takes the pistols, puts them in a drawer.

The bundle's full of currency – small value notes, numbered identically. Brad's juggler's eye flits over them and tallies, then flits on.

'We want to leave,' says Brad. 'Other countries. We're experts in that. We've made shoes that stick on walls – we reach the top! – they're stuck too hard, you can't get down the other side – you have to jump back, and leave them on. All the frontiers here have walls of shoes.'

'That's wrong,' says Khalil. 'Join the workers when they cross the frontiers – they do it every day, trudging from poor to wealth and back, and so, you pass with them, grey-blue shades, over to the other side. Keep quiet, your language isn't understood.'

The gang here's no great deal. The guys who steal – they've left the others poor, so's they can't buy the stuff, the pills, ephemera. No thing trucks on. You sell your body, and it wears out soon.

You sell your soul, they stash it in a hole; it's a paradise that smells of camphor and formaldehyde – and worse, it's dull. The brightest colours here – are Khalil's cherry, emerald.

'We may do terrible things,' says Brad, 'break the norms, all that. But it's about friendship, loyalty. Fiercer than the beasts. They lie, the gang, each in their waistcoat, watching the stars – and do those move? You'd never know, they're free, some say they form a message, in a language all diacriticals and fricatives that no one now can read or speak.'

Maybe the stars move. Maybe it's you. It's of small account.

'Khalil,' says Brad, 'times are difficult. There is no profit to be had. And you – last in. And, not because you're *takfir.* It's the unofficial rule. You're the best of us, so you're being sold – another gang. Just leave us your colours....'

'Leave me my soul, at least,' says Khalil. And Brad does. And gives the accoutrements back, to Soraya, and into the armadillo hole they go.

'Now look, Brad,' says Khalil, 'you're a criminal. You don't do deals. Take the cash the other guy has given you – and let me go. Buying and selling members – it's not at all like trading slaves....'

It's true. Khalil runs.

There'll be big trouble that arrives for Brad.

Today's a day of revelation. 'People take advantage of me, Khalil thinks. 'Regimes. Systems. Capitalism – it has a mechanism that makes it fail, and sputter if it rises. Socialism – the bosses inadequate, indifferent – falls, falls heavily, of its own inertia.

'God – has taken on too many disguises, worn too many scary masks, given too many orders, crucified the innocent – and so has lost His credibility. Philosophy? – maybe works for the guy who made it up. But to no one else. As for the everyday – it's scrambling for power, and plausible theories to justify the great division: guys who have cash and status, and those who've competed too, ending up with nothing – or much much less.

'There's nothing else, no more discoveries. Everybody knows exactly where they stand: – to have enough for now, or not. Enough? to have sufficiency twice over, for example. This trudging and adventuring, though – it brings no wisdom, leads to no respite.'

*

He trudges on.

'Suppose,' he thinks, 'I had been a Xiongnu? Not Han, but one of their enemies, laboriously engulfed into the *ethne*, whatever that may be... Which side, when there were "sixteen kingdoms", would I have been on? Or under? And now? I can't be "me" – no one is interested in that, in what I think or do.... If I'd cash, a "me" would do. Without it – I must explain, and find another provenance, or else....'

*

'You've killed someone,' says Wu. 'I see it in your shifty eye.'

'No, no,' Khalil says, 'I am not trained for battle – my eye rolls like a boiled egg, peeled naked on a plate. I have the innocence of ignorance, incompetence, combined.'

'My friend,' says Wu, 'I'm not deceived. You hide some interesting tales. You've done what Nietzsche didn't dare, the coward – misogynist and anti-semite.... You are driven by philosophies, I see. You have tried everything – especially despair, renunciation. The primeval forest – that's your home. Away with love and comfort! Share your story with me and my dear companion here....' and he introduces Rozenn. Khalil notices puff sleeves, scoop neck. Maybe wooden shoes....

'I am not reconciled,' she says, 'neither to Wu, nor to a continent. I'm free, in chains....'

'I see you're Breton, Rozenn,' Khalil says. 'Ah! – Finisterre – the end of the earth. What a challenge, what an invitation. And – to be free of the weight, the soil and stones, stretching to Sakhalin! Can Wu grasp it – you, always on the edge, the cornice, the top storey – then, the waves...? You must be terrified – escaping, with one bound, into oblivion... But Wu's perspicacious. Curious. Smarter than you. The future's China – I hear it often – also "The past is China's.....'''

'What you forget,' says Rozenn, 'is that the Chinese give everyone a Chinese name. The world – is Wu!' and at the sound, all three laugh, loud and long.

'I have read the bible through and through,' says Wu, starting a polemic. 'I bring it to your eyes: no one does any good to anyone. It's like your life, Khalil. Walking from place to place, circumstance to pitfall – and you try to read morality in all that!'

'Oh, you're wrong, Wu,' says Rozenn. 'There's miracle food, resuscitation....'

'How does miracle food satisfy?' asks Wu. 'And "Do not resuscitate" – that's what we leave – our last last lasting words. Now, a miracle belly, that's always satisfied – that would be a miracle, and a good! No lambs needing sacrifice, no fish to ladle up and fillet....'

'That's casuistry,' Rozenn objects. 'You need to find the context ... though it's true, these grand books are not about the good life lived. They're right. It's lives not lived good, some not at all ... that's what we know.'

'Listen,' says Khalil. 'This discourse makes me sweat. I know I'm *takfir*. Probably you guys are too. That isn't here or there. But – you two – what a large and splendid house you have! You can do anything – together or separate.'

'In a truly big house,' says Rozenn, 'you need do nothing, nothing at all. Or everything, everything you can. No one will criticise, no one will collect what you have done. Come – I'll show you everything.'

The rooms are immense. Some are so large there's grass and cows. Others have crags and streams. The sunlight comes pure, in through the ceilings. There's birds in cages, and birds without, just wandering round. 'You see,' says Rozenn, patting some animals, 'it's much much bigger than philosophies, or plans – five year or fifteen. You can be born and die here in any room, and never go downstairs where the machinery is, and counting-houses, and tanks – tanks of fish. You don't need eat them....'

'I can imagine,' Khalil laughs. 'They are safe! You'll tell me – it's so big you don't have Fridays.'

'Oh no,' says Rozenn, 'I thought you'd left that whimsy on the road! No, we need to build the numbers of the fish so we can stock the streams.'

'Some people,' Wu declares, 'number their rooms as if they're propositions. We prefer the wind, that blows from floor to floor and out the garden door.'

'Who doesn't like excess?' asks Rozenn. 'You can't have too much air!'

'How did you manage to acquire such a magnificent space?' asks Khalil.

'Well!' shouts Wu. 'After five minutes, you ask about our money, Khalil. How fucking rude! As if the figure wouldn't be written down and stamped somewhere. Now – if you want to dance, Khalil, this floor is sprung – don't bounce too high!'

The couple, Wu and Rozenn, is endlessly accommodating and polite. Khalil loves the Tiffany windows of the dancing room: Matisse-green – arsenic; lollypop red.... 'What does one do here?' he wonders. It's a ridiculous question. If you don't know, why ask?

'Zenobia would hate it here,' he says to Rozenn.

'Oh,' she says, 'I'm so like her! I'd love to get away myself.'

*

It's like a film before they stripe the vapid story on; the plot. The temporary people. And like the film, you can want to make love, pledge yourself, fuck or despise, discard, just anyone. They'll all be beautiful, won't answer back or bring the cops. No cost, no blame, no gain. It's the set, before the actors get their contracts, walk about, mumbling their scripts.

'I'm an actor,' Khalil thinks. 'But here, maybe it's best be in the audience, and you can do anything with anyone. No blame, no gain!'

Rozenn explains – 'Wu has a good eye for the future, and has contacts. He's much consulted. I'm the homely type. I know what really happens. It's easy: There's a mass of published stuff – states document and consume: - who wants this or that, what interests get involved. What a conflict takes and needs. The guns, the spies, all that. States buy the stuff, hard stuff and ephemeral, from everywhere and everyone. But for me – it's that I see the suffering, experience the longueurs, the inconclusive-ness.

Barracks life. I'd like to try something more intimate: murals, say. The frieze. That's easy too, if you've the talent.'

'Any idiot can start,' says Wu. 'It's finishing that's hard, and takes the time.'

'See,' says Rozenn, waving round. 'We've a tweenie in the tea-room – everybody comes in there. It's our response to class war. A sugary bun, and tea.'

The room is empty, like the rest – 'The house was here long before,' she says. 'We didn't make it happen – we help it go along. You don't need clean. Wu is passionate about the Monster racing. You should have him help you climb up on the steed....' and she points outside – a huge dumpster, wheels twice as high as stallions. 'It's info,' Rozenn goes on. 'They all distrust, despise it – but it's fuel. The system runs on it – the more you cannot trust it, the more you need. The states – they're greedy for it and we – we provide.'

'They pay you?' Khalil asks.

'Not exactly,' Rozenn says. 'We are accredited. We're like the bible, like I said. It's life, not good. It's Pascal – best take things at their word. In private – indulge your doubts. Life isn't tender, Khalil, not with anyone. We all make putrid meat. No happy end, alas. The best thing – is to be let alone. We offer our opinions – someone else assassinates and infiltrates, drops the stuff, and brews it up. Not us.'

'I'm looking for that, perhaps,' Khalil says. 'Cure? Feed? Pacify? End on the cross or kneeling – I could do all that. Even join an organisation that does it – makes things good until it's to be done elsewhere, more crabby people suffering – and raise some cash and on and on ... dodge the shells....'

'No you couldn't, Khalil,' Rozenn says. 'None of that at all. But don't fret. You're still you, and the one two three people that you meet and sing along with, it's all right, it's fine. Everything is breaking up, the big enemies are sinking in their bog, now there's dozens, bogmen, zombies, rising up to take their place and into school and college – they start small, but inside they're big as well.

'Trade, Khalil. That's the universal; stuff you need to keep you up there, on the wave. There's millions making cargo out of air, that you should buy.' She stares at Khalil. 'You don't use any of that, do you? None of the trade is for you, you don't even recognise what the pieces signify....'

'Tell him about the city, Rozenn,' Wu tells her. 'Then I'll take him for a jounce.'

'First, I thought, the barcarolle,' she says, obeying him. 'No motors – everybody singing, like in Babylon, rowing along. Hounds in the bows. But – water penetrates. Even when there's not enough – you find it in your rooms. So – there is the green. All you see is green. A figurative you, literal green. The people underground, conveyed, not seeing where it leads, the track....'

'Oh well,' Wu interrupts, 'you won't see people here, not round the house – everybody works for me. If you want to see them – go in the tea-room!'

'All green,' says Rozenn dreamily. 'You lay it out – a square. Then birds will seed it. As if there's been a camp, dormitories aligned in fives, that's overgrown. The birds bring peace, like the huts and shacks were never there; coarse plants. Bushes – no motors and no cats.'

'That's not a city,' says Khalil. 'That is a field you hope will be a garden, or a park.'

'Yes,' says Rozenn. 'A park. People will be buried there. Born too, I'm sure. The births, though – leave no sign.'

Wu leaves, quite bored. 'I'll put on my motoring suit,' he says.

'A city,' Khalil tells Rozenn, 'is full of guys with trays of baklava, and laying matrices on blanks, and shooting air, birds that pick out cards, beggars asleep to rest their last remaining leg....'

Rozenn is standing very close: their breath, you hear it whistle – there's desire, the move anticipated, wavers on the edge – their knuckles touch. Romance? Who first will tip their hand, and start?

*

The dumpster quakes. Ready for the 'off'.

'Come, Khalil,' says Wu, up in the catbird seat. 'You need this corselet, to keep your insides in.'

And he wraps a tall belt of steel and leather round Khalil.

They're very high. There's no one on the path – they're all working somewhere else; for Wu.

'At least there's music left,' says Wu, turning some on. It booms, trying to assert over the motor and the jouncing – 'And poetry. After Auschwitz, it's impossible to speak of emotions, nor useful to have them.'

'That's deep, Wu,' says Khalil. 'I have emotions, though...'

'No Khalil,' says Wu, quite kindly. 'That's lust. That's what you feel. It's not emotion, it's machinery. And trepidation. Don't worry for what comes next. Maybe they haven't scripted it.'

*

'Don't be jealous, Wu,' says Khalil. 'There's no need.'

'Jealous?' asks Wu, and laughs. 'What does that signify. If I kill you – is it jealousy? Or cast you down? Jealousy? When you killed – is that jealousy? Or fear? Indifference, maybe? Or ignorance. Please or obey someone? Who do I ask, for your motivations – the pay corps? Is lust to come in somewhere?'

'I see your point,' Khalil says. 'It's slippery, all that.'

'Rozenn,' says Wu, 'I understand. She comes from a claw of land, that ends a continent and seeks – what? Not the sea. With sea, there is no compromise. It's an obsessive, a tossing up and down: no rest. They speak, those fishy denizens, but not to us – except maybe to say "fuck off. Leave us to be." That little Brittany – where does it seek a hold, a touch, a clutch? Why, naturally, Brazil. That's nearest land. And yet – there is a flaw. Those Bretons – they went to bitter wastes, far north. She seeks an Africa, dear Rozenn – a starting point. Return, finish? But ... we know, that's false, it always was: Africa – that's misery, empires all-consuming, and populations chivvied – then, forever they're displaced. The Congo forests – possibly they see them from afar, far off, from Manaus.... But what would Rozenn do – with all those trees? She's as African as you and I, Khalil, but does she know the husbandry? Nurture the parrots and the perroquets?

'Love, Khalil – that's the last thing she wants, a poisoned fruit where all the rest have rotted or withered on the bough.... But – bough? Did I say bough? In Brittany – there's not a tree. At most a shrub, knee high. A place unlovable. There, Khalil, in barren Brittany, Rozenn flowered: – there's your love, your lust. A touch of hands, a press of knees.... That's all!

'And you? In every tree there is a tongue, a trigger – you hear the roar, the spring released that sends it up, its spirit, nucleus, the transformation from acorn to immensity. You – no tongue, only a trigger, that's destroyed your brother, your lookalike. Rozenn – she needs a nucleus, and you, Khalil – you're just a clumsy duellist....'

'Brad must have told....' Khalil, dismayed, interrupts.

'Oh,' Wu says, 'info? We are both chipped, Rozenn and I. We pick up news, it streams continually, in through our nose and ears, like blood transfused from every beast in every land, from every past....'

He cocks his head – a message? 'The serious time is here,' says Wu. 'You cosmopolitans – your hour is done.'

He tips Khalil off his perch. Khalil falls far below, into the gravel.

Wu drives off.

*

'Wu always loses,' says Rozenn. 'He doesn't listen to the info. It's his revenge – his big machine against the new, the airy ones. I must be away – but I'll take him with me. Always in my ear. A curse, a token of some emotion. Love? Nuisance? He's for ever in my head, a bullying thought....'

*

The Monsters are gathered in a line, making dark fumes, rocking and rollicking, snapping like borzois.

It's like the Battle of Jutland was; the oil, the coal, their smoke. The rocking sea.

'Wu passes on his fear to me,' says Rozenn, moving, quite far, away from Khalil.

'This is not the future, Khalil,' she says, 'nor fiction, nor science, but it's as far as you can go. I saw you fall – don't limp, though. Put on a good face, straighten out your limbs. There's no advice that's better.'

* * *

'Despots,' says Zenobia. 'That's what I must have wanted. The tops. They're there to scale, peaks that have you tumble down, or make you disappear. The canny climber, at the overhang, must jump off, glide down, or find a crevice, shiver there – and then ... onward, upward. Plant your flag on the crest – and mind your step. What a crowd....'

It's true. Before the platform, there's a battalion – snappers and phonics. The leaders look straight out, keeping a distance with the next, the brother. Maybe they're at war – if they just had the cash! – war with each other, or on desktop, punitive assaults, sallies anonymous, dumping of terrorists, subversion of theologues.... Or just a friendly feud. Those old borders. access to a sea: a river that silts up ... knick-knacks in a pedlar's sack.... Never quite nothing, always just something, rarely a substance – today and yesterday; as beneath the words, there's subsidence, cracking of facades, leaks in basements, shooting up when ads come on the screen....

'You can have any one of them,' Tabitha says, squeezing Zenobia's arm. 'Those guys – killers and liars all – the ladies too! Some with drones, and some with lads, some with jails and some with poison pads.... If you can't kill, or get your generals and slaves to do it for you – it means you haven't got the stuff, the marrow, to stand before your folks and justify....'

'I'm very close to moving in on one of them, the most presentable and permanent,' Zenobia says. 'How I've suffered, schemed and pushed, dear Tabby ... to get where any one of them's within my grasp, my aspiration. And yet – I hesitate. Remember, Tabitha – the sixteen kingdoms. What happened to those kings, the knaves, the straights...?'

'In olden times,' says Tabitha, 'sex came into deals. Not now: Cleopatra had to acquiesce, Zenobia, and didn't even get to kill a Roman. You'd be the counsellor – know everything, and survive.'

'Hmmm,' Zenobia says. 'Rising to the top means you're the cream, but these guys – they're not milk: – they're jackal's piss. Cleopatra got fucked, had to kill her sister, then herself – what kind of deal is that?'

'I see you're wavering,' says Tabitha. 'What's the alternative to power? Fragrance and accessories? Stealing stolen goods....'

'Oh Tabitha,' Zenobia says. 'You make it complicated. I want to live where there are trees, alpacas....'

'It's one or other,' Tabby says. 'Unless you have a grove or zoo.'

'I know,' Zenobia says. 'Zoos are out, but everywhere that's left's become a zoo, the rest is architecture.'

'The poor Ptolemies,' says Tabitha, her mind casting for commentaries. 'No one celebrates them. People remember Romanovs, though – and yet they had a cargo of inadequacies. Cleo – it wasn't dignified. People do glorify a fuck, but in that, whatever the position, there's no dignity.... At school, I won a prize for spelling Ptolemies – like pterodacyls, if you spot the trick. The initial "pee" secures the enterprise....'

'Oh Tabby,' says Zenobia, and laughs. 'How you make us humans sound so – human, if you see it so.... My life, my experience, had a progression that leaves me little choice. With Khalil, there was nothing, especially no cash. I'd to frequent those clubs. Play your cards well, you choose the best, the cleanest hands. Aim only at the boss – you win their diamonds, then their hearts. And in the end – alas, there's spades, they put a stone to keep you down the hole, and with some luck, some withered blooms upon the top....'

'Oh no!' says Tabitha, and now she laughs. 'Those spades don't dig – they're swords! An honour guard....'

'If you've some honour left,' Zenobia mopes. 'There is another scheme, and only one – instead of diamonds winning over hearts, hearts can win diamonds... always, only, if you choose the boss. But, of course, the structure is the same – whether it's Ur, Assassins, Ephesus or Washington. Structure, Tabitha – the basement is below, the attic up above. It's ineluctible. That's how they're built, houses everywhere: there is no other way. You live downstairs and up the stairs you go for dreams. Fiddle it around, you think you've done the trick – like, huts on sticks, on chicken legs.... You'll find the wind, my friend, will blow those feathers off.'

'There's other ways,' says Tabitha. 'But yours, Zenobia, is the strategy that reaches to the top: the perilous ascent – and then the view...! The countries, spread out like a quilt....'

'Oh,' Zenobia says, 'there is – may be – another way. Khalil, the intellectuals' intellectual – what heights he may have reached. The starry heavens ... hopping from light to light....'

'No good for you,' says Tabitha. 'Nor me.'

*

The bosses of the world – they're dressed identically, except for one or two, and one or two are women past their best, all blink and wave their little hands.

'And every one a murderer, supplier of the guns, the prisons and the cops, the soldiers, the ambassadors....' says Tabitha. 'Which one is yours, Zenobia? Which of them's your prince?'

Zenobia says, 'Oh, I'm no Mata Hari. I'm the hostess of them all. You're just my faithful herbalist, Tabby, you brew up potions, that's for sure, but that's so mild! There's cauldrons-full of venom spoken out! At these congresses – there's the same familiar staff. We travel round, we're butlers unisex, nannies and obedient slaves. The top guys fear new faces. We're their familiars. In the daytime, we marshal and we cosset – but... by night, we are their demons, dragons: we share their duvets, we're succubi and incubi, we are their retribution, nightmare, the trials and then the executions, the crowds, the axe, iron maidens, when they pay for crimes and plots.... And so we also pleasure them ... whisper of peace and compromise. So in the farewell pic – they're drained and tranquil ... we're not there.

'All of us – the *servitù*, when the bosses leave, we step forth from the shadows, woozy from the scent of deals; and smile and go our way.

'I earned my stripes, dear Tabby. I think – some paladin, commander in a fertile land where they don't scrutinise too close ... perhaps awaits me. Yet, you're right. It does disgust me. My fault is ambition and hypocrisy. The top lot's pride, and rage, and avarice. Love of applause and title....'

'Oh, don't go on, Zenobia,' says Tabitha, and she laughs. 'I never criticised your ramp. I'm just your witch! We all have peccadilloes – though you and I, I'm sure, would stop at torturing and deaths. It's your next step, however, that is of interest.... Marriage or concubinage, dear Zenobia?'

'They're so old style, my dear,' Zenobia says. 'Is it my horizon, my sweet scene? Fixing was fun – so, would ceremonial existence be too gross for me?'

'You're perverse, Zenobia,' Tabitha declares. 'You're a King Roger! You reach the top – and then resign. Neither saving worlds nor butchering the indigenes.... Nothing appeals, save your own company. You're so old hat, Zenobia!' and she laughs. 'I had it all here, in my bag.... The herbs to calm them down.... The bosses snort and fibrillate, they toast with coca and mamba juice – it makes them wild: exclusive. They'd gang up to keep you out. I'd my response ... Valerian, love-lies-bleeding, pounded up.... They'd accept you then... Drink, drink, *trinken, trinken* – sing along! Queen bee, earth mother ... they'd recognise you, Zenobia. One of them would reel you in.'

'Oh Tabitha,' Zenobia says, contrite. 'I brought you here, and now – the season's for coarse fishing, dear! I'd draw the line there, but ... there's impetus and destiny....'

'There's remedies, my dear,' says Tabitha. 'To the condition – human, but especially, ours: the ladies'. Tradition, history – and, maybe worst and best of all, there's nature. We women suffer from all three. And though our struggle starts with whiteys, mostly rich, in tranquil lands: it's questionable, where do we warriors want to end? The platform? Or the bed? The choice is dire, Zenobia. I recommend tradition's dose – a cup of poison for each boss – and then we'd ponder our next step.'

'You're right, dear Tabby,' says Zenobia – 'But I foretell – there's other battles waiting down the track.'

'One step, one battle at a time, they say. Live! Don't try to put it off,' says Tabitha. 'Find tall poppies, carpenter their box, and take their place. Or cosy up. They're corpses, strutting ninnies! That is your choice, your life, or theirs.

'Khalil took a wet and winding path: – wandering, without a port or raft; a dragonfly on a meniscus, light as air.... Living for the day alone, resolving nothing....'

'Ancient thoughts, my dear,' says Zenobia, her sadness infinite. 'False choices: – some runny jam today, more, much more, marmalade tomorrow...? Perhaps. Nature? Tradition? When we were peasants in the glebe, those were our destiny. No more! Remember – there's catastrophe around the bend – indeed, not even round. It *is* the bend, the space curved like a boomerang. You've never seen it bad like this – battalions of twisters, jumping jacks.... Too late, too late, my dear, those centuries of our complicity, complacency ... what's left, dear Tabitha...? Humiliation certain; displacement – a probability....'

'The poison, it can serve for us as well, if so we wish. It's our insurance.... To the woods, and let us gather....' Tabby says.

*

Here's the wood, the *selva,* round the back.

'It's rather small,' Zenobia says. 'Is it real wood? Or chips? A hologram, or something virtual?'

'It's a wild wood,' says Tabitha, much irritated. 'Probably like the purgatory one, though the pope says the place exists no more. Where will all the people lodged there go? It always seemed the better place for me; most like on earth – regrets and memories, sure, but – guilt is universal, wherever you end up.'

'You must guide me, Tabitha,' Zenobia says. 'I don't see a path. It's dense here, I'd not know what's harmful and what's not.... These toadstools and bright berries – they seem festive, let me try, and eat....'

'No, no, Zenobia,' Tabitha shouts. 'It doesn't matter what we take. Everything is poisoned here. Those blue and orange frogs are worst of all, but how'd you get them stable, and waiting in a cup? Just try kissing one, maybe you'll see a tiny prince spring up ... all blue, with orange hair,' and she laughs, and roots.

They fill their bowls – 'They're meant for begging,' says Zenobia.

'They're made to hold a lot,' says Tabitha. 'For optimistic beggars.'

Indeed they do – those fleshy leaves, the blood-red *cèpe*, remains of hairy gnawing beasts....

'See what I've taught you!' Tabby says. 'Now – we're prepared. It's them. Or us. And either way, it is decisive, if we so decide.'

'I've learnt so much, dear friend,' Zenobia says, holding up her bowl – an offering to higher powers. 'I've learned humility.'

She's quite convinced, it seems.

*

And many leagues away, Khalil sees far off, a line of terra cotta humps – maybe a ruin, maybe a caravanserai – free lodging, company, the songs, the dance.....

'I've nothing,' Khalil thinks. 'But I've learnt. I'm wise.'

There's no hospitality, just humps. The sand is hot, the air is chill. Khalil burns and twists, the candle flame – they say volcanoes purge the world of all impurity – Khalil is pure, in the flame space shifts, time's in turmoil. He has been on this edge before – he dies ... not quite.

'My friend,' the stranger says. 'I once put frozen lobster on a flame – it writhed and shrieked like you.... It wasn't edible, not quite – like you, half roast, half froze.'

'I didn't hear,' Khalil says. 'And you, are you an angel, come to help?'

'Oh no,' says Ahmed. 'It's quite true, good Zoroaster had them, guardians with swords, and all good faiths have avatars and messengers and spooky stars – but usually, they don't pick up the dead. That's for the birds! Hope to the moribund, perhaps, before they die, slide off the ledger, to a list, paper almonds on a paper tree, and someone else is born, unknowingly they fill the gap.... Let no one say that angels strain your faith....

'And no! I can break rules of physics, sure, but I'm not here to help. I'm usually not here, or anywhere particular, I live in space. Built space. Usually, a space that's public, though I never see my friends and followers – and it's right I don't. They follow me, but there's no place where I'm headed to. Matter: one needs, one seeks – the minimum. Remember those old rusty tales – of how a ton of grain becomes converted to a ton of steel. That was the formula, the magic, that did away with capital, with intermediation, with those moneybags! But – Capital is indispensable. Eternal too – be warned! There's no "room" for it to take up.... It's already into space. You ask – "is space, then, crowded? Stuffed and thronged?"

'The formula is false. Space is inexhaustible, by definition, it's never full, it's always empty, totally, a desolation infinite and free to float. There's everything you think of or have thought; your past, your jokes, avowals, insults, lewdness, geopolitics, pics of your cat: – insubstantial. An empty sea, full of transparent flying fish: – you drop a line – and up comes angel-food ... not water and not air, nothing you could put in a cup or on a plate. Not, really, anything, and yet ... it fills you, you can consume, eat, eat all day, arcs and hollows, arks and billows ... it's true, you swell, but that's from sitting down and eating bad. You're not up to exiting your room, quitting your chair, walking round and seeing if there's other creatures look like you, and dress and smell the same, apparently they're you, or you with breasts or balls, but you don't want to see them, you run through them like a sword or diarrhoea, know them intimately, know their lies and aliases, pseudonyms.... But – they're not there. Not anywhere – perhaps they're angels just like me, or demons – and there's no one who will tell....'

'Help!' croaks Khalil. 'Help me, friend.'

'Where can we go, Khalil?' asks Ahmed, the guardian angel, reading Khalil's tag. 'Here, it's an emptiness. There's is no one, there's no place, there's ruins but no rest....'

'Just – out!' says Khalil. 'Somewhere else. I see you're mostly somewhere else – I'd even go there, if you'll lend your arm – you are my candelabra, your hair's aflame, so, there must be ... a stick! A candlestick to take my weight, a prop....'

'Old-timer,' Ahmed says, 'while you've been lingering around, the world has changed. The messages, the friendships, they have multiplied. The old world staggered to an end – the fire, the blood, the judgment – who would wait for that? Rockets to travel to another universe? It's nonsense. So – we disembodied. All of us. And we talked....'

'Listen,' says Khalil, desperate, pointing. 'Load me on that hurdle, drag me somewhere else – I realise it's hard, to deal with my materiality.... Is there perhaps a compromise – imagination, say? Could make me light enough to fly....'

'Imagination – you need lots,' says Ahmed. 'But it won't lift a load. Had you thought – maybe to die, see what the farthest side is like, and leave your obsolescence, your materiality, to dry out here; you'd be a snack for smaller beasts, your bones will thrum and chink across the wastes, your finger tines – bush pianos: – your skull-pan a nest for desert mice....'

'I understand,' says Khalil. 'You are an angel. I am travel-stained, and bulky too. I stink, I drool. I'm not your job – but call your aides, and have them lift me somewhere safe. I know – from time's perspective, humans are both live and dead, we're thumb-prints upon an endless strip, like flies on those old tacky poison bands ... we live, adhered, we wave our arms and legs, and time moves on and there we are, quite dead, stuck on our sticky strip.... Accept it, Ahmed, you and I – we are of different substances, in thrall to sequences unlike and incompatible....'

Khalil talks on, his eyes fade ... two humble guys step up and lift him out.... Lars and Magnus. Volunteers – you have to take a side when you arrive, this is a troubled land ... or else you take backhanders, indiscriminate. From anyone.

You start as militants, or else humanitarians – then – you must survive. Somebody must pay, no?

*

'If you've no cash,' says Lars, as Khalil opens both his eyes. 'You'd be an investor.'

'But you are volunteers,' says Khalil. 'My life is free. It has no cost. Obviously, no price.'

'Volunteers?' says Magnus. 'But – the will is stronger than the deed. That's often said. What we volunteered for did not include a saving you. We need an innocent, bell-wether, who'll lead on the rest. Invest. That's needed to make the desert flower, become a power-house. Or we can dump you back, if you prefer.'

'I have no choice,' Khalil thinks. 'If Zenobia were here – she always has a choice. But then again – she chose not choosing me....' He weeps.

*

'Here, we can hunker down,' says Lars.

There is no place – but there is room for three to lie embraced against the cold. It's good, thinks Khalil, to hug another body, be hugged back – Lars and Magnus are big beasts, their bodies are like cabin trunks, and they hold tight as if the blood is roaming through all three. If only these manacles... – if they weren't so tight, and these two fixated on the cash ... but this is where we are, it's cash more cash, or else you are the wandering poor....

*

'This is your desk,' says Lars. 'Now sell.'

It's a poor place, the settlement, improvised, like bedouins have. 'You're here to raise a capital,' says Magnus. 'We'll shovel people in, you sign then up and smile, and be as civilised and cultured as you can. We must rely on you. you're too precious to be let go – you're not a prisoner. Prisoners have their feet cut off. We slept together, like the young, the very young – like people on the edge. There's nowhere higher – if you fall – what is below, in wait. The scree? Or grass, the green....'

'There's no heights here,' Khalil says. 'No edge, no grass. Brotherhood, but not with you.'

Lars laughs, says, 'Magnus took a shine to you. You could see the world with him – at least – the banks.'

Lars is the faded one, Magnus – too big to be good.

'I don't want love,' Khalil says, 'I wanted warmth.'

His feet are tied, invisible beneath the desk. He smiles, and talks of Mirò to the guys who sidle in to make a Capital.... There's always stuff that must be built and makes returns, that angels wouldn't want, but angels have a line in stewardship, it's written, though you can't pay interest, but offerings are welcomed, presents, loans forgivable, long-term loans not forgivable but everlasting, deficits, devaluations, runs on banks and currencies, and mortgages at special rates and peppercorns, factories traded, for one dollar and a milliard of debts, towers built, towers repossessed, towers with no rentals, towers made of horse and grass.... No cash is ever present, but something's written down and never paid or paid in arms and legs and prostheses and chemicals that kill and chemicals that cure, ambassadors exchanged and spies and blueprints and stolen tribal art, and Lars says, 'Your debt is nearly paid, Khalil, and then you'll be converted to our cause and you'll have a bigger desk, your feet will not be tied but you won't run, for life will be much better and besides you've no idea of where to go....See all around, it's ruined and to build it up, it will need Capital and guys like us, and keep the peace till all is vertical again, and then we'll see....'

'This is heavy,' Khalil says. 'Heavy talk. I'm grateful for your warmth, my friends, but this is not for me, whatever it may be that we're accumulating for....'

'Oh, there's so many things,' says Magnus. 'There's almost everything.'

'It would be evil, don't you think,' says Khalil. 'To establish everything as it was – classes, families, and despots? All the work, the dealing, to stand it up again, and call it different, and it won't be, it's just the first act of what ends up the same. Despot and poverty. Both; no either-or. It's like you're at the bottom of a hill and spend your life climbing back up so's you can rocket down and end up down.... That's history, I think: you're dogs, sometimes you grow, a huge dog, leading those same dogs....'

'I see it different,' says Lars. 'There's like a book of your accounts. On one page there's what you do unto yourself. And facing it, is what others do to you. Anyone can end up destitute – it's what you do that's bad for you yourself that counts.'

'You made me your prisoner,' Khalil says. 'You didn't ask. You cut my feet off. I couldn't walk.'

'Well,' says Lars. 'Gains and losses. They're not only not the same, they're never comparable. You gain, you lose: – you don't gain what you've lost. What you do, and what is done – they're different beasts.'

'You're changing terms,' says Khalil. 'It's not doing and being done to. It's what you bring down on yourself, and what occurs impersonal; malignity or accident....'

'That hill,' says Magnus. 'Suppose instead we had in mind a mountain, climbed for the first time, to the crest – then occupied and fortified at once, to last eternally.... Don't think of our countries and our names – you know that doesn't count....Follow our inspiration, Khalil.... We make the mountain, it is our invention. We climb it, put a fortress on the top.'

'But,' says Khalil, attracted and in doubt. 'It seems quite chancy – except for just what you have said. I'd go along, except.... You and Lars – you are corrupt.'

'You forget the angel,' Magnus says. 'We are its unfaithful servants.'

'Oh, Magnus,' says Lars. 'It doesn't have, need, servants. And it's inscrutable – who knows if we are faithful or just *takfir?*'

'I think the future lies in the word,' says Khalil, quite timidly. 'Our species has so many of them. It's how we coexist with strangers, how the social grows. I myself, though – I don't have much truck with words. I don't see people, those I see – I cannot trust. Besides – words lie, of course....'

'No,' Magnus says. 'Our time is short. No talk. Our end will come in a confusion, or perhaps according to a plan. Measurement, Khalil. Unequivocal. That shows us where we are and what we have – and thence – the order. How long we have to reach the end, to sort it out. The centre.'

'But Magnus – we sell the people tracts of sand!' says Khalil.... 'You're fraudsters! Despots and hypocrites, just like the ancients....'

Lars holds him while Magnus fastens on the fetters – this time they're smithied on, no keys, just metal, ends hammered into one, a start, a finish: all in one, a circle.

*

'They lost their houses and their land,' says Magnus, putting Khalil to work. 'It wasn't us!'

He whispers to Khalil – 'Lars – you see him fade. He won't last long. He won't see the end, the completion. It's a tragedy – but tragedy is always about unfinished things – the accident, the mistake, the premature, the promise broken ... all that, is Lars.'

It's an offer. What of? Warmth? We need that. Love – that's not so sure....

'You'll find,' says Lars, 'those fetters are green. They're ecological – they look like iron, but given time, they'll melt into your flesh – but you can hobble on. You should find a partner, win the three-legged race – you'd run like squibs....'

Is he proposing? Khalil asks himself... Adoption? Where would that lead – to incest? Paedophilia? I'd run, but with one leg....

'Forget the three leg option,' Magnus says. 'You're diminishing. Acknowledge it, Khalil. Your desk's a pair of pants, there's drawers, with pockets, some with a lock. Put however many legs you have inside those legs – and sit. Take in the cash. Will you end up serving Big Capital, who's always done the building here, or something modest and untrustworthy?'

'Sand, Magnus,' Khalil shouts. 'It's sand. That's all there is! Am I your prisoner for ever? Am I enslaved by what you call your state?'

No one answers. It's quite tricky, responding to despair. 'Comrades!' Khalil whispers, unavailingly. 'Is it religion? That mountain...? Or a settlement for somebody's convenience and residence.... A fraud that suits us all?'

Who is there to reply?

*

'Of course, it's complicated. We must house our bodies. Our material selves – what can we do without them,' Lars asks, 'But it's all about emotions. Where are they? Where do they lodge and sup? How do our opinions travel? On drays? On sleighs?'

'Oh,' Magnus laughs. 'Leave it to Capital. They are the belly, they churn a thing into another thing, they defecate in their good regular time – and in the end they metabolise, incorporate it all – the standing up, the knocking down, the blueprint and the writer who paints "fuck" on the facade. Or – maybe a community has taken over: what if they're bigots? Zealots and patriots? Or disordered guys who flee, and nail up two rough planks to make a barricade?'

'Set Khalil to work,' says Lars. 'Sit him in his wooden pants; behind the desk, arrange his legs that coalesce, regressing to a dino's tail.... He doesn't want you, Magnus; he wants no one, but to run, and be himself, alone.... And – now he cannot even walk!' His face – it crumples, a grimace....

Magnus takes against this – it's a provocation, after all.

There goes a blow! Returned. They wrassle, then they wrestle, like two peccaries, seeking a sharp angle for disfunctional curvy tusks – up through the other's chin and nail the jaws, the words, till out will come an unrequited bumbling....

'Shut up, bleed out!'

*

Lars and Magnus – they don't reveal their scheme. It means the promise of an old-style life, that is for sure, with favours for believers, hard times for the rest. A return, but also living right for the first time, so there must be advantages – especially for bosses, who can use the latest tech. They call it Capital, and yes it's Capital, but it could be peace, or democracy or the true faith, or the purifying lord ... they're all quite different, so don't mistake, no anarchy please, no anarchism works, nor does the rest, but you have order till it hurts too much, then you have anarchy until it hurts too much – but cynicism's out, because it doesn't change a thing, and change is permanent and deeply to be wanted, without it everything just comes to hurt too much.

*

Magnus, Lars – they don't bother to explain. Everybody – all the decent folk – knows what they want. True, they've been gulled:

routine's not pleasant, promises are always made, faking an understanding what life's really like. So – hope.

Send the daughters out of town and pack your bundle.

The Settlement

'The brutes,' Camille says. 'They tell such lies! Look – I'll cut these fetters through – they haven't grown into your flesh, not yet – see, I'll cut and you are the same as everybody else. Selling those sandy lots – I'm sure there's better jobs. Those types – they say they're volunteers, but are they fighters, spies – or oculists? They stay on, to make their buck. It's they who make our daily life so difficult – suspicion, manacles; they've friends. Friends of friends – you never find the links.'

'I'm not desperate, Camille,' says Khalil. 'My leg gave out, I rested it, stretching in the sun, that's all....'

'Oh,' she says. 'I'm with you like a barley plant beside another barley shoot. Camille-Khalil! In everything, we're complementary, we rhyme. Moon and moon, and sun and sun. And yet – in just one detail – we're dissimilar.'

'I know,' says Khalil. 'Our bodies – like coins that seem identical, but come from different mints ... our dies ... are in some detail different....'

'Oh no, Khalil,' Camille protests. 'It's all right. Sex is inescapable. Perhaps it will be good. No – it's that you're orientated too much towards ... the poor. The poverty. I'll show you – it's escapable.'

'See me as the future,' says Khalil. 'Forget the present, whatever you think it's like.'

She helps Khalil limp into her compound – he'd ended up in the alleyway, against its wall.

'We have a middling kind of life,' Camille says.

There's ospreys in the yard. 'Not many left of those,' she says. 'You need to know a source.'

'I've lots of cash,' says Khalil. 'I skimmed it off. But you're right – I should have had a better source. You have live stuff, Camille.'

'Put your fortune in here,' says Camille, pulling a brick from the wall – there's a cavern, with trinkets, seed pearls and such. Nuggets and white jade.

'You should plant those pearls,' says Khalil. 'They might grow,' and they laugh.

'It was terrible,' says Camille. 'Before they discovered the oil, they had to dive. People say it's a curse, but without the oil I'd never have seen Arizona. Before that, it was whales. The quest. And before that, it was Africans, sent westward by the wind.'

'It's still Africans,' says Khalil. 'And people like me. One day – people like you, Camille.'

'Oh,' she says. 'I'm around almost everywhere. But it musn't end like that, not like it began. Not slaves. Life before death, I say.'

Gratification's plentiful here – everything is.

'Tell me about the work you know,' says Camille. 'The ornithologists – al-Jahiz ... calligraphers – how I love Hasan 'Ali, so spare, decided.... Nothingness. The minor arts, they're called, along with philosophy – *Heech*. Nothing. And teach me, Khalil, too, about the emptiness of matter. That could be our start. All forms of wisdom, the labelling, the classification, the celebrations and bowing down, the somethings created to cover up the nothing....

'Materialism, Khalil – I can't imagine there being anything else, but there's hypothesis and axiom. Capital. Fetishism, Khalil – I admit – I like fetishes. Dialectics.... Your teachers, was it answers or beginnings...?'

'I'm not from there,' Khalil says. 'Only a part of me, I am from everywhere, but I have nothing, there's nothing that I do.'

'Here, you can do anything,' says Camille. 'Anything you can.'

'You offer me too much, Camille, but I'm not innocent. I calculate...' Khalil says. 'I skim, I dream of fornications, I desert, I spy....'

'Of course you do, you must, Khalil,' says Camille. 'Here's some dates with chocolate fillings – you will find they suit....'

'No, it's not possible, Camille. There is no garden where an unknown person offers a lasting love – to some poor relic stacked against the wall....' and Khalil makes as if to leave.

'Oh, I can judge,' says Camille. 'People. Things attempted that you hope are beautiful. It's normal, just existences maybe in shorthand, quite understandable, with some scratchy bits smoothed out. If you want, stay here with me ... this is a dusty compound, a few birds – not a love garden, unless you want to make it so ... or maybe something else ... tranquillity.You need a stream, a fountain, some tall grass. All is yours – and you are mine....You're a fine, a lovely person, it's quite clear.'

'It doesn't happen so,' says Khalil. 'It's fantasy.'

'You must have heard,' says Camille. 'Without imagination, you can't lift a load.'

'Could I rely on you, Camille?' asks Khalil. 'Is there so much cash behind you? Is there a committee who will question me, to see if I am suitable?'

'Of course you're the right one, Khalil,' says Camille, and she laughs. 'You, only you. I've told you everything. As for the wealth – look in our caveau –' and she pulls the brick out – Khalil's notes aren't there, there's only strass and cowrie shells. There's tufts of straw – those may have looked like river gold.... Deception? Theft? words that mean the same....

'There!' says Camille. 'It's always happening round here – there's poor people, they are everywhere, they watch us, and they take what's needed to lighten up their day.... It doesn't always work – there's bad trips, debts and hangovers, but mostly there are hours of joy ... the movies ... racing greyhounds ... and no, it doesn't always last.'

'I bet the committee doesn't find me suitable, Camille,' he says.

'Then don't let's ask them,' Camille says. 'Trust me, Khalil.'

'Oh I do, I do, Camille,' he says.

*

Time. There! That's another nothingness – they study it, it passes, in the beginning, it's not there, and when it's gone – the same. It seems a joke. It *is* a joke. Camille, Khalil, they learn to find it funny, it goes against the grain, but in time, it comes, the laughter. They're not idiots; they grow old, their skins go grey and brittle – but, still, they laugh.

Khalil thinks, 'I can't live up to this. It's exhausting me.'

Camille seems always eager, reflective, nudging along their speculations with some realism, earthiness ... those plumped-up dates....

*

They – the committee, perhaps – never lock the compound door. He never sees the committee of wise men – and how could they be wiser than Khalil, or any other wise man – you're wise or you are not. There's no committee.

The street is empty, it's dark, no moon, no lamps. He slides out, a cat. The wall smells strong of urine.

*

The morning shift is starting in the pastry shops. It's creative work, if you can stand the hours.

*

That committee – the wise people – might say Camille and Khalil were making a mistake, that they were seeking stasis, that science changes things, it doesn't contemplate, it knows in order to do what it can do ... and up comes good and bad, you have to deal with that. The criticism's just – but Camille doesn't want an empire, making wars and holding down – she wants to last, not conquer... No religion, no quest – no sacrifice, no death of God, or anyone at all: persistence. An illusion? A mistake?

*

Is this the moment to find Zenobia? She's findable, you press the key, don't turn it – and there she is.

Does Camille cry now? Khalil thinks of her, and cries a lot.

*

Khalil says, 'I had a career. I was a star with Mister Heinz. Then, it's all been editing. Memory is fail-safe, more fail than safe. It's better to set out your life, when it's been lived, shooting backwards through the window as it recedes, so it's not just characters coming on, good and bad, one after another. You must write a plot.'

*

'Khalil's one of us,' says Tabitha. 'He's been displaced, like us. We settled down – he's still on the move, but now Zenobia needs some help.'

'Oh no I don't,' Zenobia says. 'I have some weaknesses, it's true. That's good. Many guys prefer a star that's on the rise, that wobbles, comes and goes. The strength is always with the ones who're paid to be hard crap – soldiers, cops. The rest is intermittent – chancers like me, and militants and radicals – we're meteorites. Light burned up and out.

'If Khalil were here – he might be loyal. He's an actor, so if there's a decisive instant, he might do the murder, be the right victim. But, help means compromise: – a moral ambiguity, actor's complicity, that would make him disappear, efface himself.'

'You could live with that,' says Tabitha. 'I'm exactly the right confidant – ruthless and cruel. Let him come. You're curious, Zenobia. Go ahead with that, I'll look after Khalil. What'll he have learned with wandering? You – you only climb and wait – now you're near the top, the fruit is fatter here, but there's black birds and spikes. The drop's eternal.'

They think of the drop. At the beginning of the fall – do you feel free? You are; you are free, maybe it feels good. Swimming in the nude. Repent, regret?

'There's no time to think of anything,' Zenobia says. 'We must resist, dear Tabitha. I've been here and there, sometimes in chains, sometimes in silk. I'm well prepared to be humanitarian – I look quite foreign, that gives me strength with those who are in flight, but ... it's a weakness, clearly, with everyobdy else. I raised myself, Tabby, till everything I did was for profit. Cash. Even that sours – now, it's politics. A kind of success. You're visible, you come out from behind the tapestry. You represent. The profit is in blood now. Let's hope it isn't also ours. What do I represent? People like me. People not like me. Power and influence, persuasive friends. Friends who say "you'll do". An easier thing to manage than diving in hot seas for pearls.'

'Khalil could speak for you,' says Tabitha. 'A refugee....'

'Oh yes,' Zenobia says, sharpening pencils and filling a mug with them, 'He is the part. Of course – he's been here always. Maybe a grandfather sneaked in.... He runs – he isn't chased. He'll always seek refuge, and no one will want him in – not in their beds, not in their movies.'

'It's simple,' Tabby says. 'Your postulants. Let them in or keep them out. Spy on them or throw them back. Not back home, just back.'

‘Is it really that?’ Zenobia asks. ‘Who doesn’t want to move around? Most places – they’re crap to live in anyway. There must be something else. The tiger’s at the gates? We’re kittens in a basket, with mummy and daddy cat opening our cans....? Someone here wants slaves? Or wants their slaves kept somewhere else?’

They laugh. ‘Poor Khalil,’ says Zenobia. ‘To bring him into this!’

*

‘Listen, Tabitha,’ Zenobia says, reading off a wrapper from black figs: ‘*Language is the ultimate indispensable support of the individual, her refuge in time of loneliness when the mind battles with the problem of existence.* That’s me. But, I ask, who will come for me, to break my loneliness – those that think they’ve always lived here, or those who know they haven’t? How does language help?’

‘Oh Zenobia,’ says Tabitha, exasperated. ‘Don’t fret. You’re at the crest – descent can wait. The indigenes – they see you as a gatekeeper doing a bad job. But don’t fear them – a sequence sees them off. A massacre. Think of the Odessa steps. No, it’s your friends you have to fear. Superiors. Exile, death, humiliation – you destiny will change according to location. It’s like the dodgems, dear – you bump and scrape around – then, it all stops. End.Those are the choices; none of them is yours.’

‘This floor,’ says Zenobia, jumping on it. ‘Look – the marble’s veined, like in the shah’s mosque in Isfahan....’

‘Peace, Zenobia,’ Tabby says. ‘It’s usually put on walls – it must be cut so fine – put on the floor ... they don’t expect that it, or you, will last....’

‘Oh, I’ve known hardship, Tabitha,’ Zenobia says, still jumping. ‘We were so poor! My father, drugged, we children selling what we found in landfill so’s to fund him ... for us, no food for weeks.... I used to juggle on street corners – ah! how fortunate, that charity was an obligation there....'

'I thought your family were big,' says Tabitha. 'That's what you always said – not that you were in an act. Do show!'

She hands Zenobia two empty bottles, and one full: Zenobia makes a show of throwing them – the full one drops and cracks the floor.

'You lose your knack,' Zenobia says. 'The staff will clear it up.'

'There is no staff,' says Tabitha. 'Maybe that too is a knack, that will return....'

'I'll wait,' Zenobia says. 'There's sea here. They will come, my staff, my friends and intimates. Cargo! Rafting: cannibals and matelots.... We shan't be office guys – we'll take to piracy! That's the growing thing.... Sail away, away with them....'

The raft is beached. Zenobia sits, reflects....

'My galleon,' she thinks. 'The sails of silver, hammered thin.... We'll sail to everywhere, keep our discoveries for ourselves, and say we never found another continent and people beautiful and kind...

'It's not just tarts that must pretend....

'Those gulls...there's never solitude, dear Tabitha – there's always song and squawk.... the Mongols brought the pigeons in, good Shah Jahan, knew how to treat a girl and send her off in style....'

*

Zenobia hallucinates – you need it, a shaking of the dice.

On a raft, you're right low down, you don't see anyone, hope in time they see you. The waves – they are the time, the trough and crest are tick and tock; on, on they sweep to anywhere. What's it made of, the dialectic, marching like a hurricane, spirits and elements, winds and spray.... The seas....

What powers them? Are waves the concrete? – and an abstract's driving them, the piggy's back on which they ride and rise. What Hegel saw beneath the butcheries and hostelries – a purpose, big mind, portering the carcases and beer ... like an electric eel thrusting through the storm. What force, she wonders, moves the spume, the swash and drift – just circulation, a spin of clods and rain, a desolation always on the move? A mindless impulse? It should be concrete, what we start from, what we are. We watch, we are generals, before us – two mounted armies facing on a plain, the continents colliding ... a hundred mounted armies facing.... Then, afterwards, the plan! Those massacres – they must be requited ... have a meaning.... Watch out! Here it comes, the turning upside-down, the revelation. You need be concrete, to make a thing, thing in itself. The revelation, potentially the revolution, always coming: never comes.

And yet – she changes register – it can seem we start as abstract, bobbing and drowning in a will, a sea, an ocean. We end quite abstract too; dead, gone. Maybe that's all we leave, a will...?

'If I make landfall,' she thinks, quite lucid now, 'I'll bring them back, from ruined empires – Uighurs. And from Timbuktu, musicians, scholars. Which should we eat first, if we must? Musicians? Then there'd be no fun. Scholars? – they reproduce, they're mermen with warm eggs held in their mouths, until the birthing – tiny offspring, so sweetly tuned, their brains can push out attributes – arms, legs? Tails and fins? Or everything that swims and walks? – I'll bring them too. Oh, how I need the power – "*Je veux être reine*," ... "a magnificent man and woman, they're shouting in the square ... I want her to be queen, I want to be the queen!"'

'It's gone, Zenobia – fantasy,' says Tabitha. 'Mere quotes. There's claques for hire, that's all. They'll shout, you look demure. It's a fix. Khalil's too far beaten down – he can't be fixed.'

'Then I'll find another man,' says Zenobia. 'A lover, client, son or nurse. It makes no difference at all.'

'You're a fine person, Zenobia,' says Tabitha, eating a fig.'My! They're stuffed with chillies – those make you hop!' She hiccups. She tries to open the window, to spit out the fig. 'You're a warrior, my love,' she says, drawing back. The window's sealed. 'You'd be the best to care for everyone displaced or questing, but alas – you are too good.Your friends will trip you, have you fall.'

She cuts a fig open, takes the hot pepper out – the sliced fruit looks like two open vulvas.

'These windows!' says Zenobia. 'They're like mirrors. Help me open them –' and she hefts a floor slab to break out....

'Be careful, Zenobia, we're on the thirteenth floor at least!' shouts Tabitha – the wind swoops in and fools around, nothing stays still, the chairs revolve, the pencils flee like spillikins, the two women cling, they dance a strathspey, the room is churning, now hot, now cold and wet –

'That's why no one comes here,' Tabby says, out of breath, her coiled hair undone and flung out like a bush in autumn.... 'And look!' That slab, it leaves a hole, they see down through the floor – there's guys in offices way down, some taking bribes and others smooching secretaries, some pick their noses, others slumber in their underwear....

'If you should fall, Zenobia,' says Tabitha. 'You'd take me too, we'd twist and tumble, down we'd go, ground floor and basement, scuttle out the back among the bins – if we are spared, of course. It may be in the bins we'll go to rest....'

The thought – foretells extinction and oblivion. She weeps.

'We're lost, my dear,' Zenobia says. 'The more I win, higher I climb – the worse the fate. When I inspect the guard – is there a soldier there who doesn't think "Suppose instead of 'present arms' – I think 'take that!'", and you are gone, shot through and through.'

'Yes,' says Tabitha. 'They all think that. Each one. It's the only thing they'll ever think. Nothing can save us: not victories, not love, not sex, success or failure – we must stumble ever upward on the path. "Service before everything", of course....'

'You're wrong, I fear,' Zenobia says. 'Not service, it's just power. You need to have it, to get here, to resist, then to escape, survive. Serving humanity, my dear? – humanity just doesn't want it, not to be saved. Not by me, or anyone. That's good. It's destiny. The species doesn't trust me – and it's right. And mutual. I love the species, Tabitha – but, its good is in its architecture. That, you can contemplate, it's larger than its makers, lasts longer, you can sit in it, stare upwards at the dome.... Those cupolas, dear Tabby – they're heavens, finer than the heaven that does not exist; proportions without age, a fantasy not whimsical, ephemeral....

'The living stuff, the mortals,though – you cannot trust them. They meander, dream of dirty deeds, and waking – do them....'

'No Khalil, then?' asks Tabby.

Zenobia laughs. 'I think I'll get another tattoo, Tabby. then we can think of making my escape....'

'And me?' asks Tabitha, suddenly dismasted and appalled.

'You'll be a refugee, like me and everyone,' Zenobia says, unscrewing a gold and nacre plaque, her name, and pocketing it.... 'Let everybody come, come where they want. Who could choose who comes, and who you see and live beside, and what you do and what they do? What a grotesquerie, dear Tabitha,' and she takes the stairs that no one uses, down and down, out by the bins – and free!

*

'Duty'. 'Service'?

High up she sees the broken window.

'Tabitha,' Zenobia shouts. 'Come down, my love, my lover who gave me more than some advice....'

There's no response. She needs the work, Zenobia thinks, Tabby'll do it better than I could.

From the window, Tabitha can see the sea. The day's first rafts, full of Venuses, coming in to beach.

*

This time, Zenobia thinks, I'll have a tattoo not of a city, but a country. Maybe a continent.

*

Zenobia will see me right, thinks Khalil. If she's a governor, when strangers come, I could interpret. There must be a language I could understand.

*

Here's another milestone: – the European countries, they are full of them, the Romans left thousands, they keep you plodding on and founding empires. Khalil rests there.

'That's my stone,' says the busker, saxophonist, taking a pause, pushing Khalil off.

'Musicians are all different,' says the hornist, rather smug, and settling down. 'Actors are all the same. To me, you look like one of those.'

'I've no home,' Khalil says. 'No stage. All my life I've been here, this road, it doesn't mean a thing, all changes ... boundaries – they're rows of twigs in tempests – off they go!

'Now, I'm surrendering – seeking employment in the state. My friend Zenobia – she has a niche, she loved me once, I'm sure that means she loves me still. At least she'll put me on the payroll – what does it cost?'

'No,' says the musician. 'You're wrong – it's not religion or philosophy that binds; not politics, nor documents and cash. Still less your love and fading memories.

'Look at me – my raft drifts everywhere. My waves – are music. Music improvised, music that's wedged there in your head. It's latent in the others' mind; unrecognised until I strike it up. So, it's valueless.' He grumbles. 'You are paid only when you play; when you stop, it's penury.'

'Oh, I know,' says Khalil. 'It isn't money. That erodes: even where you've sewn it your pants, it is devalued, goes obsolete, you forget – on the dump at last it rests, in a pair of trunkless legs.... No, there must be something else, that brings a satisfaction, something that isn't air blown through a tube.'

'The something else,' the busker says, 'is everywhere. It's everything – the life you won't accept or trust.' He takes out a paper screw and eats some dates. 'Picky-pick, and choosey-choose!' he says:

'See if your friend will fund you – but beware. You're both ingenuous, I'm sure – but she'll love risk – and you, my friend, are risk's embodiment. The ground is slippery, there's snakes, you daren't fall down.'

'I don't climb,' says Khalil. 'I tend to trot. The flat.'

'You're all beasts now,' the hornist says. 'They put a collar on a wolf, a bear, an octopus – and track it. Why? Now – the humans too. Are they near extinction? Sure, they attack sheep and cows – insatiable. They get shot too, but not for being carnivores. It's easy to find your lovers now, just finger them: – a *ting-ting* in the grave, there's your first love, there are photos too.... watch the face, in decomposition, taking you in another world... Animals – beasts – God said we could do with them, all, anything we liked. Collars. Dogs. Spit or skewer.'

He points his instrument at Khalil, quite cheekily, 'Beep beep,' he makes it say. It can do jingles too – for those, you don't get paid.

'Call my friend,' Khalil says.

'Zenobia is special,' says the saxophonist. 'She was big, but fell down thirteen floors, survived, but much diminished,' and he honks. It works with geese.

'I don't much like you, friend,' Khalil says. 'But I can tell you – tomorrow, we shall all be rich. The world will be quite different, and your family, to which we'll all belong, will be what you have not imagined.'

There's nothing to say to that.

*

'I hear a hooting,' says Zenobia. '"The horn's note goes grieving to the woods" – ah! poetry! Now I have reached the night, it says. All round – the sea "blue, green, grey and pink" more beautiful than anything, they say: better than us. Tantric colours. I shall climb up again, it's all I know – but how the world will change! They'll all be rich, they say – an affliction, that; and the obedience.'

Two lifetimes, full of emotions – present together. Anticipation, mainly – some dread, some disenchantment – unreasonable expectations held, rearing and snorting, in check.

'I am the owl, the wise owl now, that doesn't hoot or fly,' says Khalil. 'I wish I hadn't had my grumpy comrade call, Zenobia. I'm wise, I know almost everything – it doesn't matter, doesn't change a thing.'

'You knew me in Paris,' says Zenobia, 'in that stark room. You knew everything then as well. Now – you still know everything, but don't know me.'

*

It sounds profound – perhaps it is, as much as anything can be. They watch the grey ships manoeuvring on the grey sea.

'Inside,' Zenobia says, 'I'm broken up. But I have powerful friends.'

'Oh,' says Khalil. 'My feet get tired. I don't believe in friends.'

Beneath the smoke, there's fire. Explosions – like creation.

'They'll sink,' Zenobia says, 'but it won't change, all will remain exactly as it was: life's in the air now, a million Ariels, flitting, whispering, from aerial to aerial....' They laugh, and see armed men and women run on shore.

'Don't fret, Khalil,' Zenobia says. 'It's just an exercise. Mastery of the world ... we started off like that, it was the quest. It's what we want and maybe we shan't like.'

'Oh,' says Khalil, much alarmed, pulling her under his rock. 'I'm not so sure, I'm not there yet. Of course, there's conquest and surrender, vice versa too. The Word, elusive: is there just one, to conclude it all – or will there be a speech?

'We need some cash, my dear, until they give us what is due. Gold, not notes, if you've the possibility.....'

She takes the golden nameplate out: 'Zenobia: Queen of Palmyra', it says.

It doesn't mean a thing.

TRAVELS WITH STRANGERS

The Concert

IT'S SIMPLE – so, they'll have rehearsed it to exhaustion. A solo instrument, and little children in a simple round.

Schoenberg? – his, although he didn't write it. The children – like in pictures, like everywhere: children, they're the camp guards and the victims. Before the world ends, there'll be other massacres, no need to write that down. We know.

'Are you all right?' asks Julia. 'There are no children. The orchestra, all straight guys, I'm sure.'

'Not crying,' I say. 'Just tears.'

'I could have known you better,' she says, then thinks how it would make no difference, maybe to shove him, me, back in the middle of the pack. Maybe he's the joker, maybe he's gay, or if not a queen, a knave; and leaving anyway tomorrow. Could be his mawkish sentiment that rants, premature nostalgia, then after all – why go? – there's money here as well....

'Home is for when you're worn out,' I say. 'Homes grow, Julia, they grow around you, a carapace, you're armoured, but too slow to cross the road, and you have beasties on you, a cargo, parasites, incurable, the spray that gets them off will kill you and your kids, your agents, bosses, guys you elect and then forget.... The sex, instead, gets less and less – endless raspberry sorbet, even a god or half-immortal would get tired of that.... Your work – is on ephemera, on inexistent things, on hope, anxiety and fiddling.... people who break.'

The City of Peace

'That is your creed,' says the bearded guy beside me in the plane. 'You must have said it many times, to many people who loved you more than you liked them. You know what *takfir* means, of course. I give respect. No blasphemy, no one wants to be an infidel, and no one wants to be obedient. Suppose you step outside: outside history, go where you aren't. If you're not anywhere, do things seem clear, and even welcoming? It could be Leibniz country, where you can ride for hours amidst the tulips, never get saddle sores ... speak Choctaw, versify in alexandrines.....'

'You wouldn't need a saddle.' I tell him. 'If only the dancer in the cornfield, at the end, didn't demand your head....'

'You mean the law?' he asks. 'Won't let you trip? No, no. you're wrong. The law is not a road, a path you take, avoiding holes and thieves; a road you think protects and guides. No – the law's a bird's flight in the air – the path it follows is its own, and what it sees is seen by no human eye.'

'So what?' I say. 'It's not your thing, nothing to do with you.... And there's lots of birds ... one for everyone, perhaps.'

'Oh no,' says the guy. 'There's just the one. You have to follow it. Because there's nothing else. Nothing, nothing at all.'

'Why wouldn't you follow it, if that's the case?' I ask. 'Perhaps I know. It is the vulture, waiting for your corpse.'

'That's wisdom,' says the guy. 'You don't need a bird to tell you that.'

*

'You'd be disappointed with Casablanca,' says Khalil, the guy. 'It's so modern, you'd find the garbage-collecting is obsessive. And there's poor persons, Senegalese, trying to hang around unseen.'

'I have a soft spot for Senegal,' I say. 'But we're not going there either. Now, take Beirut – your kind of table talk, it wouldn't go down, not at all. You are what you are, there, from when you're born. No need for birds. It's modern too – but you can catch a taxi dance. I love them. Anything can start from those, and there is nothing, ever, to conclude.... The fare's paid at the start....'

'I shouldn't tell you this,' Khalil says. 'When we land, you'll see – everything has been knocked down. But, there must be a hole, an iron case, with all the money in. The dollars – they came by tons. In bombing planes.... You might have a load of cash, already briefcased, zeroes heavy as boiled eggs – fall, hit you on the head. Enough to pay for donkeys carrying your coffin, ospreys even, bearing up your soul...You lie dead, on your back, scanning the sky in hopes another patrimony will land on you – the richest man in paradise.... More, much more, than you could ever spend on earth.... Too much to put in banks. You'd buy the banks, and put up statues to yourself, chryselefantine, coral and malachite....'

'It sounds a curse,' I say, although I'm fascinated. It's old time fantasy, for sure; much better have a card, a line of symbols than some heavy cash ... shovelling it out ... the gritty heat....

'It *is* a curse,' says Khalil. 'I'll take it on myself. We all bear little maledictions that kill you in the end. This is the big one, though. Money that will buy an empire. The new trick: you put the money in, back in a hole, or lots of them. Once you were in rags, you hoped to take some out.... Politics, my friend. Invest; clear land, to grow your food. Keep searching. Find guys desperate, who'll do your will, and dig and weed. Beneath the desolation – another curse, the oil. Guys: – for you, they'll drill. Someone must take it on, the money specially. I feel it should be me.'

I should confess. Finding is theft, even if the cash was just dropped quite promiscuous. A big challenge requires a sacrifice, a shriven guy confessing and abjuring too. It may be me.

I try: 'The past. They say it belongs to all of us, the winners, losers, combatants. It makes no sense. The past is no one's. It's not something that belongs – it's there. Of course – it isn't, not anywhere....' I say, 'What you find belongs to you, but isn't yours to keep....'

'Ah,' says Khalil. 'I get it. Your take, your trade. Antiquities. Fakes, stuff stolen, stuff uncovered, stuff dislodged. No prob of authenticity....'

'That's right,' I say. 'It's all authentic. Nothing is. Depends upon your spiel.'

'It's like air,' he says. 'You'd think it's free. In train or plane – we push our way. It parts, we leave no tracks. And yet – there's countries, deserts, boundless suburbs scoured out, fleshless – where we can't go at all. Air off limits.'

*

When we stop, the same lady meets us both. 'I'm going further on,' I say. 'But – it's a homely scene. Who are these guys, checked in and out?'

'Oh,' she says, 'they're good boys from Faluja, a militia; off to put some order into Neapolitans.'

'I'd hoped,' I say, 'to get some Afghans mustered: there's unruly doings in Saint Denis. A warlord, strong man as they called, down the road in Paris ... he can't resolve a thing.'

'It's a risky call,' she says. 'Solving the human lot. Those guys would risk, for sure, and who's to tell how they'll turn out.... They say we must begin again, the chaos here is sign of peace....'

'Oh, no one tells the truth,' says Khalil, and he laughs. 'When you have to start again, from the beginning, you find you're born with rules.' He stops, and starts again. 'No, it's not that; you're born with the law. You try to live with it, you try to shake it off. How do you get rid of what you're born with? It's called life....' and he laughs some more.

'The soldiers,' I say. 'They seem eager lads.'

'That's how we always like to see the squaddies,' Khalil says. 'Young, impressionable, correct.'

I joke with them. 'You look at me, and see there's things that need some sorting out.'

They don't protest, deny.

'You're from the museum?' the lady asks me. 'That's modern, I suspect. We're old, and everywhere abroad is new.... But, those poor Italian women! When will they be free? Should we come and bomb you, show what's what? Teach how you should behave?'

'French women,' Khalil says. 'Are freer – but there's all those fascists round....' He turns to me, 'This lady's from the Agency. They'll have told you when you bought the ticket. Her value system – it is pretty strong.... Respect it, if you can't adopt. Don't let that put you off – she's a good sort, and mostly loyal.... Nothing of her rubs off on you. She'll send you where you ought to go.'

'It's true,' she says. 'We've had our strongarm people here as well. They say it's our tradition – well, tradition is what happened yesterday – the day before that, it was quite different.'

Curating the Antiquities

Her badge says 'Orqina'.

'You get it wrong,' I say. 'I'm freelance myself, but a museum has no interest in history. It has no interest in values either. Things, Orqina: themes. Taste and relics. Collecting. Selling on.'

'I know,' she says. 'It leaves me quite indifferent. What interests me is who is doing what to whom, what drives the cart, now that the horse is obsolete. Brutality or cash? That's how it works today, that's how things are done.

'Once, every country had its spies, its Agency: but now, everyone's a spy, chooses a side.... So now, we meet you all – trade, aid, greed and myth. We ship you on. Top speed, or just economy rate – economy, there are chances you will rot in quaysides or in sheds. We don't question – but we know. The Agency is everyone's, a corp, and international: quite untouchable.'

'It's new,' says Khalil. 'But not so much. You know it all, Orqina, but you don't tell.'

'Yes,' Orqina says, trying to get away from us. 'We are disinterested. Someone must know the truth – what happens then is what you will.'

'It sounds fascinating, Orqina,' I say, twining my arms round hers to keep her still – 'I could be part of you. Employment? More than what I'd hoped to do....'

'That's so,' Orqina says. 'I could make you lucky. But – are you worthy? And – the job is dull, the worst places in the world, bus stations, airports, desperation everywhere, and guys who lie and cheat and steal.'

'Who pays?' I ask. It seems the right career for me....

'You do,' Orqina says. 'Everyone. And we go through your bags. As for you, as I inspect – no. You don't pass, not anything. Thieves are usually drifters – but you're a burrowing kind. You deceive no one but yourself. Khalil would fit us – he's ready for his tussle with Satan, and could win.'

'I hate hanging round,' says Khalil. 'I want cash by truckloads.'

I tell Orqina, 'You won't find my burrow. I have it paved with coloured stones.'

'These militias,' says Khalil, 'they come in rolls, wallpaper to hold up a crumbled house. We're not supposed to know they come and go...but everybody must.... They tip the balances....'

*

'Once your paper suit fell off,' Orqina says to me, 'Truth, Pravda, it was called – you found you weren't up to being free. No one thought to publish that: – Svoboda, Freedom. It doesn't chime. Life went on being dull, but you'd no excuse for anything. For you guys, communism was an alibi for nothing doing. Now, you don't like anything that you can't steal.'

'Oh, don't believe my passport,' I tell her. 'That's handed down from ancestors. All false memories, countries exaggerated, conquered and lost, the people trucked off here and there. You think someone cares about you – but you've nothing, no personality, can't even draw a crowd.'

'Come away!' Khalil shouts, tugging me to stumble off, 'Your truth, Orqina, is that you despatch. It's movement on a moving earth: it's trivial. The Agency is details, pixels waiting for a shape. What could be bigger than big states with bombs that wipe us out? We know all about that, how it was yesterday, how everything might change tomorrow. No present, that's clouds that fleet away. Truth is only where you are and what you do. And where it's hidden, where you dig. All you need, all you can know, the rest – love, death and loyalty, it's poet's stuff. A turn of words. In words there is no truth: you learned all that at school, and then forgot.'

'Yes,' I say, admiringly. 'You really are *takfir*, Khalil: what maybe I have been, not knowing it. You, and now Orqina, have shown me – those plausible gents and ladies, the couriers, their formulas – they're empty crates.'

'Let's get away,' says Khalil, pulling me into a car without markings. 'Leave your bag. It's useless here.'

'You know,' I say, as we bound along. 'What Orqina said: I may not have been a hero, but what I said was on the ball – communism, capitalism – both is right for you when you are there, because it's stronger than you, and the same for any other scene. Conform and suffer ordinarily. Oppose, and it's extraordinary, the suffering. Up to you. That is the choice.'

'No philosophy, thank you!' says Khalil, laughing. 'You have to be a gambler here – no one made or took a bet on what's already happened. Win and lose – that is the choice – the rest is way above your head.'

Excavating: Scraping Surfaces

On the dash, there is a tiny fan. There's music, loud, *el andalus* with beat and chugging drums. The other guys, packed in around me – they sing along in snatches. Here, the streets are wide and dusty, underneath is tarmac, maybe, rubble probably – and workshops all along, with oiled-up guys and tubes for broken cars....

It's hot. Who are these guys, what is this place – a centre ... but what of? a suburb ... who lives here? in compounds, or dozing by the road, on a chesterfield, under the sun and in the dust.... Dogs much loved, not let inside, it's not allowed....

*

'Khalil,' I say. 'I cannot understand a thing. Your plan is great. But... Nothing of this makes sense to me – not you, and not my place. Stop! Let me off, to find another way to somewhere else.'

One of the guys says, 'Wait, learn – you'll find you sing along.'

'I'm at a loss,' I say. 'I'm no use here, nothing is mine ... not even mine to steal.'

'You don't know where you are,' says Khalil. 'If we leave you here ... you're disoriented. If you take a ride, be very very careful it is someone you can trust.... Who knows, or guesses where you want to be?'

I tumble out.... Dear Khalil, I'll be back....

Away they go – no point their looking back.

I'm dressed like everyone – they stare.

No one plods along the road like me, there's dust and crumbled concrete.

A car, a guy stops, he doesn't speak, and drops me – somewhere similar. I flap my arms to show I want a plane – he's not convinced, no one else stops. Who would?

*

At last, 'Orqina!' I say. 'Send me on my way again.'

'I don't advise,' she says. 'Your plan was good, but not for you. You don't belong in being smart.'

'I can't stay here, I can't go back. Give me a ticket, where....' I say.

'Where,' she says. 'That's the right word. It's time for me to leave.... I don't believe in staying anywhere, nowhere for long....'

'It's not about aesthetics, Orqina, nor colonialism, nor stealing. Maybe I try all those, but I'm not committed to them.... They say everywhere is all the same, so being somewhere shouldn't matter, but it doesn't seem so when you're on the road....' I say.

All the booths are shuttered up.

'Your problem,' says Orqina, picking a used ticket off the ground, trotting towards a plane, 'is you're a tepid specimen. You neeed to be prepared – to run slap against the wall. Sometimes it falls, sometimes it isn't there. The running's what you do, my dear – that is the vital part.'

She goes towards her plane, buzzing, bright, with a parrot's tail – she shouts, 'You must find somewhere you'll regret leaving when you have to leave, as we all shall. I have several places so; and a space, immense. It's ephemeral, of course, but everyone should have a roost like that. You've magnets hidden in you – you summer here and winter there, and mostly you're up high and in between – all and nowhere is your home. It's what you need to know, there's nothing else, no need to learn a thing. Defecation's up to you; the route's set out.... The rest is tailings, chaff.'

Settling Down

It's dark and still – no trees, so there aren't birds. I must find a floor. I know what you do then – the floor means you can't fall further down, into the cellar, then through and through, the dinners on the grass, the shooting up, the fights, the bottle not passed on. Dissolution.

The floor is where you cannot slack, or question much. You go to work, day after day.When you are free, get a tattoo, and start to cover up your unachieving flesh with pics. Black yourself out, be like the working blacks, learn to tote bales again, and pick and pack the fruit. But, at the end – there is no better world to reach. The pain leads on to pain and ridicule. It is *le grand macabre.* A workers' state that's ruled by toffs? or working stiffs who work no more and make the rules – who'd dream of that? who'd ever dreamt, remembered, wrote it down....

Uncertainty's a privilege. It's good. Drifting takes skill and navigation. You mustn't starve, you won't – not like the guys who stand and stare at you, feet nailed to where they are. You are – *en marche*. On the road: hooked up, roughed in. Hung the cold store, outlined on the drawing board. Don't let sensation fool you – this is you, real and passing through; there's nothing more. This could be a pond, swans skidding in, their feet braced on the brake. The guy who invented planes – might she have invented swans? There's always someone saying they're the innovator. The first people. Fly away on one, your bird – a squawk, a long flap, then you're a nano-person, clinging on the feathers ... but safe, safer than in those closed aluminum tubes....

Change.... I have to change ... aha! a change machine.

'Dinars, dirhems, and yuan' – Are they what I need? And which? I push a note in, the machine takes it, that's all.

Aziza: Evolution

'Just push your note in. With confidence this time – if you doubt, you get nothing. You'll find the same amount comes out, but in a different currency.'

She's Aziza, from the Agency: 'It sounds futile, but it's the order of the world. The end of the world – will be much better than the end we've had already here,' she says. 'Ours – goes on, and on. When it really ends, the world, ends properly, you can take photographs, leave a message.'

'They say, that when you die, your soul goes off to make a tree,' I say.

'Then they're wrong,' she says. 'There'd be forests here. Instead, the trees are gone, the people too.'

'I'm fearful, Aziza,' I say. 'Evolution – it takes another turn. Better terms with animals. It seemed we'd stopped riding, hunting them: predation at a distance, the abattoir – that was enough. The struggle was concluded. We'd won. But then – the old affliction, cannibalism ... came up, flaring. We had to learn – to live again with animals, together in a troop ... those few left, those we could track down and pet and cage.... We were not liked, we starving conquerors.... Our way of living, the solid things, our cities, mountains, ice and sand – crumbled, sold, evaporated....'

'Yes, exactly,' says Aziza. 'You're right to be fearful. Evolution strides. The genders were a luxury. One – lazy and agressive, one submissive.... It must sound nonsensical.... Have you seen our city – bigger, older than Rome, and now a swirl of dust?'

'Advise me, Aziza,' I say. 'Vanity! Over and over, now, can it be cast down? Our struggle, in the void.... It is for ever resurgent, vanity....! Projects are castles made of mist: enough! Send me away, no more conviction, no more replays....'

'Your trouble,' says Aziza, 'is you don't like people much. It soon becomes reciprocal, and everywhere you go – there's only people, an abundance of them – fearful like you, or blocked, helpless in their past ... each asking you to do something to help, or hoping you get lost, disappear – quick as you like. You're a good person, I can see – you ask the questions. No one answers, and you can't. What is yours, you ask, what belongs to you? What can you take? Who owns anything – or everything? Who are you responsible for, how far....? When benificence reaches an end – the soldiers enter, shuffle the cards and deal fresh hands.... You're a good person, possibly, but goodness isn't worth a cent.'

'Then, send me anywhere,' I say. 'The questions – are always the same, and I don't know the answers. Khalil and I – we're only interested in things, in trade. But maybe people, animals – even trees, they're not indifferent.... You must know everything; if it exists, you can.'

'That is banal,' says Aziza. 'It's not about the stealing stuff. It's "what is 'me'?" and "what's a place?" The rest – the money, stuff you dig up – princesses in the perma-frost, the oil – it's all a metaphor.'

'We must watch out,' I say. 'We have to eat – that isn't metaphor.'

'Well,' she says, 'remember – the goat, caught in the thicket – that was luck for somebody! You were the sacrifice, you shuffled off your obligation, but it seemed that after that, humans are exempt. Suicide is out, so's to sacrifice someone else, or their families will kill you too – so, the sacrifice is passed on to the goat. God eats the goat, but you've escaped. You're hungry, but the service that you owed's commuted. Now, it's all down to the goat – it's food, but not for you. Don't waste it. Leave it on the temple steps – your vulture will come down for it. That way the vulture is your god – but don't tell anyone. It's not allowed. Not here, not anywhere.'

'Where, Aziza?' I ask. 'Where do I go?'

'It's old, old talk,' she says. 'It's better not to move, not go anywhere. When we were bombed and occupied and then decapitated, did we ask – 'where next'? What more can there be? Some things – they finish. Over and over, but there is an end, and after, only ghosts.That's the answer to your questions. If you insist – go somewhere, slough your old skin, tease yourself with new puzzles.... And don't ask.'

'Oh, the puzzles are dead lives, finished, that you do variations on,' I say. 'People you didn't know, even closest to you, they too didn't know what they were doing while they lived.'

She's restless. There aren't many tickets in her case....

Skiing – Falling

'You remember my friend Ivan?' Julia asks her English friend, Sandy. There's mostly sand in England now – the heat – but not why his family called him so. It would be a pleonasm.

'I haven't heard for months – he was last seen in ... I think an airport, bus station, Mosul, or Kabul – a place like that,' she says.

'A mercy mission?' Sandy asks. 'Or curiosity? That's what killed the cat, they say, they see a hole, run in and can't get out... They think they're smart, but....'

'Oh,' Julia says. 'Mercy wasn't in his stock of words. I don't know what he was – his family Russian, but it doesn't mean a thing – could be Tatars, Siberians – he was none of those. Armenians. A foreigner. There's lots of males called Ivan, circulating ... not all are terrible, I'm sure....'

'There's nothing you can do,' says Sandy. They look down the snowy slope, lean on their sticks. 'Coming up is slow and dull,' she says. 'Going down.... No time even to reflect....' She thinks – I wonder who first tried sliding on the snow, and thought it was such fun to reach a top and skitter down....

There's nothing at the peak to see but other mountains, people gliding in their baggy suits, bright as parrots' tails, swooping down like swans or falling, lying still.

She thinks: The English – they never lie aloud, they lie by keeping quiet. That way you can lie eternally, silent as the universe. How does it profit you?

'Shall I push you, Sandy?' Julia asks. 'There was nothing between me and Ivan – that's a double sense, it may appeal to you. "Nothing between" – may imply a zero or an intimacy.... I leave it up to you....'

And Sandy's gone, down the decline, wagging his bum from side to side, the part that drives the whole, the tell-tale tail – he gathers speed, and – oh no! he's gone! Into a hole – they're called crevasses, crevices, a device with special names that does for you

– a hole, a glory-hole, a hidey-hole ... a bore-hole, where the bores are despatched, disposed of – a hell-hole, and Julia says 'Oh no!'

She doesn't tell the guys whose job it is to haul the bodies out. She thinks – I'll send a message when I'm home. That's what little screens are for. Maybe he has left some cash. Death is inevitable, no one knows when, but, it will – so sadness, regret, it's quite irrational. It is the wind, the breeze, that brings you in and wafts your coracle away. We live long, it's true, longer than alsatians, less than tortoises, yet people mourn their dogs and less, much less, their tortoises. Of course, Sandy was my dearest friend, but now – there's nothing left, nothing at all, he's going home, it's good he didn't ask me in ... and so, I'll have another dearest friend, gifted by elimination.

Karine the Comforter

'Oh Julia!' her best friend, Karine, says. 'You bear a hex! We drop, we tumble, fall prostrate – all round you, and you think on! You are the conscience of the universe, you suffer, you forget. One wonders why we have emotions that must fizzle out in suffering. You ask the knotty, the impossible, and ... one day, you maybe will reply....'

'Of course,' says Julia, flattered – 'I ask the questions, everybody does. The answers – they are trivial; best not insist. The answers – they don't change a thing – the questions, they come naturally, when you are waiting at the top....'

'Tell me,' says Karine, touching Julia's neck, waiting for her to shrug off or entwine, a tingle shared.... 'Where'll be the best place?'

'It's a pity to waste one's Kazakh after doing it at school,' says Julia. 'And it's flat and dusty there already ... there's camels. That's a resource, protected. And the milk-shakes, mmmm!'

'No islands,' says Karine. 'We thought Moscow – people are used to anything, they don't panic, rush about.'

'Nothing shrill,' Julia agrees. 'Liberals – they are the worst. But we must spread out, not bunch. Wait: take the empty bus.'

Travels with Goethe?

That's what Ivan did.

He skips: 'a state of love ... at present in Switzerland ... my article ... the newspaper, the spiritual bread of life, warm and damp from the press....'

Not many got through that century, he thinks – those people, friends of no one, all a-chatter and a-bed, counts, barons, dukes, trying to make a buck restoring castles ... nothing doing. None of them has water, and in the siege, some guy opens the back door to the horsemen in exchange for lemonade.... No more strolling along the boulevards, a *tommy* on your arm. All of them – everyone; into the mixer, milk-shakes; there's prohibition. Hugger-mugger in the camps....

The bus stops – 'This is it,' says the guy.

Ur-scripts. I for 'Ivan'

'People I know,' says Anatol, as he and Ivan swap their worries. 'Bet on Moscow. But a city ... hmmm. They have nothing, and getting out's a crush, there's tented camps if they have thought of them – in short, they've lemmings. The Agency...'

'Oh, it didn't send me here,' says Ivan. 'They'll have a hidey-hole. I couldn't read the script – where the bus was going ... that alphabet!.... I guessed I'd be the only one, the passenger enchanted....'

Anatol laughs, slides his knowing finger round his jaw. 'It's brown and sandy here,' he says. 'This used to be a paradise, an

Eden. Who knows – maybe it will flood again – but if the water's salt ... too bad! That snake,' he pauses, downs a vodka. 'I love it! The earliest, those Babylonians – invented paradise, and knew their gods were beasts; they passed, with all their beauty, guile, malignity – into the shape of animals. The first sedentary people, sitting it out, they'll be the last, and glad of that. We owe it to them – they lit the taper, round it goes.... Inventing good and evil, sliding the blame on to the snake – passing the moral parcel round until it lands back on us.... It's handed on, the blame – then circles back.... The snake: I think it knows it all, what's good and bad, the goat is sacrificed, not us ... then, the boa eats the goat. The serpent holds it, Ivan, the purpose of the universe. A puzzle and a fraud, a shell game, circus, cast of trillions ... don't tread on it, the worm, it's dialectical, the good, the bad – and slowly, slowly, it digests – you, me ... the rest. And – we are free to kill each other, without guilt or punishment, a little time in rehab, or the amnesty ... the cure.'

'Oh Anatol,' Ivan laughs. 'Nothing ever is resolved. Nothing can end, it spins off where it can't be seen, emits no signal and no light.... Falls into heavy clouds invisible. This is a beginning: maybe it all is, difficult, but propitious always – going on and on, forever starting – no end to anything, but only metamorphoses and disappearances.'

'They'll all come here,' says Anatol. 'Our people, seeking refuges. It's true, the story must accommodate coincidence – but Karine, my dear friend – she'll tire of Moscow, she'll seek me out, she knows this place.... She'll bring the rest, and we shall be a little clan, and – who knows – maybe a prophet will arise. This, our Medina: amidst all this sand, our thoughts turn to divinity, the sun, creation, how to navigate the future, live according to the law.... We'll raise a stone that's sacred to the snake....'

'When's the next bus, Anatol?' asks Ivan.

Should he depart? The bus, who will it bring? He asks –

'Will everyone we've known come here, from logic of the narrative, or is it the bad sign brings them here, telling how it all ends bad, badly started, badly written, starting with a syncretism, writhing into mystic knots, and ending circular with the snake – so big, it swallows everyone, constricting slowly, arms and legs still sticking out like french fries, our heads ... you see them on the way down, a string of beads, lapis and glass....'

'Everyone we know?' asks Anatol. 'I don't believe in bad signs. Only good will come – we'll meet again, remembering good times. The ones we loved will come – Karine for me, for you....'

'No love,' says Ivan. 'Just carooms for me. Julia – an ignorant repetiteur. Khalil on the run, no cash.... The ladies from the Agency, with other tickets in their bag....'

'What difference does it make to you?' asks Anatol. 'Love or acquaintance? You have that abandoned house you stole, two dry rooms, a dry well in the yard. Rise up with the light, down with the dark – in this heat, cultivate blue aloes for tequila. Try artichokes as well – we'll have to sweat, that's how the sea got salt, from gardening....'

Lovers' Meeting

A bus – and what a display!

The ladies, rolling in, balls of fur; fur whispy, fur bouffant, with mèches, without – furs scarlet, carmine, amaranth, pillar-box and poker, bulls'-blood, magenta – 'We were wrong!' shouts Karine, as she tumbles down the step and starts to sweat.... 'These are just fantasy, we looted the wrong store. The jewellery's all gone, of course....'

Anatol hugs Karine – 'How was the frontier? Did it cost a lot?' he asks.

'O, the bus was cheap, five kopeks, like old times,' she says, pushing Anatol away.

The bus says Chinatown – Kitay-Gorod. Some ladies – they might look Chinese....

She goes on, 'The soldiers on both sides – they're similar – they share their disbelief and languages – now, the snake cult has its fans, the boisterous youth....'

'Hush,' shouts Anatol. 'That's myth – quite inappropriate. And so – the city's empty now?'

'No, no,' says Karine. 'Everyone from other cities sought a refuge there.... No room, no rooms anywhere!' She weeps. She asks –

'Now, where's our residences?'

On the shoulders of the furs there's set a row of twisted blackened snouts, and eyes of glass and lapis lazuli. 'The eyes are real,' Karine says. 'That's all.'

'We'll find you easy in your coats, if it ever snows again,' says Anatol. 'If there's anyone who looks, of course. We mostly hang out here, where the bus comes in.'

'Your lovers, Anatol,' asks Ivan. 'Do you expect some more? Did you love poor people, or are they all well-heeled, like Karine – those teetering boots – another emptied store...?'

'Of course I loved poor people. It's our obligation,' says Anatol. 'You aimed high, Ivan – relics, mercenaries – that was your line. It's not an uplift. You have high hopes, but still you scavenge on the floor. I am a friend of everyone on earth – the druggies too, however high they aim. I love believers, old and new. All nationalities: – like you and me, Ivan. No prejudice.... We'll live together here, until we can't.... An Eden – parched, short-lived, but still – more than the best we'd hoped to find.'

'Oh, but when we can't – who knows what types will come?' asks Karine, holding on to Anatol. She sobs, he weeps in sympathy, but he's fired up, with hope, ambition, all the rest.

'We'll need protection, now we are all poor,' she says. 'Maybe that means we shall have socialism – or maybe we'll be sold as slaves. The serfs – what wonders they have made. Ostankino museum – the arts, the music, golden age....'

'An authority,' says Anatol. 'For each, for all. That's what we'll have. Good, selfless people, with a goal....'

'Oh dear,' says Karine. 'Here it comes again – the state! Can't do without, can't trust it, or live underneath....'

Moscow Days

Anatol is in a rush – here comes another load – 'Oh no!' says Ivan. 'Julia! It can't be. Surely not. She runs to Anatol? His lover?'

'Sweet nothings,' Julia says to Ivan. 'What's it to you?'

'But Anatol's an idiot,' says Ivan. 'The father of his people, an Abraham, wants every woman of the tribe to bear his bunch of kids.... Beginning what he can't conclude, a man for every age and none.... Trite, a trimmer, credulous – an optimist....'

'He knows the moves,' says Julia. 'What more is there to know?'

'The hat!' says Ivan. 'Julia! Was there nothing else? Taste! Is Moscow bereft of all fandangles?'

'See!' Julia says, hefting the bright wheel off her head. 'It's tutti frutti – ripe pomegranates, even a bush – I guess it's pineapple – there's a curious peach to boot.... Abundance, richness.... Besides, the sun here brings the apples on, and in a day they plump and rot.'

'It's better so,' says Ivan. 'We have such little time, things speed up.... We have a politics to do, before the end, some conclusion, a good show, questions resolved.... I'm sceptical – that owl, does it have conclusions, or just hear its dinner squeak?'

'Oh Ivan,' Julia says and laughs. 'You don't believe in plans, but act as if there is a plan. Remember the scientist who says –

"I've studied many games, especially of football, and I'm sure the purpose is to put the ball into a net, using head and feet – not hands, which would be easier. That is the purpose. What the purpose – of the purpose – is, I'm not so sure. Cash, ritual, diversion, exercise – a training, maybe for a hunt? Fun – unlikely.... Solidarity and resolving conflict? What a joke....! All these come to mind. But then, we're far from what they really do with heads and feet, and why they're watched with ribaldry, respect.... Analysis, reflection – useless. You'll never see what all's about. You have to set your head on straight: – sarcasm is the winning mode. The whole? Accept. It is ridiculous.

'The joker in the sky, behind the scenery: – oh vanity! he says, and giggles. "Now, what will they believe, those gangly apes – a talking animal? A cow? A mouse? What's the least likely as a messenger? A message anyway that's far beyond their grasp. A worm? No – it must be a bigger sort: a snake. With black and amber rings – see, it speaks, and climbs up trees and runs around. So very limited, and venomous! Surely the guys will not believe it knows what's good and bad...." He laughs and laughs, and so he tries it on: and – lo! it works.'

She stares at Ivan, wondering at his tears. 'We could have had great sex,' says Julia. 'But you were into manifestoing. Think, Ivan! What next? We came by bus, but soon they'll come in trucks, and then on foot, whole nations....'

All Roads – No Rome

Khalil shows up – and Ivan asks, 'The dollars, Khalil. Did you find the drop?'

'Yes,' says Khalil. 'Of course I did.'

'Well?' Ivan asks. 'Me? Maybe a share, at least a tip....'

'You're not one of the squad,' says Khalil, cold. 'Besides, the dollars here aren't worth a snit. For you guys, currency – it's carrots and it's cabbages: potatoes your reserve. You've all regressed. You're primitives....'

'How did you carry it, the cash?' asks Ivan.

'I dug it up,' Khalil says. 'And then I buried it.'

*

'What I think,' says Anatol to Ivan, 'is – we went along with everything as we could. We weren't chosen. No one selected us, we're none of us the kind of people you feel sympathy with. No one worries about what happens to us, any one of us.

'Things go on elsewhere as they do, have done; everyone complains, some want to help, improve, they say, the others just whine and wheedle on. It's all quite arbitrary – now, we're in this paradise, but it won't last. Maybe there's lots of paradises scattered round. We'll stay in here and dig and plant – and then, for us, it fizzles out.'

'You have Julia,' Ivan says, 'and Karine.'

'High-born ladies, or they've studied how to be,' says Anatol, quite glum. 'But I'm not their special favourite. Not any more.'

There is uneasiness. 'Then,' says Anatol. 'There is the stream. Our Drina, Don and Mississippi. A thread....'

'Spun? Held?' asks Ivan. 'Or a thread of voice: songs and stories?'

Anatol pushes onward, past – 'Another paradise, perhaps, nearer the source, could block our trickle. Otters, beavers, too – whatever they may be. We ought not expect great change.

'Even if we make the seas run dry – still, it's better than a massacre. It's pardonable, – a failure of imagination, impatience. Hastening extinction – it is painful, but it's humble too, the hands thrown up and in. The banker – immovable, always deals. The animals – they're long gone here. We're carnivores, we don't protect.

'Don't watch TV. You'll never know how the cattle plains, where once the Indians roamed – long ago, they went to dust: the hills – to ash. We have the time, Ivan, to reflect, to elegise. It's nature: this way, it all *is*, we're buried in it.

'If you missed your fun – you're not alone – the coypu and the glutton – they'd no time for it....'

'I knew you were a trimmer, Anatol,' says Ivan. 'Now, I see you are a bosses' man. A fatalist.'

'No, no,' he says. 'You're wrong. Opposition – it is noble. Revolution – hope and justice. What can detract from that? Principles – have no time limit. Indeed – the less time you have to quiz a history, the better it will seem.'

Gardening Delights: A Future Eden?

'Those are weeds, Ivan,' Karine says. 'Didn't you have a childhood? A garden? When you're young, you grow only weeds, you're proud of them. When you've grown, you recognise them, and grow aubergines instead: and lilies too.'

'They're not weeds,' says Ivan, pulling them up nonetheless. 'They cure all sorts of ills.'

'No,' Karine says. 'They disguise themselves. We know all about that. They're weeds because they don't do anything but grow.'

'It's just nomenclature,' says Ivan. 'Everything has a purpose. Those lacy things – they give you shade. A pattern for your underwear.'

'You need grow things above the ground,' says Karine. 'In the dark – potatoes – tarnish your soul. Remember the picture of the horse: it looks out at a sacred landscape. Now the horse is sacred too.'

'We stay down here and dig,' Ivan complains. 'Life everywhere else – ramps up and skids along. Aside from these allotments – what do we have? Flash clothes that's much too hot.'

'Everybody has a gripe like that,' says Karine. 'Grow, mature, Ivan.... If you can't find wisdom, find a good end.'

'This greenery and love-your-destiny,' Ivan says. 'All the toilsome stuff, the puffy rhetoric: a useless aria. It does nothing but cut us off from all we want to do.'

'You're ignorant, Ivan,' says Karine, turning away.

Julia doesn't take much part. 'Maybe the cops one day will come,' she thinks. 'Ask questions, and there's answers I don't want to give.' Her world is colour, and geometry, that's what she prefers. No blame, no sacrifice, no doubt of what's alive, and what is not. Sandy, disappearing in his crack, a gecko in a sky-blue coat, back into lasting lethargy. No mind left on that ticks, no corpse, resentful of a push ... the shove left, maybe, in the mind....Telling the truth, like telling lies – either, makes you anxious, insecure.

'The music, Ivan,' says Julia. 'It wasn't Schoenberg. I looked it up.'

'I know,' says Ivan. 'Mahler guessed, Schoenberg knew. That's why I said.'

'What does that all matter?' Karine asks. 'Julia – music? It's not your thing. Ivan – don't be an aesthete just because you failed to be a crook. Anatol is right – we are not liked, and we don't like ourselves, but we've no plan to change....'

'My folks were black,' she says. 'They hoped so much I would be white.... Uncertainty – makes you be disloyal to everyone.'

'Mine worked so hard – they hoped I'd be an idler,' Julia says. 'It's easier than being black. Then I met Anatol – he made some cash, but not so much you'd get a charge if somehow he had lost it all. He was a debt collector – it means you get quite rich if you are not in jail.'

'Why ever would he collect those?' Karine asks. 'It sounds quite desperate.'

'It's so,' says Ivan. 'We are of the middling sort. We're stuck. It's hard to envy us – though I confess – I envy Khalil. Somewhere in his ruined land, he knows there is a fortune buried, where he's marked and mapped....'

'Cities and nomads – that's where civilisations start. The Caucasus is different – there's everything, and everybody here – the cities ephemeral, nomads all sedentary,' Julia says. 'Two lots of monks, a Sufi band – there's one or more of everything. Choirs and strong-arms, nothing has been left out....

'Once, these valleys and the hills were green and infinite, the lake – full of pink fish.... Now, there's Abkhazia dried up, Elbrus – a small pond....'

'It's not about the heat, dear Julia,' Karine says, quite irritated. 'It's about us.'

*

'The agency,' Khalil says. 'It gives you points. When you have enough, you go, you stay. That place is right for you. New names, new everything. You stop your wandering, and drop your old world in a ditch.'

'It's where we've come from,' says Anatol. 'That's what we are. Not where we lodge now. We're the best there is – we'd be an army, but we're smart, other people – we pay them to do that stuff ... left-right and blancoing. Who'd come after us, from envy or to harm? Paris, Berlin, New York and Moscow – we've built them up, they are our masterpiece ... the other metropolises all racing on, the other cities that we visit, all beginning to be easing past their peak, getting seedy, hot and wet.... And now we're here, we're still the best, if you are poor, you'd want to be like us, if you are us – there's not much more to try.'

'I'm not convinced,' says Julia, laughing. 'It's true, young guys all over follow us. What's left to try? Puttting our finger in the sun. It's seeing how it works: that never ends.'

'It wasn't up to us, that people left this place. It is our challenge now,' says Ivan. 'We've loved each other – in a way; I – not so much, but for sure, and there are prospects too .... we're close, suspicious, inseperables, like parrots in a cage.'

'We're clean here,' Karine says. 'We've decided, there is no taint laid in us from a past. The past – it doesn't smell or taste. It's gone. The little stream ... if you want more cleanliness, you can wash in it. If you think your body's worth it, you can have it gleam to someone that you think is worthy – just lob them a shot, a frame. You must convince yourself, things are tied together, one thing is never isolated, it's linked to everything, all the good and bad, a twig in a bundle, like those woody knots in oaks, like nests, houses for someone, only they are not. Just accumulations: windspew.'

'We must watch out,' says Khalil. 'Maybe we have post-capitalism here. A mode of being. Plum in the species-nature. Not productive. No surplus, just day by day, jogging along. That's paradise. We're vulnerable. Our economy is based on theft, or call it peaceful occupation. We pushed no one out and lied about it – the land was poor, unworkable. Central, our Ganga, our stream, quiet, parsimonious it flows. For ever – until we came. "A state of things so destitute of thought is imperishable," is what the philosopher says – and corrects at once. We must beware: what we've taken will be taken from us – "likewise by theft or force".'

'We must concentrate on ourselves. Only us, and what we do,' says Julia. 'Find patterns. Don't change them, ever.'

'Yes,' says Anatol. 'Build a dam. That's what they do. But – we've no cash, and none of us is interested in it: what there is, here, we just take. But a dam.... Forget the despotisms – those, we can't afford.'

'Everyone should read the book,' says Khalil. 'Shapes. *Formen.* How slippery is everything. Metamorphoses.'

'Yes,' says Julia. 'That is what I love. The basic blocks. Snowflakes and lace – the ephemeral is manacled to the same shapes as all the rest, the great illusion, those eternal stars blooming one morning in the black ... or – was it light?'

'None of us likes cash,' Khalil goes on. 'And each has reason to dislike the state. We're not big on solidarity, and what we have seems primitive. But, read the book. You'll see, there's every kind of oddity, of systems in transition, fleeting, mayflies, lasting for days or centuries, that glow like northern lights or flights of moths and butterflies. Or fireflies. It isn't socialism, that's for sure. Not on a timetable we don't have. What we have's unique: sophisticated primitives, withdrawing, and withdrawn.'

'Does anyone have more lovers coming in the bus?' asks Karine. 'Maybe we should block the road. Is this the future, Khalil...?'

'No, no,' says Khalil, 'none of that futuristic stuff. We want to hide, not make publicity. This is our present, forget the other genres – they're fantasy, tinsel, nursery tales. Conjecture, "maybes": – May bees buzzing round the wilting flowers. Uncertainty is our air, our atmosphere. What can we accomplish – we can never know. On illusion we have based our faith, our loyalty – and so again, dear comrades – onward, onward.... Again, again: there is no other path, it's endless – and yet.... tomorrow it will peter out, perhaps....'

'That's very clear,' says Karine, 'And it lets me out.... Betrayal, abandonment – it's just a blink, a smudge, a dot that changes vowels....'

'Oh do tell, Karine,' shouts Julia. 'What dishonourable deeds ... the deaths, the babies screaming in the refuse bins as you run off....'

Karine ignores her. 'Khalil,' she says. 'It's a wonderful idea you have. We humans too – we slip away, we slide back in, from day to day quite unrecognisable – unrecognised. Our eyes wear out – today: – it's humanity that's dim, tomorrow, maybe our friends are in long boxes, mustered in the shed. Who's there to recognise? Tears or rejoicing? Who invented mathematics? Who invented chance? No one, or one of us who's now unknown, who's no expectations of us, nor we of anyone. We are the living, but we're also dead, and so we can't make rules or legacies for anyone that can be guaranteed. Death cancels contracts, but since we live in the knowledge of our being dead – nothing holds. In the midst of universal death – is there a glimmer? Nothing at all....

'The ground plan, Julia – it's laid out in grains of rice – the wind blows them – the mice have banquets.... *Grundrisse,* Julia – what enthusiasm! What a hope!'

'Oh Karine,' Khalil says. 'That's quite the wrong way to begin!'

The Book

Karine persists – 'A book about us, to make things clear. That's what we do, write when they'd leanred, that's what the old ones did. But if we write the book, or one of us – it's not about us, it *is* us. We are the book. While we're alive, we are its context: dead – there's only text. And us. Where are we from? Not one place. Do we tell our story? – not at all. We're not reliable – that's how we have survived. Who knows what we propose, who knows this Caucasus – that none of us knows, that no one knows....? Besides, what kind of book? To inform, inspire – or is it a chronicle of what we wanted, and we failed to make? What we couldn't have. Or is it a conjecture? – about us, about who reads us, about where we came from, why we settled here...?'

'Oh Karine, no one will read us. Our stories, anyway: are they separate, or can we make a tale so vague it fits us all ... expresses all of us, what we are or'd like to be? ... or something else?' asks Julia.

'We should block the road, and dam the stream,' says Anatol. 'That way, we'll have a context. We can't leave, but we can live – before, we couldn't live, but we could leave. Now – the only way to leave is by a rocket – to somewhere else entirely, quite irrelevant.'

'Yes,' says Ivan. 'Block everything.'

'Boredom,' says Khalil. 'That's why we don't go to the sun. No one will sacrifice some years – ah yes, the limetrees, little tables, youth, the boulevards, *diabolo menthe* – just for five minutes walking on the sun amid the flames and storms. Karine – perhaps we'll have no state, but for now – we've a dictatorship. We decide for you. Your garden – it will flood. Don't build an ark – grow rice, or carp. Don't cry, don't drink tequila; you'll be the first of us who's destitute. Wait, watch how we shall treat you!...'

'The people downstream,' Ivan says. 'Suppose they have a cannon, aimed at us....'

'Oh boredom!' Julia shouts. 'No more! Let's do just what we can – no story overtold of how we start, and slowly, tediously, all history starts with us again *in nuce.* Tempests and droughts, then time wizens out our kernels too, blights the nuts, and we grow more wise, bereft, more stupid.... No cautionary tale, no Shangrila, no dénouement. No! Let's do something absolutely new and different.... Experience the ephemeral, our day as mayfly, then it's done. Find something else....'

On this, they all agree.

Living with the Future

There's always new passengers on the bus. Juliette – she looks a bit like Julia, but she's new – not to herself, of course. She's quite tired of herself, in fact. Conversation – makes things seem fresh for a while ... Ivan! What adventures – exciting things you might have done yourself....

'It's such a choice!' says Juliette. 'Ivan – are you sure it's right for you? Is it right for anyone? There's so much predation anyway. Signing as a mercenary – well, yes, I see it has a logic, but suicide, that has its logic too.'

'In the foothills,' Ivan says. 'I learned to do most things, that mostly turned out bad. At least – not good. Besides – I shan't be on the killing end – I'll be a communicator. Every side must have one – some sides live the truth that no one tells – those communists, those millions killed by their own boss ... not quite forgotten, but not celebrated.... "Someone," they say, "must tell the tale." Does it avail? – you tell me, Juliette.'

'You're wrong, Ivan,' says Juliette. 'You mustn't try to learn a lesson. School is finished and forgot. If by chance you do remember, some taradiddle – you must absolutely not repeat it, not in any of its details, no excuses.'

'Where people come together, very fast you see everything that's ever happened since they straightened up and started picking apples off the tree and taking pomegranates from the snake,' says Ivan.

'Think of everything you see as new, unused,' says Juliette.

'Being a soldier,' Ivan says. 'What they call a mercenary, is exactly that. Mostly they're Africans who serve. You go where you are called – that's all. Like everybody else – except there is more pay. You are worth more, and so you get to choose, and you are safer than the guys under the bombs, safer than the guys inspired, with paradises in their eyes.'

'... an extreme wandering,' Juliette says.

'Seeing others' deaths, then mine,' he says.

'Telling....' she says hopefully.

'There isn't to tell,' he says. 'I have nothing – I have no child, no lover, the choicest things they say you might possess. It's good. Karine – a loser, and a sheep. Julia – a goat with its wisdom sucked out somehow.'

'You are the bird of death,' says Juliette. 'Except – you cannot fly.'

'No, but I can walk, and sniff the ground. Get lifts in trucks,' he says.

'I can smell all of you,' she says. 'Your friends, tucked in your little mode among the green hills, folded tight like baize cloths. You have the gift, you can transmit – every sweat, your faded clothes – I see it. I like Karine best. She will have a loom now, make fine throws. Khalil – is my hero. He's single-handed – he can knock you down or write you down, and fail at everything and convince it's all worked out....'

'Khalil's a thief,' Ivan says. 'He has an aviary – birds come to see: he'll eat them all, inside ones and out.'

'Is that everything?' asks Juliette. 'I know about you all, your rural interlude, coaxing some creatures back, though they'd come anyway to drink.... Julia and Anatol – they could be friends. They're nothing much, I bet they're famous and have strings of friends. Travelling by bus, you learn everything there is to know about the guy beside you, and the deepest things.'

Road Block

There's been a fall of rocks. They all get off the bus and sit around.

Ivan says – 'Suppose I told you – I'm the survivor. We had a fight, the others died, some lingering, some could be saved but fuck them all. And here I am.'

'Oh,' says Juliette, 'I'm not at all surprised. What would you do anyway – cut a stele, bury a tablet for them? Confess to someone – what?'

'If you've a country,' Ivan says, 'if a country has you, it requires you to do anything, anything at all. Being a mercenary – it's much the same, but there's a difference: you have a little choice. Religion – is perhaps a little easier still; the interpreter is often you. Principles? They say we all have those – it isn't so. And they aren't like a country – there's no document, the history is all in boxes somewhere, or on shelves, and you never get to them.'

'I understand all that,' says Juliette. 'With some tools, we could shift the stones here – but there's a squad. You wait for them, because you've paid – or, in our case, you wait because you haven't paid. It's like those plays – Iphigenia comes to mind, or maybe that really happened, and these stones – they could be always here. You pay a tax and skirt them – or there is another bus, the other side.'

'I don't know that play,' says Ivan. 'If you don't have a theatre, it's a bit snob to hit me with it. But yes, we could stay here, buy a donkey and some hats and wicker shoes. Is that what you'd want to do? Really? Dig in the sun?'

'Basic training, everyone does that. Someone buys the guns,' says Juliette. 'You must do what you're told, or they can shoot you, but you have a choice. Khalil used his choice, over and over. Julia, Karine ... when they have guns, I wonder if they have the choices they once had. Animals – once, we girls, we were much closer to them than the guys, and we were more a prey, although we got to pluck and skin the catch....'

'You're drifting, Juliette,' says Ivan. 'Nothing and no one is like that. You're sinking in the fable. They'll send another bus and we'll climb over – and be off again.'

'Come on!' says Juliette. 'Let's climb over this heap anyway and go on along the road, and hitch....'

'I'm for waiting,' Ivan says, pulling back. 'They put me to rest under a pile of stones – a much smaller hump than this. Some thought I was a goner, they all wished I was. It seems that I'm reluctant.'

'Oh, you can't speak for everyone,' says Juliette, 'about if it is worth while. Even just a few hundred like you had. You don't look like someone who would wander into suffering from principle....'

'No, no,' says Ivan. 'There's always a Karine whose land gets in the way, or someone who takes the risk and all the consequence. There's always someone it all falls down on.'

They stare at the stones, cocksure in their heap: it tells – 'no further'. 'Don't tread. We're prone to slip.'

'See – the rocks have three sides or seven,' Ivan says. 'It makes me think of Julia – she noticed things like that.'

'All rocks are five or seven,' Juliette says. 'Like snowflakes. That's why buildings fall. You think, "if only", two and four, not difficult – then you realise, it's foolish.'

'Julia was keen on shapes,' says Ivan. 'If they fit together, they're not worth much – separately, people kill for them – cut emeralds, carnelians....'

'Julia was glue,' says Juliette. 'The social sort, like "*In hellen Träumen ich dich oft geschaut.*" You dream what you think of other people and have never said, or else they drift away, have a bigger house or none.'

'Wasted lives, you mean,' says Ivan. The light is going. 'Sell up all you've accumulated. See what it will fetch, whether you bet right. My body, Juliette, that's for sale too. You won't need it, get rid! Best to leave cash, hidden in its hole. Khalil was right.'

'Once you mentioned Anatol,' says Juliette, as they climb the rocks. 'He was a diplomat? They say civilisation can't exist without war – maybe he failed.... Let you all down, one way or another.'

'Oh,' Ivan says. 'Civilisation. I don't think we had any more of that when we left than when we came. Anatol – he turned to melancholy. You see a distance, but the near is dim. Wealth and poverty – they both gnaw at you. You invent new stuff, you catalogue, you hunt. War and peace – it all brings bitterness. Win, lose, – another game? Anger and frustration – in the end, the master loses one, then the next, the next. Just playing – even *Go* – taste fades. War, peace – both are a bore, you're frightened, that is all.'

'I know all that,' says Juliette. 'But Anatol. He sounds a jolly sort. Tell me, tell me everything.'

'He was the best there was,' says Ivan. 'I've already said.'

Archaeology – Those Blocks

'Arslantepe,' Juliette says. 'That's special. We could visit there. Ancestors – they buried them beneath the floor, and they lived mostly on the roof. The first palace, Julian, just think!'

'I think of you, Juliette,' says Julian, an archaeologist. 'Your body. Not all of it, just bits.'

'I wish everyone was homosex,' says Juliette, much irritated. 'It would save time. We could go there easy – take the bus. I spoke to someone who'd once lived way up north – ruins, quite a fascination.'

'No,' says Julian. 'What little there's to see – it takes an hour, and then you're bored. It's not a holiday.'

'Then we shan't go,' says Juliette. 'At least, I shan't go with you.'

When there is him, it isn't necessary that another human should exist, she thinks. He blocks the light.

A Gathering of Scholars

So, that's how I'm here,' says Juliette.

'Quite the wrong place,' says Ivan. 'And Arslantepe – they burnt it down. I'm sure they were quite right.'

They climb on to the stones – 'I hope this is not an ambush,' says Juliette, 'or a kidnap.'

'No, that's over,' Ivan says. 'They did a deal. I'm sure they were quite right. You should have gone, though – holidays are when you see the sites.'

'Oh, Julian was a bully,' Juliette says. 'Just like you. A pacifier – like your Anatol, a puppeteer. Intolerable.'

'I don't need to judge,' says Ivan. 'I want to be where things happen, not after when it's of no account. Even if you're put on trial, you find what people think of you. It's interesting....'

'Don't think of it,' says Juliette. 'Only the clever ones can think like that, and they'd no business being there.'

'Look!' says Ivan. 'Asphodels. I've never seen one, and here they are in crowds. You'd see lots in Turkey, I expect. I only saw the mountain there, from very far, without the detail pencilled in. The asphodels are beautiful, but a terrrible portent too. The mountain – it must hold a truth, people go there on expeditions, looking for the ark. I think – the asphodels: they don't know anything. You know nothing of them, including why they're beautiful, if that is what they are. The mountain, then – may hold a truth, you wouldn't say it's beautiful – besides, it doesn't matter. It's big. People tend to think big things are beautiful....'

'You're rambling,' says Juliette. 'The key to this is meaning. Not beauty, not truth – but rather, what does each mean, has come to mean....'

'You're probably on the right path,' says Ivan. 'It's people once again – their fingers poke in everywhere. Trying to decide, to lay things out. This place – it's full of different flowers. Best not to touch – there's asps inside, and tiny birds that came to drink and fell....'

'Spiders,' says Juliette. 'If you dislike them, do you have to like the flies?'

'I confess,' says Ivan, brushing her off. 'We fell down on meaning, when we five had worked the land. We didn't agree on what it was we had, how we came by it, or what it was we thought we had, or wanted. Mostly – we could not agree. It tired us – we hadn't failed, but everything became more difficult, day by day.... In the end – you never make it, never reach the goal....'

'Inequality,' says Juliette. 'There must have been a lot. You may each have grown your own, but there's the water, and the seed ... some have everything, some need....' Ivan joins her thought –

'Oh, we had little corporations, guilds. No state, no project, no single meaning. If you were poor, you could paint your face and dance – the others didn't have the time, and thought it looked ridiculous... Then Anatol: – said it didn't work. None of it, and us. That's how it all began – or, you might say, Juliette, how it all began to reach its end.'

The Search Continues

There's no bus the other side. They walk.

'The question was,' says Ivan. 'For those of us alive, if we should pray for those who died that they be born again as human beings. It wasn't what the locals used to do, but they were gone, long gone; it wasn't what we did, but we were all from somewhere else. We had to choose, to put it in a ritual – from missing them, to hoping they'd go on ... somehow. In some other way.'

'What did you decide?' asks Juliette, not much involved.

'Some did, some didn't,' Ivan says. 'It is the choice.'

Karine: Her Whole Story

'If you aren't wanted, not in a country, any country, they put you on an island. It's quite new – they're artificial, and they go wherever they are wanted – way up north, or to perpetual summer. You can grow anything you want, and eat it, smoke it, sell it – it's that you can't get off. There's corrugated and tall grasses, and a flat spot where they play football.

'In the end, they say, everyone becomes a woman. You have the fear; but at least you're sterile. Perhaps it shows, being a woman's not so great.

'The end – it's hunting you, and you'll be caught.

'When they flooded my land, and I was destitute, I knew a bird would come – "Away," it had to say, "try somewhere else."

'In the beginning, there was a game of pool, an exhibition, probably – the first shot was so powerful, there was just the colours, spots and stripes, set up in a shape, like a single eye, that flew apart, quite beyond your sight, beyond the laws, it deafened you and blinded you. The balls went "smack" against each other, like flesh, then the cushion; some fell on the floor and rolled. It happened like it does to everyone.

'Juliette took Ivan on all her campaigns – to bad places before disaster, to disaster, then the bad place bandaged up. There was no kind of sense in what she did – she took no sides, and gave no help. She contemplated, tried to find the lesson to be learned. They were precious soldiers – too costly to be used in battle; still, taking risks. Ivan wanted risk – if he survived, it meant a temporary pardon, forgiveness. A respite.

'Juliette – she had no conscience, knew she wasn't responsible for anything. Just chance and other people's plans.

'I chose to be free, though if you've money, you can be free and pay others to do most of your living for you. Then you're not free, but you're not free anyway if you don't have cash – and there's always people who see you abandoned and they think "poor thing", or "dumb thing" – and climb aboard you – the mule, the beast who won't walk someone's way.

'My Chinese friend, called Liu, like in the opera, who's never finished anything – is quick, so quick, does everything faster than me – the outlines of a language, being famous – you just need what it takes to start it off.... Too sweet, too lovable, you can't stand living with her. Suppose she dies – you'd have to die too. She says, "I'm going back. I love unfinished things – they bring regret and hope. You can't, Karine, go back anywhere. Don't let them put you on an island, but if they do, I'd come and visit, if I can – you have to come from somewhere, but you don't; your destination's unattainable, besides, you don't know who to ask."

'"I'm not so stupid, Liu," I say. "It's just the time we're in. There's those who want to cling, and shove the others off, and those who want to make the best."'

Jealousy. Karine's Speciality

'You think I'm slow,' Karine says to Anatol. 'Not everything moves in step. There's portents – what they portend, you don't know it when it comes. Music – it runs ahead ... what it foretells, there's no one there, not ever, no one who listens. Too difficult, it defeats your hum and whistle. Anyway, what can you do? If a warning's big enough, you can't run. No time to dig a hole. Best not listen. Stop your ears, or they'll pull off your head.'

'You *are* slow, Karine,' says Anatol, no longer amused by her. 'Where we were, we could have had a city. Civilisation.We had agriculture – that, you couldn't do. Religion – that you don't believe. And trade. What can you make, Karine? What then? A prophetess in a cage, ranting in tongues?'

'Go, Anatol,' says Karine, who couldn't say she loved him, not ever, not even with her fingers crossed, not wanting him to stay.

'You like Liu, more than me – and there is money there. You must be quick – it turns to leaves or snow if you let it hit the ground.'

'The mountains – that's the best part,' says Anatol. 'Matriarchy, polyandry. That's the way – it sets you free; and who's responsible – they sow and reap.'

'I'm sure it was mistaken,' Karine says. 'The flood. If there's no law, no measure – then you all must run, and go on running, climbing – all your history. A flag, a frontier – those won't stop the water, or the fire. No one's guilty of anything – it's all been wiped clean – the gold melts in the fire, the notes – dissolving in the waters.

'Go, Anatol. Find Liu, find someone who loves you. Why the fuss? You'd never know. It's all inside, it's you, Anatol – you invent the universe, and set it on your back ... salamanders tumble in your hair, your knees go "crack", gum arabic drips in your eyes. It's worth it, Anatol, I'm sure. You bear the weight, complain, and hope Liu will wipe away your sweat.'

He's ready. Can't wait. Buses – they must go down there. Or caravans. Singing: the sweet company of camels....

'There's stone houses up the hill,' Karine says. 'There's journalism, naturally, or fame. To eke out. But – I could use branches for a summer roof, then – some corrugated.... You need a flock – the deaths are easy, it's the births require a skill....'

Can a Good Day Be A Bad Day? Karine's Not Sure...

A settlement, an Irrelohe – they're abandoned everywhere. Everyone's a prophet now, Karine knows nothing. She doesn't know – you can be free to buy slaves. Free to get the documents that get you out of jail, or on the plane, settlement, deportation – little fences on an endless field. Prophecy requires a skill, some figures and convictions too. Not musing on. Being a hermit – that's good too, has a history, an engraving too.

She waves and waves – smaller and smaller as Anatol marches off, the light has gone, her face is dark ... an ageing lady, black, no documents. No diploma – the hardest case you will find here in this place – though she could start a civilisation, kowing about trade, religion, and agriculture, a history, philosophy as well but, Anatol thinks, where would you start? Where do you begin with her? Where could you end?

For Karine, it's a good day. A start.

Karine: Keeping On

Almost always, you've enough food for another meal, or else there's guys sat round who'll help you out, or if you need, you take. None of that is here. The stone houses – people were clean, they took the roof-trees, unburied their familes and bundled up the bones. All long ago, not written down. The bones, all white, even if the people were black or brown....

There's food abundant. It just grows, it's there to eat, and only if you take it to the market, turn it into cash – there's grief. It must be so, thinks Karine. Anyway, she knows – planting, and all that.

Good birds sing all day – just shoo the bad ones off, and pick the fruit. You won't live long, it's true – but then, when you're just bones too, it won't be written down, nothing will, no when or how, besides, Karine has had one life, even more, as if she's survived poor Anatol, who left to go – somewhere within the wall, somewhere in China; that too, not written down, or not so's you could read.

For longer life, hunting is a better bet – if you don't fall down a hole, get lost, or find a beast bigger than yourself. Karine wouldn't make it, so – better not think of it.

Mostly, she'd be feeling desperate. There's a good side – you don't hunt, so you won't fall into mines or quarries, there's no one round to give you a virus or to do the other things. Karine worries that she may be pregnant – you probably can't be pregnant from a flood, but it brings all kinds of stuff, plastic and fæces, and it reaches in you everywhere, and as the years go on, it's more likely that something will have attached itself: – you'll have conceived. How'd you bring it up, unnamed artistic shit in a coke bottle ... and every day you feel warmer, colder, at dusk; the memory drops, the mnemonics drift away, you can't remember, and there's no point anyway. You've nowhere to fall into, except yourself, like a bad egg making a bad omelette.... It's good there's no one around – intruders, but how you miss the people you never met or who went into their hole – years, many years ago.

Karine's Basement

A few days are enough. More, make it seem an inconsequential life. Not time, it's all the colorless same, but seasons – they give life a shape. Seasons could go on for ever, time makes you die, often much sooner than you'd hoped. Under the stone house where Karine camps, there's certainly stone steps that lead down to a vaulted space, where the old timers played rude games, made sacrifices, pushed into the future and the past, where they weren't. But without fire, she couldn't see. It's black as black, there's water, you can't see how deep, still less whether there's a chance it will go away. If you can't see it, it never will recede, you can't see the gross pictures on the walls, or if the walls are rough stones or smooth. Do sightless things swim and eat each other down here, where Karine never went?

Anatol, now – he's seen, counted, documented. When the bus has stopped, everyone awake gets off, the driver often waits to see if Anatol's back on. Anatol has a ticket, that's a document, and he explains many times how he left Karine, until he's replete with it, and other passengers are bored.

Then, he's noticed everywhere. He could be rich – once he was. It sticks for ever, the look. Wanting to know about everything, then moving on, forgetting.

'When I was just a speck,' says Karine. 'They took me off the Capo Verde, sold me. My Armenia – once it was green, but now it's burnt. All summer we wandered, looking for the grass.'

Probably, it's not relevant – it's not about the grass or countries, it's about us. Civilisation – lives by trade. Once, it was religion, architecture, agriculture – Karine is quite ignorant of those, although she uses them, like everyone, quite uninvolved. The *camorrista* who should have traded her grew quite attached – trade makes us stick together, but you should exchange some stuff.... Otherwise, you try to have it all.

The *camorrista* was ignorant of architecture; Karine did not believe. You wouldn't eat the agriculture if you knew what it was growing from.

Yet, she ran – it's normal, if you didn't, there would only be one civilisation. And that's so. Just how it is, just one.

'I'm lucky,' Karine thinks. 'I have no regrets.'

Anatol: A Sequence of Adventures

With two planes you can reach anywhere in the world. Anatol says this to guys who're seated next. Even a German lady who plays kneesie with him in a DC3. The story of Karine has slipped – from sick wolf she has become a brilliant frippery, a kink in the brain from Kurdistan whose shining images fade on the bar's table top as she cadges booze....

'What you need,' says a guy, 'is this camera. It's to capture extinct animals. Tie it on a tree – it seeks out Karine's heat. Her picture comes to you as she looks out her doorway, till she's extinct.'

'Yes,' says Anatol. 'That's exactly what I need. And it will show her eyes....'

'Sometimes only those. But persevere,' says the guy, Marcel. Karine comes to the door, often she hopes to stop the seasons, keeps her eyes closed. If you saw the picture – there's no glow. Nothing's given away, not for free, not even a camera on a tree, but Anatol is satisfied.

*

'That's settled,' says the guy who instals those cameras. 'Now, we'll be in the air for hours, you won't see the ground, you don't know where they're taking us, or if you land where you had booked. Tell me, speculate a bit – if you're ready for the revolution,, and its mess, the amputations, the blood, all that – if you have a good grip on your philosophy, if you're that type ... you've put on your boots and goggles.... What comes next is crucial, but the philosophy – it doesn't serve, not any more. It's set out for someone else. Let's say – for everybody else. What you need now is not philosophy, it's the outlook, world outlook, the *Weltanschauung*. Where do you find that? Not in philosophy – that's a technique, like twirling on a mat or lifting weights. No: – you find it in the book that tells you all about the past. And what you mustn't do. That alone is what the book's about. Not doing that, not again, not for necessity, not for pity, not for good taste, not for a new boss or an old, not to wear fox fur on your head, not for your poem or your tiredness.... If you do capital, when you've been told don't, not at any cost ... it's better not to have the revolution, at least, you call it something else. Dictatorship, but leave the proletariat out. What is it that isn't capital, that isn't capitalism that's been awaiting us, growing inside us all, our collectivity, a cyst that would burst out like an angel from our head? ... the culmen, our goal, awaiting for ever, our epithalamium, that's wriggled inside us like a second secret penis looking for our womb ... and finish off so: the growing barley, building palaces, laying out some stalls, buying the slaves and soldiers, all of that, the start ... human history, the civilisation, digging conduits, making ordnances, giving out the medals ... everything we've been preparing for to reach its top – and then, just for a blink, it's all wiped off. Hiatus: a different end, a different beginning.... Like texts that you don't save – they go, quite irretrievable, no memory, nothing – just ... a space. The smell, the smoke? Hell? Or overload? Maybe, you've burned out the whole shoot. Wait! There's no water to pour on anyway.... Then, there may appear – a new picture: everything not as it is or was, but as it now appears....'

'I know all that,' says Anatol. 'How does it appear? And if it doesn't? Is it politics or economics that's on top? The classes disappear – but the dictators – they're bosses who say they're proletarians....'

'Then there's a problem,' says the guy. 'If there's no new view – you're at a loss. Back you go, to where you have been told you are not to go. When you're shut out from the garden – don't go back. Be thankful for the gifts you stole.... Take those wise apples in a sack....'

'See!' shouts Anatol. 'We're coming down! I see the ground, Marcel!'

'Let me finish, Anatol,' Marcel says. 'Either there is something, a picture, a guide. Or there is nothing. Or – you may decide to do what you've been told is wrong. At all events, you've gone much further than the dinosaurs. Your friend Ivan – stuck at the crossroads, like Balaam's ass ... choice! Don't waste time with that. Karine – choosing extinction....

'You, Anatol? What's your vice? A tourist? In that case, you'll need a camera. I'll take a card....' he laughs. 'Even if it is the joker.'

Then they alight, never see each other, never again, but as they touch the ground, they both are laughing....

Ancient Indigenes

There's peasants, guys in bib and brace, with straw hats – maybe they are engineers – sitting round. They look like Zapotecs, descended from the civilisation everybody knows, those babies sacrificed, the citadels – there's strings of tourists, like at the city, Monte Albàn, the grand centre, fortress of the civilisation, stones incised with hieroglyphs that you can't read and no one will translate for you.... They play that ball game, where things go bad, very bad, for who lose....

For sure, these people are not Han. But who? ... where? Those faces – they look like....

'The cart, the cart!' they shout. There's two cups screwed on a bendy pole, on at each end, the driver sits in the far one, you hope you balance, the pole is long, elastic, the cups spin round. The horse trips on – sometimes you're at the horse's head, sometimes it's the driver's turn, he thwacks the horse as he goes round – faster, faster, wavering – on one side there are trees with spikes, on the other, there's a gorge. If you fall, or if your weight and his – or hers – is out of parity, or whack, the pole, the cups, the whole caboose, falls down and you – the end!

'Luck, luck,' the guys all shout, they're on their bicyles behind.

'A special guest,' the driver shouts, 'must come in style, and show the luck is coming too....'

Here in the village – luck is boss. There's guys who're playing cards, and guys who wait for telegrams to tell which horse to back – there's trotters, gallopers, even electronic ones who don't eat hay, donkeys and ostriches too...there's coins that's tossed and hands that's read, the kids throw cans high to see if one falls luckily.

The place is neither rich nor poor – the luck, it circulates, there is no certainty, of course, unless you think there's lucky ones who generally win and hide their cash – unlucky ones who sift the dust to find a tiny coin – 'a find, a find!' they cry – the guys here bet on birth and death, the length of goats' horns and the length of days, of piglings' pizzles and the hours of rain....

'I had not thought,' thinks Anatol, 'The world view could be this, so logical, haphazard too – and yet secure, conservative, with those who lose in equilibrium with those who win.'

Here's Liu's stall, selling tourist suff – the folklore of the place...

'Dear Liu,' thinks Anatol, 'this is the place – my devotion should assist me, and with her I can forget the arid years, get lucky....'

Liu, Anatol's Best Friend (Probably Han)

'You're stupid, Anatol,' says Liu. 'No one believes in luck. There's chance – you can't do anything with that. People here – they don't believe in luck – they bet, they think they'll win because they're right, they're quick and smart. They bet to live because the rest is predetermined – by someone else or by cause and its effects.'

'How terribly banal,' says Anatol. 'I thought I'd found a place which had – the outlook.... You – with the luck, and Karine, without any; I thought maybe you'd taken it, and set up a tourist stall down here using her luck. Then, there's polyandry....'

'Why are you interested so?' asks Liu. 'You want to join a flock?'

'It's curious....' says Anatol.

'No, Anatol,' says Liu. 'It's you who's curious. Besides, you could have befriended me back there – and now you're here.... Some don't bother what it's called – polyandry, polygamy, or chance and luck, and betting that it's all for kids, passing on your hopes, your failings too.... Spinning your wheel, Anatol, cutting the deck....'

'I was sure,' says Anatol. 'Dear Liu – that we two had something special... You – filled with pathos. Me – seeking an order.... I came ... two planes, enough.... The lucky cart....'

'I remember, Anatol,' says Liu, 'your favourite quote – Engels saying the bourgeoisie "have their women in common".... What does that mean? It's true and false, like everything, and all that you believe: – grow into it, Anatol. While you're here – you can make bets.'

'It was for you I came, Liu,' says Anatol, much confused, 'You, who never finish anything, but are so quick – you're infinite.... That's the definition! You – the image of infinity!'

'Oh Anatol,' Liu shouts. 'Infinity! Use your camera. Steal anything, everything, steal the red and steal the green. Infinity's a setting on your camera. Then go! *Go*'s another game of luck where there's no chance. Another obsession, Anatol. Replicas – gardens and floods, and now the snaps. You've beaten time, you don't proceed – but, Anatol, you're stuck. Take your prints and make your cash – bleed it out, Anatol, everything you think you see: filter and bleach. Drink blood like everybody wants. It's not about us, Anatol, the polyandry – it's the cheapest way to settle big sisters with the brothers, and everyone will do the work they're better at.... Dig, Anatol, try to be perfect – don't flood the garden of your friends again....'

'It was necessity,' says Anatol, abashed.

'There!' says Liu, in triumph. 'There you have it. Necessity. Not invention. You invent necessities, dear Anatol. Excuses, alibis. It's not a drama, there's no orchestra, there is no end, no climax, no resolution. Now – go: go away....'

'I shall miss you,' says Anatol. 'Miss you terribly.'

'That is exactly right,' says Liu. 'Gardens. Happy families – they're made to be missed – terrible is right: the Word. Remember

where you did the wrong, poor Anatol. Invent it, if you can't remember. Take your snaps – that's all you'll get from us.'

'It's an aberration,' thinks Anatol. 'Not at all what I had hoped, not an analysis, not excitement – but there's emotion, life – a kind of conquest, I suppose.'

'No, Anatol,' says Liu, betting she can read his thoughts. 'The conquest comes when – if – the wheel stops its spin.'

*

The plane – it flies itself – Hegel was right, the Mind has taken over. Anatol looks down, thousands of Fausts are toiling, and there's Mephistos too, every place, every country has a bunch, blancmange of spawn – the heat has brought them on – 'Maybe,' the guy beside breaks in. 'You made a gaffe. This chatter about gardens – here, there are mountains. Nothing sticks, no grass, no undressed flesh, no picnicking. People haven't learned yet how to romanticise the agriculture, and, without a near-original sin, no one believes that leisure and free fruit existed in the past.'

'It's good,' says Anatol. 'You've set me right. Now, I must think of where it all went wrong, and what I did....'

'No, no,' the guy says, preparing to sit elsewhere. 'You all did well. Prepare – the worst will come; before it does, the bad will drive you on.'

Julia – Readying for the End

'We know how to end the world, Anatol,' says Julia. 'No one knows how to end capitalism. It's the way that everything works. It's like they said it was and would be, but if you graft, or if you organise, you can coax more cash from it. And there's entertainment! Winners! and losers!'

'I didn't get lucky with Liu, Julia,' Anatol says ruefully. 'Karine is nearly extinct – she's unique by now....'

'You want everything, Anatol,' Julia laughs. 'Ivan was right – you have a choice which means you're bound to lose a half at least of everything. Usually, of course, you make your choice and nothing happens. Nothing at all. Sex and love – you can buy sex, but love's a chocolate biscuit – eat one, and you'll go through a packet, then a crate. They'll never tongue you back....'

'I feel responsible,' Anatol says. 'For the gardening. It exploded. Our shells are hard, but we all fell on our backs – waving our legs.... Most couldn't breathe....'

'Forget all that,' says Julia. 'All you read and marched about, and then betrayed. We jog. It's called a rite of separation. We do one thing to get away from all the other things. If they attack us – we run or if we can, we get our gun, or pay some guys. Till then, the big guys aren't interested, not in us – they've got the big plan, how to end the world. When, how quick. We know, we were there, and quickly we forgot, or said we did.'

'Liu was busy,' says Anatol. 'To find that out cost me all I had.'

'Well,' Julia says. 'You could briefly stay with me. Don't knock on any door that's closed. I'm always busy, I have friends. Busy people – they're all I want to know. Not sex – gossip and quips – what you call intelligence. Find a safe place for us to go, Anatol – we'll be the first to throng along.... There's just the one door anyway – I'm open plan. Just – go away when I don't want you in.'

'I want to have a project,' says Anatol. 'A project for oneself, just one. That is antiquity, gone by. Bring other people in – and you are lost, completely. You don't just cluster into them, you disappear as "you". Suppose, Julia, instead of living, each of us, embodied – there is a story, something like. There is some verisimilitude: every morning, if we wake, we have it: realism. If we die by night, we can be fantasy.

'What would that story be, I wonder, each with a part, but structured in, nailed together like two-by-twos.'

Even fables have an end

*

'Wonder on, Anatol,' says Julia. 'I have mine, my wonder-tale. In my story, you are plump and rich. And – now, you start to leak. It needs more characters. The poor and the perverts – those are plentiful. I fit everywhere, my inspiration is a peacock's tail. I want invites from high-born rationalists – rare birds.... I think they only eat together, a flock of chatterers, egging each other on, evoking glory days – moas and dodos ... maybe they don't eat at all, just fleet behind the arras, gulp something down, leave you to guess.... Or brainless, just cogs and keys, winding each other up, self-regulating, but rich enough for butlers.... Ah, Anatol, the rich, the reasonable, what have we lost? Perhaps it's good that no one now has servants spying on them, or even knows what servants were. Anyway, I'm sure I'd have been one of them.'

'A story, Julia,' says Anatol, quite irritated. 'Not a pantomime. You wander, there's no thread, no hero in distress. Make it like Karine, even if it's sad and dull. A shape, a purpose....'

'A barrel rolling down a hill,' says Julia. 'Beginning and end – both inevitable.'

'I like brusque people, Julia,' says Anatol. 'You know exactly where you are. There is no depth to fear.... Liu was a skitterbug. Courage! – you always see when there is none.'

'You missed your opportunity,' says Julia. 'With her. You should have chanced your luck.'

'They don't believe in chance or luck,' says Anatol. 'Though I'll regret leaving – it seemed another world of my invention, as if I'd spent my life decoding Cretan, just one word, then found a crowd of people making jokes in it.'

'That's nonsense,' Julia says. 'There, everybody bets and luck is tops. You could have stayed and been forever in the way.'

'In a cold light, Julia,' says Anatol. 'Liu bet on me. She won. That she could send me off within a day....'

'You see?' says Julia, laughing. 'She had the luck. You lost your chance. Both were unlucky, I expect. It's all in there. It always is – each episode contains the past and future, all of it, makes you look foolish while it's going on. Something, someone, somewhere – knows more than you, much more.'

'Well,' says Anatol, 'none of us is dead yet – you can say we have all life ahead. I have a project, Julia – but where do I sleep here? I'm your guest, but I can't enter, and you have the one room, your open plan....'

'Think of death, not sleep – avoiding death's the thing,' says Julia. 'Sleep will come unsummoned and inappropriate. Besides, who cares who dies among us? – even if we cuddled up, grew flesh.... It's a convention – grief for unknown cadavers, it lasts five minutes or a day....'

Back to Khalil, and the Wars

'It's Khalil's plan,' Anatol tells Julia, and he's proud. 'He trusts me, more than he did Ivan. After, and in, a war – there's stuff you can divert. Material that can't be used. Arms obsolete and food uneaten, magazines and manuals, cans and cannons.... Buildings destroyed, their basements still inhabited. Landscapes bundled up in loam. The dead. The irretrievable, the hurt, the dispossessed, the inconsolable. Then, more banal, there's stuff abandoned, left beneath a film of tears – there's caches, holes half-dug and branches strewn, jewels entrusted, dropped in squirrel homes, relatives adopted, graves marked, unmarked and desecrated.... Khalil thinks – we can be vultures, angels, doing the work of scavengers and treasure-finders. Retrieving, thieving, rehabilitating, erasing memories and writing memoirs....'

'Dung-beetles Inc.,' says Julia, admiring. 'Scavenging. And then – laid out on the market stall. What nobody recalls, the memorabilia: helmets and ration cards.'

'That is the underside,' says Anatol. 'We settle accounts with history, and launch the new. The story with an end without a plot.'

'Terrible,' says Julia. 'Truly – terrible. And so – you avoid the metaphorical, the dirt, the lying and the spying, and shovel up the real, then bury it....'

'You know Khalil,' says Anatol. 'He's poetry. How conventional you are, dear Julia.'

'If you aren't, no one can understand,' says Julia.

'Talk of lying, Julia,' says Anatol, 'who are you spying for? Whatever could our secret be – or are you just the spirit of the time? Somewhere some info must be worth a buck?'

'No one can know as little as you do, Anatol,' says Julia. 'There must be another story pumping on inside. Inner Asia, China, everywhere – no money – yet you fly, you always land and stay and leave. You don't spy – you're what the others spy upon! Everybody knows something the others don't – that's not interesting. What's interesting is what everybody knows – the one who doesn't, that's the suspect.'

'I've told you our secret, Julia,' says Anatol. 'What's the use for you? Informers don't get money – it would break the bank. They get praise for patriotism.'

'Well,' says Julia, 'something breaks the banks. Maybe....'

'No, Julia,' says Anatol. 'We are clean. Reconstruction. Shapes. Right angles, verticals, stones – every cut. All your favourites.'

'I'm intrigued,' says Julia, pushing Anatol away. 'Khalil will take the ruins, flatten them, make a desert. Purity. Nothing, no return. But you, Anatol – you want to stand them up, make it as it was, exhume and resurrect. Khalil accepts the end – for him it's "finish", not rebirth or revelation. You'd start it all again, as though next time there'd be a different end. It isn't so. There's battle coming, you and him.'

The End of Archaeology – Modern Ruins Everywhere

'You should put our experience, digging in the wild – into your story,' Anatol tells Julia. 'You'd be responsible for the writing – but not for anything that happens in it. The world news, Julia: that gives a part to everyone. When we came, there was just us. Catastrophe – we'd fled from it, and it seemed it had occurred already everywhere we ran. We didn't realise, it circled like a stork. Round it came! We ran, scrambled, scratched faces, trampled on each other.... There were lurches, then quiet. After: – Americans, everywhere: and in Georgia. And Russians in Chechnya and everywhere. Best to say anyone is anywhere, they infiltrate and pry, they all have eyes set in – a diadem – around their head. While they eat and write reports – they shit like horseflies. They have white coats and leather shoes – but they're not doctors. We are prone. It's like we're hooked up to machines, thousands of them, not to keep us live, but to see if we are dead.

'Ivan felt responsible, but it ended there; sensation. No inventiveness. There was no other basis to any of his choices. Used, secondhand – it's travel down a trodden road, if you call it all antiquities. But our experience – the occupation, the landscape and the farming, the intelligence and the stupidity, the falling-out and the dispersal, waiting for the cataclysm and fighting to survive – it could be an epic, Julia.'

'It's been an epic, Anatol,' she says.

Khalil

'It was hard, Khalil,' says Tasha, 'For you. Not to be let in to Argentina. It was for religion, I suppose. Or colour?'

'Not colour,' says Khalil. 'I love black girls like you, Tasha. There was Karine – old enough to be my grandfather. What an *amplexus*! – neither of us would confess the depth.... We feasted Bacchus, his days – they're called the *Orgia* – did you know? No, it was my surrealism kept me out. At the time there were too many of us. My village – up in the snows, the monks, old believers, dressed in red. And people sensitive as nowhere else. Buddhists mostly – salt of the earth. Leopards, there were – a few. The black-necked cranes: or are they storks? I'd hoped to see them all in Buenos Aires – they were just hanging on where I was born. And then – catastrophe. The glacier died. No water – we had to leave, abandon everything, all of us, trek down to the plain.'

'That's terrible,' says Tasha, not holding back her tear. 'And so – later, you lived it all again – some details differed ... disaster again, and you kept out....'

'No, no,' says Khalil: 'It's not enough for episodes to be the same because, or if, a detail differs. Everything was not the same. Indeed, quite different. It's me that is the same, except – of course, you will object ... *panta rhei*....'

'Oh no, Khalil,' says Tasha. 'You are identical. Still looking for a landscape flat where you could start to dig – treasure. That's your goal, I know. And if not treasure – water, barley, pomegranates too.... Those dragon's teeth, printed on dollar bills the cowboys sowed – dropped in iron boxes that split all those heads....'

'Yes,' says Khalil sadly. 'All unattainable. Dig them up, then bury them. Vanity. Our ancestors – they knew it – the orgasm that is everlasting. That's what kept them going – those sieges, the prayers, the young mortality, those *chaises percées*. I'm not embarrassing you, I hope?'

'Well,' Tasha says, 'you are. Somewhat.'

'Imagine,' Khalil says, 'all the treasure we've dug up. Gold sovereigns, the emeralds, the cabuchons, the little telephones – all from the earth, the earth *desnuda*, millions of us, digging, nothing edible. All of us, on the ladders, all slaves, black more or less, Sebastiao Salgado's miners, Tasha. All of it smashed, like golden Easter eggs, and trampled down, back in the ground. Up and down – dig up, cast down. Remember the Haitian army that conquered North America? They took the treasure, and they hid it well. Up and down, Tasha, that's how the money goes. Compared to me, why – you're not even black, not a smidgen, not a song or dance....'

'It's true,' says Tasha. 'I'm not black. But – I can't follow you. We'd maybe not hit it off – your sweep is huge, I can't connect – though I respect, of course. You are a genius – I don't understand a word. Of course, I know the photo – the muddy gold – it's not always miners who are black who dig it up, the treasure, and the whites who trash it, throw it down. I don't believe it's that at all – I think you like things neat and flat. Flat – is neither up or down; not dug up nor trashed.'

'You're there, dear Tasha,' Khalil says. 'We don't have a choice. Ivan was wrong. Things can be different – but you never choose how. All that is built – you could tell Anatol – is made to be a ruin. That is architecture, it's what the mason has in mind, the plasterer, the bricklayer – how will it look when it is bombed and mined, how will the photo catch it in the second before it's trucked away. By me. Maybe by me and Anatol. For fill.'

'It's true,' says Tasha. 'Berlin – stands freshly built, on dust and broken bricks. Knock the world down, set it up again – design a grid, a back with ribs. You can buy a person really cheap. Begging to be bought – if they would dig.... You'd think that everybody can....'

'It's not so easy,' Khalil says. 'You can get yaks and horses – they'll do the spade work for you – but it's water! That's the precious stuff you need. Sulphur, salt and alum, nitre – some come in deposits, like your cash, but water....! Without that, it's all useless, and you have to leave.'

'I know about it,' Tasha says. 'We were warned. The plagues – they come, unremitting. No one knows why the punishment.'

'Yes, that's the punishment,' Khalil says, and laughs.

The End – Thirst? Or Blindness?

'What's it about?' asks Tasha. 'It's not about water, not about us, not about our feelings. What is left? Anger is no use – shortens your life. Laughter – probably the same. You know it's the end when they stop talking, dancing wild and singing small and high – when it ends you know there's no more to say, it must be why, Khalil, you talk on and on. When you're out of words, it is the end. If only there was no water, none, anywhere, we'd know it's been resolved, a conclusion is in reach. But – it's always more than that. Then you could ask – "What was it you wanted to achieve? Not dumb survival. Not nature – we separated us from it. What then?" But say it's all a linger, suspension, dragging on ... deflation, stasis, tragedy and crash....'

'I'd love to give you the right answer, Tasha,' Khalil says, sliding an arm around her waist. 'But – it's my affliction, this goddam blindness. They say it is hysterical – do I seem that to you?'

'Only a tiny bit,' says Tasha, pulling herself away.

'How often is there a miracle, I wonder,' Khalil says. 'Light! Let there be! One that helps the person having the mirage, not just the tourist guys?'

There's no response to that.

'One thing we can do together – or maybe there are one or two,' he says, grimacing sexily. 'My dear, while I await my cure. The tango. I'm a whizz at that. Morally and ideologically it's the pits, but I'm a super whizz...!'

'Exhibition or competition?' Tasha asks. 'I'm a medallist, you know.'

‘Of course,’ says Khalil. ‘I feel it in your bones. Tum-ti-tum-ti-tum. Ah, the piste, the strut! Of course, the dance isn’t what one does if one wants discoveries, but then – what’s the point in communism or any other plan or stop-gap, a regime, empire or a Reich – if we can live only a handful of new seasons, scudding years? And – then, it’s all gone. Down we go, hole in the ground, the black mouth, Tasha, swallowing all dreams.’

He weeps.

‘All the same,’ says Tasha. ‘You have lovely eyes, Khalil. See that as a compensation.’

‘Yes,’ says Khalil, running his hands over Tasha as if seeking a path. ‘Eyes. That’s what you need, and all is clear. With full sight, we could avoid making our old mistake again. It’s not that hard to see what life is all about and for, and what it needs: it’s all around, striding and crawling, flying and flopping.... Starting over, it’s the obvious choice, always available – flatten everything. When the slate is clear, you see exactly what there is to do, and on you march, nothing to stumble over. If it wasn’t evident, it would be a puzzle, a conundrum: a bad joke, with no one left to laugh.’

*

The conclusion proposed – re-burial of the sought-after treasure – is a commonplace, except that no one does it. The renunciations – they don’t lead to success and joy. They may seem what we have already – suspicion of those we say we love, dissatisfaction with a rare satiety. Do you dwell on the end, accept it, hasten it? – the end’s the end, it doesn’t depend on Karine, nor Khalil. Nor Julia, nor Anatol.

It’s adventure. Taking the bus. Making it reach the next stop.

The Blue Armchair

The agent, impresario – is familiar with the world of cash and smash. That world terrifies Ivan.

'I-van' says the agent, slowly. A woman wouldn't start like that – it's history, patriarchy, tradition – culture – that makes it so. Do away with it, history: it leaves a smear, a scum.... But there it is, it was. Ineradicable.

He taps – tum: tiddle-iddle tum tum.

'I – Van. You, the "I" just like the rest. Like me – "I". But Van – a famous lake, location trepidating. Your friends? Round the lake? Or on the bus? You want to sell your friends, who could be anyone. As what? A movie? Or a song? Not to disappoint you, rather, it's a good sign it has been done, over and over. Real ones, your chums, or barn door skins? Beware – there's lots like you, it seems like everybody ... thinks their stories are unique, significant. And you've few deaths, just many big useless plans. But – friendship is important, so they say. A family is chance. In friends, there is a particle of choice....

'I lose my friends,' he says. 'When money talks, we all join in to shout each other down.'

Ivan says – 'Dear friends, met randomly, they tramp with you for a while, then fade away. What stays – is solid. You call them visions – those are what you see through many pairs of eyes.'

'Situations? An intimate take? Seeing the invisible? Guns hidden in the thatch? Anger beneath the crust?' the impresario-agent asks. 'Selling your friends – yes, Ivan, that's an interesting take. Your enemies – do you sell them too?'

'No,' says Ivan. 'That's intelligence. Forces, laws, that you can know. Spying – everything permitted. Get it wrong, you pull the whole world down; and get it right – the same. The search for truth, advantage – it's like knowing nature and its rules. Natural laws – you know them, but can't change them. Why are they there? It's good – everything's predictable. Nothing is. God can raise a dead man here and there, but the laws go on, as laws. Not justice.'

'Intelligence. Hmmmm,' says the impresario. 'Do you need that in my job? Who needs it – you? Where does it end – killing the right people?'

'Certainly you can't say it's right to kill the wrong ones,' Ivan says. 'If those are your categories – keeping relativism out the way. No ifs and maybes; good and bad mixed – out comes designer grey.... Besides, you might ransom the bad guys, or befriend them. Send them to camps or pardon them.'

'I'd shoot them down,' the impresario says. 'So's to be sure. But – my question is – what can we know? They say if you know everything: the why and what – you would be God. Only God knows the game, the rules.... Does He? Everything, outcomes? In that case, it doesn't seem a game.... That's the limit, anyway, that's what you can know, and can't. Best not bother, I should say. Fatalism, I suggest. Each to her place, her own.'

'No,' Ivan says. 'That's the challenge. Maybe you would be God, but you're right: maybe He has no idea what to do next. Re-write the laws? There's all those stars to fix, re-wire, and worse – the murky stuff between them. What are they all for? Is that another stupid question? Seems all questions are! Of course, if you can go so far as knowing laws, you all, we lovely animals, you humans – should reach that fine cognitive spot. Or else the ones that know, and then decide, have better grounds than dullards or the mass that never went to school....'

'Or didn't bother much,' the impresario agrees. 'Or was a wiz at games,' and he flexes.

'The trouble is,' Ivan goes on, 'if the laws are there, eternal and pre-determined too – why? Did God make them? Or some crew – dinos, maybe.... The challenge is to know what God did and knows – but it's a limit too – on you, what you can know. And God, what's His take, his story ... what's in it for Him? Or – forget Him – for us?'

'Of course,' says the impresario.

'And then there's logic,' Ivan says. 'Where did that come from? Is that part of law? Or mindless nature? And, we're scientifically inclined to ask: where does that Mind come in? Whose is it? Mine? Yours? Inherited? If science works haphazardly, trial, error, fantasy – where does it end? To make life comfy – or to make ourselves extinct? Law-bound and axiomatic – what's the sense? Uncertainty steps in.... I'd digress – mathematics: has some real odd bits.... And language. Is it a machine? A tool? Does it shape according to those laws, or is it little boxes we use to differentiate our thoughts and so ... indispensable to them...?'

'Yes,' says the impresario. 'There's thought. Where, why? Where does it go on, what feeds it, how do we know about it, and its rules...? I see your game, dear Ivan. I've been thinking too. Your idea – to me it seems quite duff. I'd prefer it if your story is all tarts and spies. Spice! Like – Khalil, – looking for the treasure box. People love to see those dollar bills stacked up. People being shot and shocked. And Julia – hot and cold, and Juliette – maybe her daughter. Someone's, for sure. Karine – the Russian spy, or was she from Brazil?'

'She could of course be both,' says Ivan, losing patience. 'Like Anatol. He could be a spy who's turned, or even doubled up.'

'A series?' says the impresario, unenthused. 'Odd bodies in strange parts. Some strange person with strange unanswered questionings. A mystery, not revealed. Love and combat, a philosophical twist – all tiny, screened on those little oblongs that they hold.... Not ordinariness, that's for sure....'

'Oh no,' says Ivan. 'I didn't complicate. All sorts can ride a bus, and of course we skirted round the wars. The point is that these little wars are just the prelude to what we don't admit.... It's Montenegro and princesses, and the Archduke shot. The prologue – all wagging tongues, no words you want to hear.'

'Yes,' says the impresario. 'You could do the final, the decisive war, I guess. Views and situations, comments from the smaller guys. But then – there is intelligence. Will it, won't it happen? Choice...? Do it or not, survive – find out the why, last judgments, first ones too....'

'Oh,' Ivan says. 'I don't think anyone has got far along that road. They've given up. In one's materialist stodge – there's always an idealist sugarplum. It's the way it's put, conceived, there's no way round. Uncertainty. We can't know if our knowledge has a limit because so far we find it limitless. If we don't have a mind, and just a brain – there's all that goes on purposefully in places we can't even see, that doesn't seem to have a brain.... How do you account for that? If brain's a mechanism, how's it programmed, who by? And so we're at the start again....'

'I have no answer, Ivan,' says the guy. 'Suppose I give you lots of cash – for your intelligence. Tell me how you want to lay it out, and what it is, how many people have to learn some lines, and what it's all about. To me, it is a symphony, an opera – when it's finished, executed, there is nothing left at all. They're things-in-themselves, but evanescent. There's pawprints on the page; that's on the shelf, without a sound, enfolding voices that have climbed the stairs and tumbled down – and silence, silence.... Is there a win? A loss? A quiddity? Life or story, it's aesthetics, right? Questions of taste. Or touch.'

They stare at each other. 'These blue armchairs,' the impresario says. 'I find they cool you down. We should sit and think, sleep if we must. What does it all mean, Ivan? What will it all have meant, if it all blows up, up and away....?'

'Nothing in the beginning, nothing at the end,' says Ivan. 'That's what it means. Music. You mean you to yourself, just like the music means it to itself. It's carpet. Shiraz?'

'Then there's Julia,' says the impresario. 'You belittle her, your twinkling star.'

'Yes,' says Ivan. 'I don't know what she thinks. I speculate. I'm dross. I'm vindictive: because she doesn't love me as I'd hope. And likes other people much much more.'

He'd like to explain, smooth himself out of accusations. Prejudice, discrimination ... that's the charge....

In the other blue armchair, the impresario dozes, quite quietly.

Ivan wonders, should he leave? If he knew where Khalil had left the cash, he could steal that, and wouldn't need to sell his friends. Or, he could ask them, go ahead, notwithstanding if they should refuse.

'We could be the last people,' says Ivan. 'The last, decisive act. Then the soft curtain, dropping soft.'

The impresario does not stir. 'We pick at each other, as if we were crows, we sort each other like we were ripe grains,' says Ivan, louder. 'We should expect the revolution – but that's been done, over and gone.'

'Yes,' says the impresario, waking suddenly. 'I see it all, your little plan. You put some sense in it, and I'll shape it into spectacle. There's so many of you, your absent friends, you'll be the public too – when each one's scene is done, go to the back, sit in the dark, and see it all unfold.'

'You're sure you grasp the plot?' asks Ivan.

'Oh yes,' the impresario says. 'I'm a professional. I've put on shows like this all over. They're self-financing.... At the end, Ivan, you'll have the chrism: of the artist. The creator. Just like me. You'll have said it all – not that your friends were representative or special, even coherent as they got on and off the bus – but you're an artist through and through, from those first tears, those premonitions – how they reverberate! And yes! Those Montengrin princesses – a touch of genius there – the "greatness in the miniature ... *multum in parvo*".'

'Oh no,' says Ivan. 'That wasn't in the script. I don't repeat myself, nor history! There's no need for portents, hints. Now we know how to end it all, everything's translucent. Or, better, we know we cannot stop what we have started. All of us – Anatol, Karine, the rest – they have a robust stature: they're mediocrities, like the tsar, tsarina, but they're magnified, arriving casual at the end, swooping in like owls, following the squeaks and rustlings. Polishing everything off.'

'Good,' says the impresario. 'As you know, I put on scenes, like yours, and I'm your agent too. Your friends are of the modest sort – it goes down well. You may as well write up just what you have. Nothing special, no big effects. Don't take the bus again – adventures everywhere are much the same.'

'No Lake Van, then?' asks Ivan, quite disappointed.

'Oh, it might make another book or film,' the impresario says. 'But – repetition, as you know, is a dangerous ploy. You take the buses, but the details slightly change, your descriptions get meatier, the women more farouche, the men more louche! But that's already had its day: avoid the gendered rhetoric. Taking the bus – is metaphor enough.'

'I can go now,' Ivan says, partly relieved, partly questioning. 'But – did it please? To me, it seemed a little inconclusive....'

'Yes,' says the impresario.

'Which?' Ivan asks. 'Please, or inconclusive?'

'Naturally,' says the impresario. 'Someone else can play your part. If you're tired, that is. You've done all that's required.'

'I didn't put my country in,' says Ivan. 'Politics – only in a general way. Perhaps I didn't stress how awful are the massacres, waiting in line for execution; long lives lived in bidonvilles or short ones pushing carts – cripples, beets – or just the family.'

'No, certainly that's a lack,' the impresario says. 'But they're a scourge, misfortunes are. They've always been, and mercifully it's coming to an end. Let's say – we'll all be rich, just for one day! It will wipe away the years of penury, we'll live like lords, and pay our way – money for bribes and miracle cures, and maybe there's a race or two – are you a greyhound man, or horse?'

'Then there's sex,' says Ivan.

'Oh,' says the impresario, twirling his moustache. 'I think we're old enough to remember all that stuff. It's all on little movies now, if you've forgot. Then there's the crash – losing the money you thought was yours....'

'Oh, none of us had enough cash to bother if it went,' says Ivan, laughing. 'The food! There's no descriptions, not a ladle, not the funnel that you use on geese.... A heel of bread: enough.'

'Enough,' the impresario joins in.

'I didn't make you cry,' says Ivan. 'Perhaps you empathised. Did you laugh?'

'I'm with Bergson on that one,' the impresario says. 'Laughter, musical comedy – it's without thought. Quite mindless and irrational. A hitch in the expectations, that is all. Haha! – and it's done! If you've no expectations, you don't laugh, there's no transgression of your good sense, of routine.'

'What makes a success?' Ivan asks, emboldened. 'What's expected?'

'You ask me?' laughs the impresario. 'Something unexpected, that's for sure. If I'd a plan, I'd do it all myself, or not at all. All the stories, all the dramas ... not leave it to you puffed-up Homers bringing in your tales! Mostly – what happens, it is "more". "More" of the unexpected, but no plan. The same, reheated.'

It's not encouraging.

'Remember,' says the impresario, after a long pause, 'I'm a special kind of guy. I'm an agent – I evaluate you, judge what you've got, and whether it is promising. Then – I'm the impresario. I put you on the stage. And yank you off – I use a hook,' and he laughs heartily.

'Of course, it started in Iraq, then...' Ivan starts...

'Ah yes, a huge Balkans, like I said,' says the impresario, 'Boundaries! And the poor Kurds. Ladies-in-waiting, I'm afraid. I'm sure they had their day, but no one remembers it. Anyway, it's like they say about the revolution in France – too soon to tell.'

Coda

Despots – bodging the universe, Ivan thinks.

Despots sailing their leaky ships, their galleys, fiery seas all round.... You can't beat them. You're a fish, though, unseen and silent, living far below, in another element. We – friends and passengers – we had so many plans; associates to find the cash and cart it out, then in the end, or maybe from the start, Julia was lost ... then, others too.... I didn't learn about myself – what was there to be learnt and what good would it do to learn?

Selling the story, trading in the vision? Trading us, as it happens. I don't see much money in it, Ivan thinks. Maybe the show'll be put on somewhere, somewhere far away. We were in the midst of everything – what shape, what structure, did it have? did we give it? We should have grasped more....

Lovers' meetings. That's how it's supposed to end.

*

Khalil's tango – it's a marvel, leaves you breathless.

About the author

John Fraser has lived in Rome since 1980. Previously, he worked in England and Canada.

www.ingramcontent.com/pod-product-compliance
Lightning Source LLC
Chambersburg PA
CBHW020550310726
48979CB00008B/1157/J

* 9 7 8 1 9 1 0 3 0 1 6 6 1 *